STAY DEAD

ALSO BY ANNE FRASIER

Writing as Anne Frasier

Hush, USA Today bestseller, RITA finalist, Daphne du Maurier finalist (2002)

Sleep Tight, USA Today Bestseller (2003)

Before I Wake (2005)

Pale Immortal (2006)

Garden of Darkness, RITA finalist (2007)

Play Dead (2013)

Writing as Theresa Weir

The Forever Man (1988)

Amazon Lily, RITA finalist, Best New Adventure
    Writer award, *Romantic Times* (1988)

Loving Jenny (1989)

Pictures of Emily (1990)

Iguana Bay (1990)

Forever (1991)

Last Summer (1992)

One Fine Day (1994)

Long Night Moon, Reviewer's Choice Award, *Romantic Times* (1995)

American Dreamer (1997)

Some Kind of Magic (1998)

Cool Shade, RITA winner, romantic suspense (1998)

Bad Karma, Daphne du Maurier award, paranormal (1999)

The Orchard, a memoir (September 2011)

The Man Who Left, New York Times bestseller (2012)

The Girl with the Cat Tattoo (2012)

STAY DEAD

Anne Frasier

Published by Thomas & Mercer, Seattle
www.apub.com

Amazon, the Amazon logo, and Thomas & Mercer are trademarks of Amazon.com, Inc., or its affiliates.

ISBN-10: 1477820132
ISBN-13: 9781477820131
Library of Congress Control Number: 2013920783

Cover design by Cyanotype Book Architects

Follow-Me-Girl Mojo

Queen Elizabeth root

Rosebuds

Lavender

Spikenard

*Name paper: Write the subject's name seven times in black ink.
Rotate one-quarter turn, write seven times in red.*

One hair from the subject's head

Put all the above in a red flannel bag. Dress the bag in follow-me-girl oil and carry it close to your heart.

CHAPTER 1

The voice on the phone was hesitant. When Homicide Detective Elise Sandburg heard it her heart began to pound, and all of her war wounds throbbed. She reached for the pain meds beside her hospital bed, popped a pill, and downed it with a swallow of water.

Elise, the detective who'd stared down many a gun barrel, who'd trailed madmen through the underground tunnels of Savannah, who'd been captured, caught, and tortured, was now quivering in fear, brought down by the sound of her own mother's voice.

"I need to talk to you about Anastasia," Grace said.

Anastasia. The other family outcast.

"Your aunt . . ." Grace's voice trembled. "She called me last night."

Which was a very strange thing to say, considering Anastasia was dead.

In that moment Elise thought, *Oh, how the tables have turned.* She was no longer the crazy one in the family.

"I wondered if you had something to do with it." Grace plunged on. "That's what you people do, isn't it? Conjure up the dead?"

It was hard to shake the rumors when Elise's own mother believed she had some sort of power. Grace's question shouldn't have been a surprise. The woman's conviction would always be the source of their estrangement no matter how many years passed. Elise was the dark mystery her mother brought into her home, someone without her DNA, and the older woman had quickly come to regret taking in an abandoned baby. A baby everybody else had been terrified of helping. Elise had to give her credit for at least stepping up and saying she'd do it. She'd take in this child people thought should have been left on the grave where she'd been found. But a little love would have been nice.

"You're contacting me after five years to ask if I brought your sister back to life?" Elise asked.

Silence. Then, "Yes." The admission came as a quiet whisper.

"You know I'm in the hospital with stab wounds, don't you?" Not to mention dehydration, bruised ribs, and a severely sprained ankle.

"I saw something about that on the news."

Right.

"So, you haven't brought your aunt back from the dead?"

"No."

"Oh." She sounded disappointed.

"What did Anastasia say when she called?"

"I was so shocked to hear her voice . . . You know how that is. When your heart starts pounding and you can't think."

"Are you sure it was her?"

"Yes. She told me not to tell anybody, but she wanted me to know she was alive and that I shouldn't worry about her and that she loved me. Oh, and that she adored you. You were always her favorite, you know."

Elise did know. "Why are you sharing information told to you in confidence?" And with her, of all people.

"Because of her daughter. Melinda. The plantation has been left to Melinda."

"That doesn't seem so unusual," Elise said.

"I think it's strange that she left nothing to me. Nothing. Not even the cuckoo clock. And now here she is, calling in the middle of the night to tell me she's not dead."

"You went to her funeral, right?"

"Yes."

"You saw her dead body, right?"

"The service was closed casket because she'd been in the water so long. The funeral director said she looked awful. He couldn't really do anything with her, and he didn't want her family and friends to remember her that way."

"What do you want me to do?"

"You didn't cast some spell on her?" Grace asked with a combination of hope and disappointment.

"No spell." Elise thought about telling her that's not what root work was about. Not her daddy's root work, anyway, but she didn't see the point. She'd tried a million times before.

"Could you go to the plantation and check it out? See if anything seems odd?"

The only thing that seemed odd was Elise's mother. But some of Elise's best childhood memories were of the weeks spent on her aunt's property. It was a healing place. And who knew what Melinda would decide to do with the property. Probably sell it. Elise wouldn't mind visiting one last time. And she could do with some healing.

"I'll look into it."

Elise's looking into it had something to do with the fact that she and her mother hadn't spoken in so long. It wasn't that she wanted to spend time with Grace. She knew better than that. Even an occasional conversation over coffee came with the promise of fresh emotional trauma, but Elise wanted to reestablish a distant contact. Like this. A phone call once or twice a year. And if a Band-Aid on the relationship meant poking her nose into Aunt Anastasia's affairs, she'd do it, plus it would give her a place to recover while her house was in shambles.

CHAPTER 2

Crisis belief. It was a powerful thing, Elise thought, as she lay in the reclined passenger seat of Detective David Gould's car, her broken body supported by the pillows he'd stuffed around her earlier, her crutches wedged between them.

"This is insane," David said, revisiting his earlier attempt to talk her out of recovering from her injuries in a house she hadn't seen since she was a kid. "You're on some heavy-duty drugs and shouldn't be by yourself."

Funny that David of all people would make an issue of drugs, but he *was* the expert when it came to pharmaceuticals.

"Come stay at my place," he told her. "I'll take care of you." Then his shoulders stiffened as he most likely realized his poor choice of words. Nobody took care of Elise. *Elise* took care of Elise. And really, his gloomy apartment with vines that blocked the sun and a Siamese cat that peed whenever it got upset? How could that possibly be any better than the plantation house where she was going? How could it possibly be any better than . . . than . . . well, than almost anything.

They hit a bump, and the dashboard hula girl did a shimmy. Elise groaned, and David let out a muffled sound that was part apology, part annoyance at being put in a situation where he was causing her more pain.

"You brought your gun, right?" David asked. They were both thinking about the remoteness of the plantation. It was near Savannah, but hidden the way so many things in the area were hidden. Isolated, secret, on a twisted, tangled dirt road.

"Yes." She would have said more, but pain was making a harsh revisit, and she didn't want David to know. She dug her fingernails into her palm to keep from making more noise.

"Why the hell go to your aunt's?" David had argued back at Elise's Victorian home in the Garden District of Savannah where they'd stopped to pick up some things after her four-day hospital stint.

"My house is full of men with power tools and hammers, not to mention an asbestos abatement team." She'd had to shout over the sound of those very power tools and hammers. Elise was just happy the construction crew had finally shown up even though they were three months late. Did anything ever happen at a convenient time? But recovering in her own bed would have been nice. "I'd say it's serendipitously fortunate," Elise had told him. "Not that my aunt's dead, but that her house is empty."

She hadn't told him about her aunt's supposed return. She'd considered at least sharing her mother's request that she check out the plantation, but it had been hard enough to talk David into driving her here today. Let him think she was coming to the plantation in order to put the past week behind her, and because her home was a hard-hat and toxic-waste zone. That's all he needed to know right now.

From her low perspective, Elise could see blue sky and rapidly moving clouds. Live oaks and Spanish moss created a strobe of light and shadow that was hypnotic. She wanted to roll down a window and smell the world beyond the car, but the afternoon was unusually cool for early November in the South. And even though she knew it was the medication, she suddenly felt close to tears.

The kind of feeling you get when your senses are flooded with the overwhelming beauty of the moment. It's a feeling that comes out of nowhere, probably the same kind of euphoria a dog feels before it begins tearing madly around the yard, just high on life. Or the drunken woman at the end of the bar who suddenly loves everyone. That's the wave that came over her. She loved David. She loved her teenage daughter, who was at that moment on a short-term foreign exchange in Sweden even though Audrey had begged to stay in Savannah after her mother's ordeal.

Elise would heal, but the near-death experience made her question all of the turns in her life, and the choices, good or bad.

Should she have become a detective? Should she have exposed her daughter to the seedier side of Savannah? To the criminals and the murderers? Maybe she should have become . . . what? A doctor? A *real* doctor. Or a veterinarian. Or a florist. Or a farmer. Or an artist. Or a writer. Or a bookstore owner. Or a café owner. Audrey could work at the café too, and they would both wear white aprons, and if a customer stepped in and said, "Hey, did you hear about the murder last night in Forsyth Park?" Elise would just shrug.

Too bad, but she had beans to grind. Too bad, but she had a latte with a whipped-cream heart to make. She would be all about bringing a bit of comfort into her customers' dark lives. She wouldn't be stepping into those dark lives. She wouldn't see what those lives looked like from the inside, from the hearts of murderers and victims. She would return home smelling like fair-trade coffee, not a body that had been lying on a living room floor for three days in the heat of a Georgia summer.

Elise never thought she'd become one of those women on a quest for the meaning of life, the meaning of *her* life, but she suddenly found herself looking inward. Who was she? Elise Sandburg, detective? Elise Sandburg, daughter of a root doctor? Elise Sandburg, the woman abandoned in a cemetery as an infant?

The cemetery incident alone could do a number on a person, and she'd spent the bulk of her life trying to prove she wasn't a weirdo and a misfit. And in so doing, she'd denied her heritage. Shame? Had it been shame? Maybe. But also fear. Being the daughter of a root doctor carried with it a responsibility she hadn't wanted. Years ago, with her father's death, the mantle had been passed to Elise and she'd done nothing with it. Just watched it drop at her feet.

How could a detective believe in mojos, in root magic, in hoo-doo? And she didn't *want* to believe. But as much as she denied belief, a part of her wondered . . . was it real? Or did the simple act of believing make it real? So much of magic and superstition was belief-based, and yet root doctoring was supposed to be in a person's blood, passed down from generation to generation.

Elise should have died. She'd been beaten and tortured and stabbed, but as she lay there bleeding out, thinking of Audrey, thinking of David, she'd called upon a chant that had been taught to her years ago by an old woman who'd lived down the road. Knowledge she'd put aside. Swept aside. Kicked aside. In that moment, when she should have been embracing death, saying good-bye to life, she'd turned to the old chant. If it really meant so little to her, why had she reached for it in what she thought to be her final moments of life?

Crisis belief. Yes, it was a powerful thing.

She didn't die. A chant—root magic saved her.

Nonsense. She'd lived because her blood had excellent clotting properties. She'd lived because she'd outsmarted her captor. She'd lived because she was relatively healthy and she'd been able to endure the abuse her body had taken.

Root magic hadn't saved her. Elise had saved herself. And the man she'd outwitted, Atticus Tremain, aka the Organ Thief, was now in a coma that he would most likely never awaken from. A depraved sicko who'd been obsessed with her. A man who'd left a string of bizarre murders in his wake, removing body parts ranging from hearts to genitalia. *That* was the truth. *That* was real.

Elise wished she'd killed him, especially since they hadn't been able to directly tie him to the murders, but he was as good as dead, she tried to tell herself. He would never hurt anyone again, she tried to tell herself.

They hit another bump, and Elise stifled another moan. "What do you see?" she finally managed.

Would David understand if she told him she was trying to find herself? Find Elise? Yes, he would get it.

"What do I see?" he asked, throwing her question back to her, turning his head slightly, but not enough to make eye contact. "Crazy. I see crazy."

She laughed, because he'd always been the impractical one.

"And total isolation," he said.

"That's what I want."

He stopped the car in the middle of the road and lifted his cell phone. "No bars."

"There's a landline phone. I gave it a test call yesterday."

"Did anybody answer?"

"Just the ghost."

"Ha-ha."

"The place *is* supposed to be haunted, you know."

"Did you ever see anything?"

"No, but people have reported hearing voices and music. Personally I think those people were high."

"What isn't supposed to be haunted around here?"

The car dipped down a steep grade, then turned through a pair of stone pillars and rusted iron gates that probably hadn't been opened or closed in years. Elise's breath caught on the pain as the car stopped and David shut off the engine.

He sat behind the wheel, looking through the windshield. "Holy crap," he finally said in a voice that held both horror and amazement.

CHAPTER 3

David helped Elise from the car. He was dressed for work in black slacks, white shirt, black tie, and black knee-length wool coat. Unlike the more casually dressed officers at the Savannah Police Department, David had been reluctant to part with his old FBI threads. Elise was a sloppy contrast in her black hoodie, black sweatpants, and black plastic walking cast. Once upright, hobbling on one foot, she understood his reaction to seeing Anastasia's place.

Whenever Elise thought of her aunt's house, she pictured it as it had been all those years ago, not like it was now—a Southern plantation swallowed by vegetation. Plywood over windows, dangling shutters, rotten support posts, crumbling tabby brick. Beautiful decay, a house devoured by nature.

It had never been well kept, and had always looked neglected, but that neglect had been deliberate. But the Lowcountry had a way of swallowing a place if a person wasn't careful.

Vegetation crept out of the soil and wrapped around footings and pillars and shutters, vines climbed up past the second-story porch all the way to the gabled windows and chimney of broken brick. And yet the building itself didn't seem to cower. Quite the opposite. Even in its crumbled, decaying state, it seemed to stand defiantly against a brilliant blue sky.

Maybe it was a Southern thing. That magnificent and ornate defiance that permeated the very buildings. A sense of place that set itself apart from the rest of the country.

"Smell that?" Elise asked.

David inhaled. "What is it?"

"Sassafras."

She closed her eyes and took a deep breath. "I love it." Rather than coming from one place, the scent seemed to be everywhere, with no specific source. "It's a favorite of root doctors."

David snorted, then asked, "Love spells?"

"You could say that. Good for treating STDs."

He laughed a little more seriously, and then they both turned their attention back to the structure in front of them.

It wasn't a *Gone With the Wind* plantation and never had been. For Anastasia, it hadn't been about the past but about a good space for her artists' colony. It hadn't been about preserving history, but rather about creating her own. In its day, the plantation had been known around the country. Maybe not by the mainstream, but by struggling artists looking for a place where they could live cheaply while they honed their craft.

Elise made a sound that conveyed her dismay, and David's hand touched her shoulder. "Let's go back to Savannah. This isn't habitable."

Despite his words, he handed her the crutches and she wedged them under her armpits. "I want a closer look," she said.

It wasn't just that the house was in shambles. The decay also served as a painful reminder of the passage of time. The clock was ticking. It had been ticking all along; she just hadn't been mindful of it.

"Wait here," David said. "I'll check it out and come back with a report."

Elise and David were both picturing her trying to navigate whatever they would find inside. Elise imagined broken furniture. Dead rats. Piles of trash. "No, I want to see it while I'm here." Her plans were already shifting. She already imagined camping out on David's couch.

"How long has your aunt been gone?" David asked, surveying the house while exotic perfume continued to drift to them from unknown places, the scents comforting and at odds with the visual image.

"Two months." Elise hadn't even known Anastasia was dead until a week after the funeral.

"How'd she die? I don't think you told me."

No, she hadn't wanted to tell him. "She drowned," Elise said with reluctance. David's young son had drowned.

Elise went on with the story, hoping to paint an unfamiliar picture for David in order to take him away from the scene of his own terrible tragedy. "She was a strong swimmer, but she'd been drinking."

"Drinking and swimming never mix," David said, taking the drowning well even though he'd flinched at the D-word, the memory of his loss shooting through his veins before he could get full control of it.

Elise could almost visualize the night of her aunt's death. The meal around the table, along with drinking and talking and laughing. Those events were often followed by a dip in the indoor pool. But sometimes they would take lanterns and make their way to the Ogeechee River that bordered the property. When Elise was a kid, it had all seemed so magical. Looking back as an adult, she realized those late-night skinny-dips had been laden with alcohol and drugs.

She went back through her memories until she heard her aunt's voice and the laughter of the men and women who surrounded Anastasia with what her soul craved. Admiration, love, art.

Elise regretted losing touch with her aunt over the years. Elise's parents had cut off ties after finding out about the drinking parties and the skinny-dipping and the strange men who came and went. Elise was forbidden to have any contact with Anastasia, and as the years passed Elise almost forgot her aunt existed.

But she regretted not looking her up once she became an adult. It was so easy to let these things slide. It was the way of adults. It became easier to let it go than to restart something that couldn't be restarted. Because those reacquaintances often didn't move past nostalgia. Those people, once removed from your life, were hard to put back. You could try, and you could think it was going to work, and you could enjoy the company and the reminiscing, but it was hard, if not impossible, to make them a part of your life once again. And so opening that door invited in a certain bittersweet melancholy, and a reminder that life was fleeting. And those moments that seem bigger than a movie? Even those moments fade and become part of our mental scrapbooks.

"What are you thinking about?"

David was watching her with concern. Elise had witnessed that concern a lot lately.

His face was the first she'd seen after those of the recovery room nurses. Her daughter had been there, along with Elise's ex-husband, who'd flown in from Seattle. That had surprised and touched her. But Elise's eyes had latched onto David. *Because he would understand.*

These were the emotional pacts and bonds you made with partners. And when he flirted and told Elise her Southern accent was like Tupelo honey on a hot and lazy afternoon, she laughed while stashing his words away where she kept everything about him. Close to her heart, but not in her heart.

Partners couldn't be lovers.

She wasn't sure if that was a rule or something that simply made sense. Sometimes she thought she and David should just do it. Just go away together and spend an entire week in bed. Finally have an answer to the question they both wondered about. What would it be like? Them? Together?

Maybe it wouldn't be so great. Maybe they'd regret it. And then they'd have to see each other every day. And work together every day. So awkward. Or worse, maybe he would leave. Go to another city. Another department. And he wouldn't come to her house on holidays. And she wouldn't look out the window to see him helping Audrey with her softball pitching.

Instead, he'd go into the scrapbook with people like Anastasia. People she'd let go, that she didn't hang on to because the magic was gone. She didn't want the magic with David to be gone. She didn't want to lose him. She couldn't bear that. So this . . . this . . . whatever it was that they had . . . it was okay. It wasn't right, but it was better than losing him.

"You're doing it again."

"What?"

"Thinking. You get that look on your face that I haven't seen before. What's going on with you, Elise?"

"Too much medication." That was probably it, she told herself. She'd hoped to cut back, but she was still popping pills like a junkie.

Up the porch steps. Not easy with crutches, but she ignored David's outstretched hand. *I can do this myself. I can take care of myself.*

"The trim is blue," he said in his investigator voice.

"Haint blue." It kept out evil spirits. Or kept them in. "That wasn't there when I was a kid."

"Maybe she suffered from dementia in her later years." David tested the doorknob. "That would explain the condition of the house and the paranoia about evil spirits." The door swung open. Surprised, he stumbled inside.

Anastasia had never locked the doors.

Thank God the inside didn't reflect what they'd seen outside.

"Somebody's been taking care of this place," David said with surprise.

The interior had kind of a gypsy-wagon or vaudevillian feel to it that hadn't changed since Elise's last visit. Back in the 1800s, wide wallboards had been covered with starched fabric, then coated with paint. At some point, the cloth was removed to expose rough, unfinished wood that had turned black in places. Wood you could smell. The old kind of wood that hinted of men in frock coats and women in mourning gowns.

Along the dark walls were framed and unframed paintings and drawings, given to Anastasia in return for room and board. Some of the work was hideous, but much of it was colorful, and Anastasia had loved color.

"Okay, I take back everything I said." David stood with hands on hips, coat hanging open as he surveyed the space. "This house is cool as hell."

"You *would* like it." After all, he lived in one of the most depressing buildings in Savannah. David had a dark soul for someone who was always cracking jokes. She often wondered if the joking was a recent trait, a screen, or had he been funny before tragedy entered his life.

Even though Elise hadn't been to the plantation since childhood, the open layout was the same, which was saying a lot considering the amount of renovations that had taken place over the years. Even much of the artwork hadn't changed.

The first floor had been gutted and remodeled, most of the work done over time and for free by the artists who visited the plantation. To the left of the front door was a kitchen with white farmhouse cupboards, a farmhouse sink, and mosaic countertops. A strange chandelier with gold cherubs hung above a round wooden table. To the right was a narrow church window and a staircase that led to a solid blank wall—another remodel, Elise always assumed.

In the adjoining dining area was a hand-hewn table that could seat twenty people, and very often had. Walls were floor-to-ceiling bookcases, packed with hardcovers and paperbacks and more pieces of art, from sculptures to ceramic bowls thrown on a potter's wheel. Past the staircase was an upright piano surrounded by comfortable furniture. Deep couches and chairs in dark shades of greens and reds, the colors echoed in lampshades. One large section of the shelves was dedicated to a stereo and what had to be at least a hundred record albums. And there, near the stereo, was the infamous cuckoo clock.

Elise pulled the chain, raising the pinecone weight, then she tapped a finger lightly against the leaf-shaped pendulum and the ticking began. She turned to David with a smile. "Still works."

Beyond the sitting area were large windows that overlooked the outdoors. Through the windows, Elise could see the stone path that led to the Ogeechee River, and the dock where the drunken parties had been known to end in skinny-dipping. Beyond that was a small island with a cabin where Anastasia had taken her on picnics.

"Someone must have aired the place out," Elise said. Not only aired it out, but left a bouquet of flowers in the center of the round kitchen table. Along with the flowers was a note from Melinda, Anastasia's daughter.

"She says she put clean sheets on the bed in the main room, and milk and fruit in the refrigerator." Elise returned the sheet of paper to the table. "That's nice."

David inhaled. "I smell chlorine."

The pool. Where Anastasia's body was found.

"It's this way." Elise hobbled in the direction of the chlorine. "You stay here." She moved toward the glass door that led to the enclosed room, opened the door, and stepped inside.

As with most childhood memories, the pool was smaller than she remembered, but one end was deep enough for a low diving board. Her aunt would swim laps in her rubber cap with pink flowers, pausing to hold up her arms to her niece.

"Jump, Elise. Come on. I'll catch you." Red lips. White teeth. A beauty and charm Elise couldn't resist, that no one could resist. "Come on, Elise. I'll teach you how to float. Better than that, I'll teach you how to sink. I'll teach you how to let the air out of your lungs so you can sink to the bottom of the pool. It's magic down there. Down there is the land of tea parties. Of mermaids and castles of the deep, and fish that glow in the dark."

"They must have drained and refilled it," David said from behind her.

"You shouldn't be here," Elise told him. She didn't want him driving back to his apartment full of thoughts of his son. She didn't want him reaching into the cupboard for oblivion once he got home.

"I'm okay."

The water was crystal clear. They were both relieved to find that it no longer gave off the aura of death. In one corner of the room was a white chaise longue with a black swimsuit draped over it. The swimsuit looked like the one Elise's aunt had worn all those years ago. And Elise suddenly got the feeling that Anastasia had never died, that she was still there, that maybe she'd just stepped out for groceries and soon she would be back with wine and bread and the makings of salad and lasagna.

When Anastasia was around, Elise had felt challenged to be a better Elise, and she was pretty sure other people felt that way too. Strangers wandered in from the road after having hitchhiked across the country, carrying a suitcase or a duffel bag, many with guitars. They'd heard of her. They'd heard of Anastasia and the plantation.

"Artists need help," Aunt Anastasia had said. "Artists have to stick together. Are you going to be an artist or a drone?" she'd asked Elise.

"What's a drone?"

"A drone is someone who does whatever she's told. A drone doesn't think for herself. Being a drone isn't a bad thing. The world needs drones."

But Elise had the feeling being a drone *was* a bad thing. This was a test. "I want to be an artist."

Anastasia smiled at Elise, and Elise jumped into her arms.

"Did you have an adult who was a major influence in your life?" Elise asked David as they both stared at the pool.

"You."

"No, not me."

"Yeah, you."

"As a kid."

"My mother."

He and his mother were close. Elise liked that about him.

"My aunt was the only person who accepted me for who I was," Elise said. "She was the only person who wasn't afraid of where I'd come from."

"See, I think that's what this is all about. You had a near-death experience. That makes people reevaluate their lives. I get that. But the thing to keep in mind is that sometimes it makes us behave in uncharacteristic ways that don't make a lot of sense."

"Like this," Elise said. "Like coming here. Now."

"Like this," he agreed. "I've been where you are now. I know how it messes with your head."

"The plantation has been handed to me. It came when I most needed it, and you shouldn't ignore something like that. So what if it's irrational and out of character? What difference does it make? I'm a big girl. So I spend a week or two here and when I'm ready to go back to my place I go back."

"You'll go stir crazy."

"You don't know that."

He shook his head, resigned. "I'll get your suitcase."

Down the hall from the kitchen were three bedrooms. The wooden floor creaked, and walls were bare to the laths and decorated with more framed art. At the end of the hall was a narrow door that took a person to the cramped servant stairs and the second and third level.

If things were still as Elise remembered, the second floor would look like a boarding house, with six rooms on each side of a narrow hallway. A couple of the rooms had been used as art studios back in the day, and Elise recalled walking in on a painting session for which her aunt was the model, lying in a pool of sunlight, completely naked. Nudity was an unheard of occurrence in Elise's house. She'd gasped, and Anastasia had gracefully lifted a hand in languid greeting.

Now many of the windows were broken and boarded up, and Elise couldn't help but wonder if the couch where Anastasia had reclined was still there. And the painting? What happened to the painting?

Beyond the studio, another flight of stairs led to a third story of mice and dust and planked flooring—an area of the house where Elise had been forbidden to go.

"Are you sure you want to stay in this room?" David asked, hefting her plaid bag onto a padded vanity stool.

"It's fine." Elise surveyed the space. Windows that overlooked dense trees, a sprawling king-size bed. More artwork on the walls. She remembered being read to in this room, cuddling up next to her aunt, and Anastasia's two dogs at the foot of the bed.

"This will be the handiest," Elise said. "It has a bathroom, and the kitchen is just down the hall." She pointed. "Phone next to the bed."

"So, no talking you out of this." David stuck his hands deep in the pockets of his coat.

They both knew that wasn't going to happen.

And then he did something very strange and very uncharacteristic. He approached Elise in a way he'd never approached her before. With serious blue eyes that transmitted more than friendship. Eyes that held a question she didn't want him to ask. He reached for her in this tender way, a way that seemed to project and evoke longing.

There it was. The thing between them. Elise's breath caught as she thought about how it would feel. His lips on hers. And more than a kiss. Much more. What would it hurt? What would it hurt to drop the screen of friendship?

David was old-world handsome. Classically handsome. She didn't hold that against him, because it came in handy when they interviewed women, and sometimes men. Dark, straight hair with streaks of light brown that would vanish whenever he got a haircut, then reappear as the sun did its work. Beautiful skin, and an angular jaw that needed to be shaved again by late afternoon. Like now. And a mouth . . .

That mouth turned up slightly at the corners, and he whispered, "Someday . . ."

For a brief second, Elise saw something in his eyes that was too deep and too scary. With David she always got the sense that he was hanging by a thread, and if he ever let go . . . And now he was inviting her to come with him.

She pulled back a little, but his hands were still on her arms. "Someday what?" she asked, hoping he would follow her lead to the land of safe.

He didn't. "You. Me."

"Highly unlikely."

"What are you afraid of?"

"I'm not afraid."

"You know what I mean."

They stared at each other for a long time. And then they both laughed. Maybe too hard, but that's how they did these things. That's how they handled it.

The hair she'd put in a ponytail before leaving the hospital began to slip free, and dark strands fell around her face. David took note of her dilemma and came to stand behind her. Once in grooming position, he tugged the band free, swept back her straight hair with his palms, and redid the whole thing in a matter of a few seconds, giving her shoulders a there-you-go pat. He took rejection well.

CHAPTER 4

That night Elise woke up thinking she was home. Thinking she was in her bed in the Garden District. She stared into the darkness, barely able to make out the shape of a painting above her. For a disoriented heartbeat, she thought the painting was a door, and she wondered what would happen if she opened that door. She got the sense that if she opened it she'd find something she didn't want to find.

So odd. She didn't remember a door in her room. And then she became cognizant of where she was. The plantation. Aunt Anastasia's bed. That realization created a cascading sensation as her brain struggled to rearrange the puzzle that was the space surrounding her in the darkness.

The bed, with its feather topper, was almost too soft. Elise liked a firm mattress. And it smelled. Not bad, but like the vanilla and lavender oil Anastasia used to concoct.

"Try it, Elise. It's so refreshing."

Elise would put her finger over the brown bottle, tip it, and dab the homemade perfume behind her ears.

"The ears seem like a silly place for perfume," Elise had said. "Why do ears need perfume?"

"Because men like to smell a woman's hair," Anastasia explained. "They want to bury their faces in your hair and press their lips just here"—she touched her niece—"just below your earlobe."

"And you want to taste good for them?"

"You want to taste delicious."

And maybe the bed smelled a bit like wine and smoke, as if the years of Anastasia's life had soaked into the feathers. Elise remembered her aunt pulling her close, and the smell was like that. Like her arms and her clothes and her hair. The pillow, where Elise's head was resting . . . Anastasia's head had rested there. Elise found that knowledge both comforting and disturbing. She wanted to stuff the pillow under the bed, and she wanted to hug it and inhale deeply.

At one point, Elise drifted back to sleep and dreamed that a bouquet of gardenias rested on the small marble-topped table next to the bed. And later, during the night when she half woke, she could still smell them. That sickening and cloying and wonderful scent. She imagined shiny black ants crawling over petals.

Pain. Her pain medication had worn off. That explained the dreams. The weird thoughts. The constant waking.

With the crutches under her arms, Elise thumped down the hallway and was halfway to the kitchen when she heard a splash coming from the direction of the pool.

Her first thought was intruder, but her second was more logical. Someone else had probably been given permission to use the house. Or maybe her aunt's open-door policy was still in play. But that theory didn't keep Elise from returning to the bedroom to grab her gun.

She'd never tried to use crutches and hold a gun at the same time. She briefly contemplated putting the weapon between her teeth, but finally opted for slipping the shoulder holster over her nightgown.

Back down the hall, she leaned her crutches against the wall so her hands were free. She pulled out her Glock 17, then, favoring her good foot, lightly putting weight on the walking cast, she approached the pool room. Except for the cast, except for the shoulder holster, except for the gun, she would have looked like some heroine from a gothic novel in her white, sleeveless gown—a present from her daughter. Elise wondered if Audrey had been trying to tell her something. *Be more feminine, Mom. Be more like a regular mom.* Bake cookies and wear nightgowns made of cotton and a bit of lace.

Sometimes Elise thought she'd failed Audrey just as much as Grace had failed Elise. The long hours of work. The way she was never as present as she should be. Watching a softball game, her mind would wander to the cases on her desk. To the most recent crimes she and David were working.

Another splash.

The door to the pool room was inches from her shoulder. Deep breath, gun braced, Elise swung into the room, scanning with her eyes and the barrel.

In the center of the pool was a disturbance left by a diving body. As Elise watched, a black question mark rose to the surface. She blinked and stepped closer. Just a swirl. Just a shadow.

And then, not a yard from her feet, a person exploded from the water. Elise's eyes and mind processed an aqua swimming cap with yellow flowers. A black bathing suit. The bathing suit that had been on the chaise longue earlier, and a woman all long and willowy, with white arms.

"Hello, Elise," the woman said with lips as red as cherries, with a voice that was familiar in tone and inflection and softly Southern accent. "Welcome back to the plantation."

Aunt Anastasia.

CHAPTER 5

This is where the woman in the gothic novel would swoon, then awaken to find some handsome lord in a black cape towering over her, possibly trying to loosen her corset in order to revive her. Elise didn't swoon. Instead, she kept the gun pointed steadily at Anastasia's head and demanded to know what the hell was going on.

Anastasia casually pushed away from the side of the pool, did a lovely sidestroke to the ladder, climbed out, grabbed a towel, and began to dry off, lifting her long, lovely legs one at a time. That's when Elise noticed how young she was. Maybe in her late twenties.

Without looking up, the young woman said, "You can quit pointing that thing at me anytime."

Elise remembered the gun in her hand. She lowered it. "You aren't Anastasia," she said.

"Of course not." The woman pulled off the swimming cap and shook out a cascade of red hair.

Elise had never been attracted to females, but she was smitten right then and there. This had to be Melinda, Anastasia's daughter, born after the family rift. Elise could see she had the same power as her mother. The uncanny ability to make a person—any person of any sexual orientation—fall head over heels within seconds.

Elise was glad the power had been passed from mother to daughter. The passing of the mantle. Not of root work, but something just as strong. Something people might have called feminine wiles fifty years ago. And just as Elise had sometimes diminished before her aunt, she now felt herself become less feminine, less attractive, older, more awkward, in front of Melinda. At the same time, she knew it wasn't the lovely woman's fault, which made her adore her all the more. And yet Elise was suddenly excruciatingly and painfully aware of her dark, drab, shoulder-length hair. Her body beneath the gown. Not willowy, not fat, but not as toned as it used to be. Riddled with scars that she laughingly referred to as her war wounds but that she now saw as defects. Not glorious things of which to be proud, but ugly damage.

And she thought of David. And in that moment of clarity she understood one of the reasons, maybe the biggest reason, she didn't want their relationship to change, to move beyond what they had. She didn't want him to see her body. And she particularly didn't want him to see what Atticus Tremain had done to her.

It was different when you met someone at your peak, married, and grew old together. Midthirties certainly wasn't old, but Elise's abused body was on the downhill slide, and it would never be beautiful again. She wanted to be beautiful in David's mind. She wanted him to imagine what it would be like, what she would be like. And that imagining would be so much more than they could ever have.

It was very unlike Elise to have such thoughts make their way to the surface of her brain. She didn't care for them.

"I'm sorry if I startled you," Melinda said. "I live in Savannah, but I often drop by to do laps in the pool."

"Your mother loved to swim too."

Melinda tossed the towel over the chair. "Listen." Her face took on a let's-be-frank expression. "I know why you're here. Aunt Grace is contesting the will. You have to realize how ridiculous that is.

I'm Anastasia's daughter. And she and my aunt hadn't talked since before I was born. Why wouldn't she leave everything to me?"

"Grace led me to believe that they'd reconnected in the past several years."

"Not that I know of. My mother never mentioned her. Her sister didn't exist as far as Anastasia was concerned."

"You've had no contact with Grace?"

Those lovely brows drew together in puzzlement. "None. Ever."

Elise filed that away to ponder. "How long have the windows been painted blue?" she asked.

"Windows?"

"The windows and doors are painted blue."

"Ah, I'm not sure."

"Did your mother say why she painted them that color?"

"We never really talked about it. I just thought it was an artistic choice."

"Structurally the building is in bad shape, yet she painted the windows and doors."

"I'm sorry. I don't know. My mother did a lot of things that could be considered peculiar."

"Did she ever voice any fears? Of people? Of . . . well, evil spirits?"

Melinda gave it some thought, and then shook her head. "Anastasia was fearless."

"That's how I remember her," Elise said. Which made the blue trim all the odder.

CHAPTER 6

The morning after David dropped off Elise at the plantation, he got up before dawn to jog. Located in a rough area of downtown, his apartment was on the third floor of an ancient building called Mary of the Angels. Like all of Savannah, it had a dark history. Mary of the Angels was a sad place that had once housed children orphaned by the yellow-fever epidemic, and was later turned into a home for TB patients. People claimed it was haunted, but David said that was bullshit.

By the time he'd tugged on his gray sweatpants and black T-shirt, laced his shoes, and hit Forsyth Park, the sky was beginning to lighten and birds were singing.

He'd started running after his son was murdered. Back then it had been the only way to wear himself out enough to sleep, and the rhythmic pace hypnotized him, lulled him into oblivion. Now he ran because he liked it, and, no matter the time of year, he preferred early morning to take a tour of a city he'd come to love.

Never dreamed he'd ever say that, but the place had gotten to him in so many ways. Even the smell. *Especially* the smell. He couldn't place it, and people from Savannah didn't seem to notice it at all. Whenever he asked about the source, fingers pointed to the paper mill and its billowing clouds of smoke. But this wasn't the mill. This was organic, and like nothing he'd ever smelled anywhere else. Maybe the closest it came was to a greenhouse, but that wasn't it. No, this seemed to be mixed with the marsh at low tide and the wood from ancient buildings, the sandy soil that reluctantly held the tombstones in Bonaventure Cemetery, and the draping Spanish moss that made even the most horrid of crime scenes appear placid and peaceful.

He sometimes found himself sniffing a handful of live-oak leaves, searching for clues to the source of the perfume, because it could almost be considered perfume. But he knew the smell wasn't coming from the leaves. It came from everything, reaching from the past, from the blood and tears and antebellum gowns to the organic coffee and patchouli emanating from the café across from Forsyth Park. A new world perched atop dark history.

Savannah was considered one of the most haunted cities in the world, and David might insist he didn't believe in ghosts, but he understood the ghost thing. The souls who'd come before could be felt in every tabby brick, every trunk of every breaking tree, every narrow street, every blooming square, every pane of glass. And when you were staring at a headstone lovingly and intricately carved by a man who'd been dead for over a hundred years, you could feel a certain . . . *imprint*. You could imagine the sculptor's hands moving over the stone.

David would always be an outsider here—he knew that—but his Yankee eyes had never seen such a dark, gritty, beautiful place.

He hit his favorite high points: several of the squares, River Street, then back through Forsyth Park. Street sweepers were out sweeping the night's fallen leaves, the homeless were waking up, and a few tourists were already visible, standing on corners clutching whimsical maps as David wrapped up his run.

Back in his apartment he was heading for the shower when a knock sounded on the door. He answered it to find a woman named Strata Luna standing there in all her spooky glory. Behind him, his cat, Isobel, skidded around the corner to vanish into the bedroom.

David hadn't seen the woman in months, and as far as he knew she'd never visited his apartment. And why was she out at this hour? Strata Luna, Savannah's most famous madam, belonged to the night, not the mornings. But then again, she probably wasn't someone who paid much attention to the clock, and she could pretty much do whatever she wanted since the entire city was afraid of her. Hell, the entire police force was afraid of her, which was why they looked the other way when it came to her business. But David silently accused her of being all theater, with her black veil and darkened car windows. She didn't scare him. She'd never scared him even though it was said she could kill a man with her gaze.

As he understood it, she was of Gullah or Geechee heritage. Both, although different, had become interchangeable, Gullah the more widely used, and even the locals weren't sure of the difference anymore.

With a dramatic gesture that carried with it the scent of exotic oils, she lifted the ornate veil from her face, folding it back so it fell over her shoulders. Black gloves vanished into the sleeves of her black dress, the dress itself full, falling to the floor. He found himself staring at her luminous brown skin, almond eyes, and full, red lips.

"I have something for you," she said.

He backed up, never taking his eyes off her as she floated in. Her dress rustled. Like leaves. Like paper.

She stopped in the center of his cramped apartment, inhaled, and turned to face him. "This is a nice place."

Vines covering the windows. Clothes tossed over the chair and couch, both pieces of furniture well shredded by his cat. Dismal, but it suited him.

"You're the first person to ever tell me that." Most people begged him to move. Most people wondered why he lived in such a depressing place, a place where years ago hundreds of people had died. Of course she'd like it.

Should he offer her something? Orange juice? Water? She'd served him tea at her pink plantation house. He didn't have tea.

"I'm here to help you," she said.

His mind tripped along, trying to figure out how she could possibly help him with anything. His first thought was a girl. One of her girls. Yeah, that was probably it. For a moment he actually gave it some consideration, and then he remembered what had happened the last time he'd used the services of Black Tupelo.

"I'm fine," he said. "Really."

"I'm not talking about sex, but if you're interested I have a couple of new girls I think you'd like."

"No. Thanks. That's okay."

"I'm talking about Elise. I worry about her, and I want to help you. I know things haven't always been . . . well, that wonderful between us. And I know you suffered, no thanks to me. I want to do something for you. Free of charge. Out of the goodness of my heart. Well, not really goodness. I want to pay my debts."

"Can you be a bit more specific?"

"I've brought a mojo."

He almost laughed, but that would have been rude. "I don't believe in that stuff."

"You don't have to believe for a spell to work."

He had to admit that when Elise went missing he'd actually thought of contacting Strata Luna to see if she could help. And then he'd gotten the call from a strange number, and he'd heard Elise's voice.

"It's me," Elise had said.

And he'd dropped to his knees. Just dropped to his knees.

He realized Strata Luna was still standing in the middle of the room. "Would you like a cup of coffee?" he asked. "Glass of orange juice?"

"I can't stay. My driver is waiting."

He let out an internal sigh of relief. He couldn't exactly imagine shooting the shit with this woman. They had absolutely nothing in common. Well, that wasn't true. They both would forever grieve the loss of a child.

"The mojo is for Elise," she said.

He looked at her blankly, and she went on to explain: "A follow-me-girl."

A love spell? "So why are you giving it to me? Shouldn't you give it to her?" And who in the hell was Elise supposed to fall in love with? He backtracked in his head, trying to think of someone she might be attracted to. There was her ex-husband, but he'd remarried long ago. Seemed a good relationship. And that guy had been all wrong for her. All wrong. So who? Somebody in the department? Mason? He'd split up with his wife. Oh, God, no. Couldn't be him.

Strata Luna was talking: "Elise is a strong, independent woman. I understand that. Who needs a man? Beyond sex and the occasional back rub? And a cup of tea brought to bed?"

"Riiiight." It came out as more of a question. No need to point out the obvious—that she was talking to a man.

She let out a resigned sigh that seemed to imply he was too dense for the room. "Have you ever thought about you and Elise together?"

Weird that her words echoed the very thing he'd said last night. "She doesn't think of me that way," he hedged, fairly certain the woman would know if he lied.

"I can help."

"I don't need your help."

She began moving around, looking at his shelves of books, wiping at the dust on his TV. "I started thinking about this when Elise was abducted. She's an independent spirit, but she needs somebody in her life. You're both single and close to the same age."

David felt his heart soften a little. This woman who claimed she cared for no one, claimed she needed no one, was worried about Elise.

Strata Luna gave him an eloquent shrug. "You don't believe in spells, so what does it matter?" She tucked a gloved hand deep into a fold of her dress and pulled out a small red bag secured with a drawstring. The scent that had followed her inside was stronger now, and he realized it came from the bag she held in her black-gloved hand. "Take it," she whispered. Her voice was dark and smooth, the tone like nothing he'd ever heard. And for the first time, he began to doubt his lack of belief.

Truth be told, Elise gave David's life meaning and made his world livable again. And almost losing her . . . that changed a person's perspective. It made him question the role he'd been okay with before her abduction.

He didn't believe in spells and mojos. He didn't believe you could make someone love you. But even though he didn't believe even a little bit, he humored Strata Luna and took the bag, fingering the smooth velvet, inhaling the scent.

She actually bestowed a smile on him.

God, she was beautiful. Some people said her beauty was the reason for the veil. Without it, men fainted in the street as she walked by. David felt a little woozy himself right now.

"Sleep with it under your pillow," she told him. "Every night. And before another full moon, Elise Sandburg will love you with the love of a thousand poets."

Strata Luna left in a swirl of black.

Love. Right. David closed the door after her. He didn't believe, but he'd keep the mojo anyway. He liked the way it smelled.

CHAPTER 7

Elise spent the bulk of her first full day at the plantation settling in and roaming the house and grounds—as much as she could with a cast and crutches. By evening she realized she'd done a little too much roaming, and pain drove her to bed early. She shook a full dose of medication into her palm and popped the pills. She'd reached the point where total oblivion was welcome, but she'd settle for anything that cut the pain in half. Just cut it in half.

Once the pills were swallowed, Elise propped her leg and cast over a plumped pillow and lay there in a sweat, staring at a crack in the wall while doing the breathing exercises she'd learned in Lamaze classes. Doctors had said her ankle wasn't broken, but the tendons and muscles had been so worked over that healing could take a long time. But it wasn't just her ankle that hurt. It was bruised ribs, a shoulder that had been dislocated for most of her captivity, and a multitude of cuts and stab wounds, none of which had been deep, but all meant to inflict pain and disfigure her. And her back . . . God, the mess he'd made of her back . . . She hadn't been able to do more than glance at it in the bathroom mirror. Maybe someday . . . or maybe never.

The phone next to her bed rang and she answered. David. He asked how she was. He asked if she was ready to leave the plantation.

Elise told him no in a voice she hoped wasn't edged with pain. Had she overcorrected? Had that sounded too perky?

"I thought about coming out there tonight, but I had to work late," he told her. "Then I had a missing person's case dumped in my lap. They wanted a homicide specialist's opinion."

It was weird to think of him working cases without her. She didn't like it. Almost like hearing he was seeing someone else. What an odd thought, but that's kind of how it was with them. Those late-night visits to alleys where they bonded over dead bodies. But even if she'd been in Savannah, she wouldn't have been able to be involved in any cases. Doctor's orders. Not just the doctor who'd treated her in the hospital, but the psychiatrist assigned by the department had ordered her off the force for six weeks.

Elise's immediate reaction had been concern about boredom. She didn't know what to do with herself when she wasn't working. "Savannah will be the murder capital of the world by the time I get back," Elise had told Dr. Kicklighter. But it seemed things were going along fine without her. Elise didn't like that.

She told David about last night and how she'd mistaken Melinda for Anastasia. "She looked and sounded just like her mother." The pills were kicking in. Elise felt her body begin to relax.

"How about I come and get you tomorrow?"

Elise was having trouble forming thoughts. And once she got the words lined up in her head, she felt too tired to bother saying them. "I'm perfectly fine here," she finally managed.

"What about groceries?"

"The cupboards and freezer are well stocked. I microwaved a burrito for dinner. It was surprisingly good."

"Your voice is slurred," he noted.

Just move along. Nothing to see here.

Elise didn't like being out of control, but he was right. She could feel the thickness of her tongue and the heaviness in her arms. She could feel warmth seeping through her veins. "I had to take something," she confessed.

"See, this is why you should stay at my place," he said. "When it comes to pain medication, you're an amateur."

"We can't all be pros like you." She realized she was talking with her eyes closed, and she forced them open with a wide blink.

"Which means I would have made a good guide. A guru."

"Let me ask you this. Would you go swimming in the very pool where your mother drowned? Does that seem odd to you?" Elise asked.

"People do weird things after the loss of a loved one. Like becoming fixated on funeral homes and cemeteries. Or the place where the death occurred."

Elise sat up straighter, a pillow against the headboard and her back. "Did you use the tub?" she asked bluntly and without a filter. "After your son's death? Did you ever use a tub again?" This wasn't something she would normally ask. Too personal. Too terribly painful.

David was quiet for a long time, as if trying to decide how much he wanted to share. When he spoke, the words were without emotion. "I never used a tub before, but after . . . I used one all the time after. I would stay in it until the water turned cold. I would submerge myself and look up at the ceiling through the water. I would imagine what it had been like for him." His voice broke.

"Oh, David. I'm sorry." *So* sorry. Why had she brought it up?

"Maybe she's doing the same thing," David said, pulling himself together. He was good at that. "Maybe she's putting herself in her mother's place. Maybe it makes her feel closer to the person she lost."

Elise heard a splash. "Damn. She's back."

Then she heard laughter. The echoing, high-pitched kind that sounded like colored kaleidoscope glass. Far away, undefined, with a texture that never quite solidified. This sounded like a party, not a grief-driven visit.

"Who's back?" David asked.

"Melinda. I have to go. Call you tomorrow."

Before he could ask any more questions, Elise hung up. Then she hefted the cast off the pillow. This was a maneuver done with two hands supporting her thigh, cradling her leg as if it didn't belong to her. She swung the leg and cast to the floor, her good leg following. Then, balancing on the foot without the cast, she reached for the crutches and positioned them under her arms.

She moved toward the door, paused, and waited for a wave of dizziness to pass. The pills had taken care of the pain, but they'd also done a number on the rest of her.

Elise had gone her whole life without a broken arm or twisted ankle. Gunshots, that was different. Knife wounds? Oh, yeah. But now she'd been taken down by a sick bastard who'd spent days humiliating and torturing her.

Don't think about it.

How could she *not* think about it when she was dealing with the remnants of that ordeal? *Bastard, bastard, bastard.* The things he'd done to her. The things she would never tell anyone, not even Dr. Kicklighter. And David. Especially not David. Or her daughter. Oh, God. Not her daughter. Audrey could never know. Elise would change in her eyes. She would become this other person who'd miscalculated. Who'd made a mistake. Who'd been overpowered. If her daughter knew, Audrey would no longer see her as strong and tough. She would no longer see her as the person who would protect her.

A mother should be able to protect her child and her home. And now Elise didn't know if she could continue to be a homicide detective if it meant putting Audrey in danger.

But she was a cop. That was her identity. Who would she be if that were taken away? And what would she do? She had no other skills. God knew her body was too ravaged to be a hooker. That was a little joke she liked to tell her coworkers. And then someone would finish by saying that wasn't at all true. "Have you seen the women we arrested last night?" And everybody would laugh.

But even if looks didn't matter, Elise would have made a crummy whore. *You expect me to do what?*

So there she went. The bad whore, bad cop, bad victim . . .

Still dizzy, she made her way down the hall. It was hard enough to maneuver with the cast when she wasn't under the influence. Put a gun in her hand and she turned into a ballet dancer, but otherwise she was just your average klutz with an array of bruises to prove it.

With the crutches under her arms, Elise moved down the hall faster than was wise, but she was mad. So much for her vacation. So much for her sabbatical and her days of self-discovery. Nobody else knew that this was supposed to be a time for serious reflection and soul searching, but still . . . Deep down, she knew she'd never discover herself at the plantation. The real Elise was back in Savannah. At her job. With her daughter. And David. Her mind always went back to David.

Maybe this was an escape. She'd seen something in his eyes that had her running. Or hobbling. She would run later. She would run like hell once she quit wearing the cast.

Or not.

Oh, my God.

Was it more enticing to think about how things could be between them? Could anything live up to her expectations? Round and round she went. And the next time David called she would talk to him in her all-business voice, or mildly friendly voice, and maybe he would never know that she thought about him, thought about them, all the damn time.

No wonder she'd come here.

She hadn't come to find herself. She was running from David. She was running *away* from herself. Not toward herself. Oh, how people were full of self-trickery. Some of the worst criminals she'd ever encountered thought they were doing something noble. One thing she would work on while she was here—stop lying to herself. Or at the very least, stop believing the lies.

The momentum, the forward thrust of her body dangling over crutches acted as weight and hurtled her forward. It was kind of like riding a bike down a steep hill, but instead of running into a tree at the bottom, she smacked into the pool-room door with its steamed glass. She paused, then opened the door and inched her way inside.

There she was. In the pool. Swimming in her rubber cap, turning her face to the left to take a breath with each lift of her elbow. The front crawl. What precision. Elise admired it beneath her annoyance.

The tile under her one bare foot was wet and cold, and she suddenly wondered what she was doing there. David was right. She should just go home. This had been a silly idea.

Melinda must have spotted her, because she broke her rhythmic crawl and switched to a breaststroke, making her way to the edge of the pool to surface at Elise's feet. Just like the previous night.

"Hello, Elise."

Elise's mind recoiled.

Same eyes. Same lips. But this time they were surrounded by wrinkles.

Elise thought about the blue paint around the doors and the blue paint around the windows. Was this a slip-skin hag? She'd heard of them. Spirits that could slip themselves over people. Even dead bodies. And what if the evil spirit was inside the house? What happened then?

This is where root magic and Elise had parted ways long ago. Elise had never believed in this kind of thing. Of people being brought back to life, and spells being cast. She believed in herbs for health and healing. But then why were the doors painted blue if not to contain or repel?

Elise suddenly imagined being in a cemetery with David, making love. Bonaventure? Yes, it looked like Bonaventure with the Spanish moss and land that sloped to the water's edge. She wasn't wearing the cast, and, in the moonlight, her body didn't look as ravaged. The marble was cold under her skin, and she wondered whose grave they were desecrating.

"Don't look," David panted when he noticed the turn of her head as she tried to read the stone. "You don't want to know."

"What are you?" Elise managed to ask the woman in the pool. She was surprised by how little her voice betrayed her inner thoughts and fears.

This was Elise's aunt, but her aunt was dead. Nobody could be brought back from the dead. Those were the truths she'd clung to, a lack of belief why she'd never take up the mantle to carry on her father's work. Her belief stopped here. Right here.

As Elise stared, the woman in the pool raised her arms and told her to jump, told her she'd catch her. Or did Elise imagine that? Had her lips moved at all?

As Elise watched, the woman pushed off and did a sidestroke to the ladder. Elise stared some more as the woman climbed out of the pool. Same black swimming suit. Same cap. But the body. Not a young woman's body. This body was old, with loose skin.

Slip-skin hag.

A slip-skin hag overtook sleepers while they dreamed. This didn't seem like a slip-skin hag. But what . . .?

Elise took an unconscious and understandably awkward step back. The rubber ends of her crutches made contact with the wet surface. She tried to catch herself with her bad foot. Plastic cast hit tile and it was like metal against ice. It was like stepping into a frozen rink with dull skates.

Elise flew backward, feet out from under her. She saw walls and roof and recessed ceiling lights. And then she was airborne, arms flailing. She thought she heard someone scream, but that could have been her.

CHAPTER 8

Elise hit the surface of the water, flat on her back, the wind knocked out of her in a loud, unfeminine *whoof*. She sank like a stone. Silence engulfed her as water covered her head. The cast filled and acted like an anchor, dragging her to the bottom of the pool. It was ridiculous, but she imagined how she must look. The cast, weighing her down, her body swathed in the white nightgown, her face surprised, her hair a seaweed cloud, all dreamy and beautiful. And she thought about David. David again! He'd been so against her coming. She could be in his apartment right now, wrapped in a blanket, a cup of hot tea in her hand, an annoying and charming Siamese cat at her feet.

She hit bottom, and she swore she heard a dull, echoing thunk as the cast—that horrible cast—scraped the pale blue bottom of the pool.

Elise thought about the tea parties she and Anastasia used to have in this very pool. Had her aunt died like this? In the deep end? At the bottom of the pool where she'd loved to go? Had she come down here, had a tea party, and forgotten to surface for air? Just forgotten because it was so peaceful and lovely?

Elise sensed that Anastasia was with her, and then she was. In her black bathing suit. Elise made a drinking motion, pretending to hold a dainty cup and lift it to her lips. Anastasia laughed, and bubbles escaped. Elise wanted to stay there with her. Drinking their tea. Just the two of them in their little private world. Mermaids. Beautiful mermaids with their seaweed hair, their slightly distorted faces.

With burning lungs, Elise mimed her tea. It might be okay to stay. Just stay.

But what about her daughter? What about David? What about the sex they'd never had? In the cemetery? They had to have sex in the cemetery.

But this was nice. Really nice. Elise was surprised, because she'd heard that drowning was unpleasant.

Once again her thoughts went back to David. How horrible that must have been for him to find his child in the bathtub. She imagined him pulling the blond-headed boy from the water, David's face ravaged with anguish. Poor David. He would never get over the loss of his son. Of that Elise was certain. But he loved Elise. He loved Audrey. She and her daughter weren't David's son, but they were important. They gave him a reason to live.

Anastasia tugged Elise's arm. She pointed up, toward the surface of the water. Elise stared and shook her head. Anastasia's gestures became more deliberate and frantic. She wanted Elise to leave. Pointing. Her mouth moving. *Go! Go, Elise!*

Would a slip-skin hag do that? Would a slip-skin hag tell Elise to leave? Would a slip-skin hag try to save someone's life? No, she would try to drown her. She would try to suck the life out of Elise and take over her body.

Elise brought her unhampered foot under her, bent her leg, and gave herself a terrific push. She shot upward, traveling through the water like a bullet. Her head broke the surface and she gasped for air, arms flailing, her clothing tangled about her, the cast, filled with water, pulling her down again.

She fought the weight of everything. Of the cast and her clothes and the drugs singing in her veins.

With strong strokes, she made her way to the ladder. With a flailing hand, she touched cold metal, gripped it tight, and pulled herself to the edge. She waited a moment, catching her breath, arms entwined in the rungs of the ladder. Then she heard her name and looked up to see Melinda standing over her.

"Oh, my God. Elise."

Elise glanced around. "Where is she?"

Melinda's brows drew together in puzzlement. "Who?"

"Anastasia. Where's Anastasia?"

Melinda shook her head and offered a hand to help Elise up, water dripping from the young woman's black swimming suit. As if she'd just left the pool moments before Elise reached the ladder.

"Elise, my mother isn't here." Melinda sounded both hurt and confused by the question. "My mother is dead."

Elise squeezed her eyes shut and grimaced, not at Melinda's words, but at the incredible pain in her bruised ribs, shoulder, and ankle.

CHAPTER 9

Elise's smartphone buzzed, indicating a Skype call from Audrey.

She hit the "Answer" button, and her daughter appeared, with her dark curly hair, beautiful skin, and cute glasses, and immediately started telling Elise about how awesome it was in Stockholm, and how much she loved Sweden, and how glad she was that Elise had insisted she go. Then she paused and said, "Oh, my God. Are you in a hospital?"

Damn. Elise hadn't thought about the IV rack in the frame.

Shortly after her little dip last night, David showed up, concerned about how she'd sounded on the phone. By that time Elise had already changed out of her wet clothes and had shooed Melinda away, but David wouldn't rest until he'd taken her to a nearby ER. And now here she was, waiting to leave.

All was well, the ER doctor going so far as to recommend she quit using the boot cast, citing it as being too tight and a big part of her pain. He'd wrapped her ankle with an elastic bandage and told her to stay off it for several more days, then gradually start putting a little weight on it. He'd even told her she might be able to shift to a cane soon. Which meant once her car was released from the evidence lot she'd be mobile again as long as she was able to kick the pain medication.

"I had a little accident," Elise told her daughter. "And they kept me overnight for observation even though I insisted I was fine." She shot an irritated glance at David, who was hovering near the bed. She'd been discharged, and it was just a matter of waiting for the wheelchair escort to take her to David's car.

"I'm getting ready to leave the hospital now."

"I shouldn't have come to Sweden! I should be there with you!"

Maybe Elise shouldn't have insisted Audrey go on the foreign exchange, especially when she actually *wanted* to be with her mother. It hadn't always been that way, and until recently Audrey had lived with Elise's ex-husband, his wife, and their twins. But then Thomas took a job as an editor in Seattle, and at age fifteen Audrey didn't want to leave her friends in Savannah. It seemed a good time for her to move in with her mother even though Elise knew Audrey would be better off living with Thomas and Vivian, with whom she could continue to experience a normal family life.

Being a parent was so hard, Elise thought. Much harder than being a detective. Maybe she should have allowed Audrey to make a sacrifice and not go abroad for two weeks, but Elise wanted her daughter to see the world beyond Georgia.

"Would you like to open a coffee shop?" she asked.

"Whaattt?"

"A coffee shop. You and me. In Savannah."

"Mom, are you on a lot of medication?"

"Yes, but this is something I've been thinking about a lot lately."

Audrey stared at her as if she'd lost her mind. Elise looked up from her phone to see the same expression on David's face.

"We'll talk about it when you get back," Elise said. "Think about what we'd call it. Nothing like the Coffee Cup or the Beanery. Something different. Something that hasn't been used."

David's phone rang, and he answered it while Elise and Audrey wrapped up their conversation with plans to talk again soon.

They all disconnected at the same time. "A homicide," David said.

Elise dropped into detective mode and started gathering her things.

"You aren't going. And what's this about a coffee shop?"

For a moment she'd forgotten she was on leave. "I'm not staying here. I'll come along. Just not in an official capacity. And the coffee shop. Why does everybody think that seems so strange?"

"For one thing, I can't imagine you making lattes all day. I can't imagine you waiting on people. Ringing up drinks. Cleaning. *Smiling.*" He was getting too enthused with his list, wrapping up for the big one: "I can't imagine you being nice for hours at a time."

"Well I can," she argued. "I can be nice."

"And why am I just hearing about this coffee thing now?"

"Will you miss me?"

"You know I will." But she could see his mind falter. He was thinking about the coffee shop, wondering if the idea wasn't so irrational. Wondering if he was being selfish to hope she wouldn't leave the department. Wondering if she might be better off away from death and murder. Because really, who wouldn't?

"Let's go. I don't need a wheelchair." She was standing on her good foot, trying to act as if nothing hurt when everything hurt; the coffee shop was something she would think about later, dream about later. "Coming with you today will be a chance for me to get back into some action without people worrying and watching me."

"*That* I get."

Nothing worse than the whole department waiting to see if you could handle a homicide after being through what she'd been through. And it wasn't as if she hadn't wondered about it herself.

Could she handle it? Dropping in without being scrutinized would get her past that tough first day.

"Back in a sec," David said. Tired of waiting for a hospital escort, he commandeered a wheelchair from somewhere, and within minutes of the phone call from Savannah PD, Elise and David were in his car.

"Tell me again how you ended up falling in the pool," David said as he maneuvered the black Honda out of the hospital parking lot and aimed it toward the bowels of the tourist district a couple of miles away. Elise sat in the passenger seat, her injured leg stretched out in front of her.

"I was walking. And the pool was there."

He shot her a look, then turned his attention back to the street. "This is exactly what I was talking about the other day. I don't get how I've been labeled the smart-ass of the team when you clearly out-smart-ass me."

"Oh, come on. You're better at it. So much better. If they gave out awards, you'd win every year."

"The pool," he reminded her.

"I slipped," Elise said, resigned to telling the story. "I hit a patch of wet tile with my cast and I just slipped." She didn't tell him about thinking she saw Anastasia. She didn't tell him about having a tea party in the deep end of the pool. She didn't mention Anastasia at all. "I'll admit you were right about the drugs. I don't handle them well." It had to have been the drugs.

"You're coming to my place."

She wanted to get back to the plantation. "Let's talk about that later." She couldn't quit thinking about going back there. To find out if the black swimsuit had been returned to the chair. To see if there was any sign that Melinda had been there again.

Melinda.

She was trying to scare Elise away. That was obvious. Why? Because she had something to hide. But now that Elise recognized her tactic, she could approach the situation with a level head. Now that she knew it was a trick to drive her off. How childish.

Who'd been excluded from Anastasia's will wasn't any of Elise's business or concern, but that didn't keep her from wanting to get to the bottom of things, especially now, when Melinda seemed to be going to the extreme to keep her away. Elise wasn't the type to be chased off, simple as that.

CHAPTER 10

Fifteen minutes later, Elise and David pulled up not far from the statue of the Waving Girl on Savannah's River Street. River Street was a heavy tourist area, with shops and taverns in part of what had once been the Savannah Cotton Exchange, and a riverfront with hotels that overlooked cobblestone alleys, cable cars, and cargo ships. The Waving Girl was a Savannah icon, a tribute to Florence Martus, a woman who'd taken it upon herself to welcome every ship that entered the Port of Savannah. It was said that in over forty years she never failed to greet a ship, day or night. That kind of singular dedication confounded Elise, while at the same time filling her with a sense of admiration.

Not far from the statue, police cars were parked at odd angles, lights flashing and sirens letting out a few squawks. Detectives Mason and Avery were already there. It was hard to miss Avery's red hair, and Elise realized she'd started looking for it in situations like this where there were mobs of people in dark clothes.

Mason and Avery had worked together for years, but lately Elise detected a weakening in their partnership. Mason had always been the leader, but over time Avery seemed to have gained confidence and maybe that threatened Mason. Not making things any easier, Mason had recently gone through a divorce, and Elise knew it was hard to leave that kind of pain at home.

Upon seeing Elise, the men glanced at each other. Nervous.

"What?" she asked. "I'm just here as an observer. Not on the clock."

"What do we have?" David asked.

Avery spoke first. "Maybe you should just go look." He glanced at Elise. "And maybe you should just stay here, Detective."

She wouldn't have them coddling her. She'd seen a lot of dead bodies in her life. A lot of homicides in her life. Not that she was immune to death, but she could handle it. Like she'd always handled it.

Avery caught David's eye, then gave him an almost imperceptible shake of his head. Elise could almost hear the silent dialogue. *Don't let her go. She's not ready for this.*

Without a word, she pushed past them, moving fast on her crutches until she reached the area where the crime-scene team was snapping photographs and collecting evidence.

David followed to stand with hands jammed in the pockets of his black knee-length coat. "Water seems to be a recurring theme in our lives," he noted in a deadpan voice.

"It's pretty common knowledge that water is good at erasing evidence," Elise said. "Even the idiots seem to have figured that one out."

Avery joined them, catching the tail end of the conversation. "This one was too stupid to take into account the tide. Looks as if the body was dumped over there"—he pointed across the harbor—"near the hotel, probably in a nice hidden cove, but the current carried it right here, to one of the most popular tourist spots on the waterfront." He laughed, then, remembering the bystanders, bent his head to hide his face.

"Stupid criminals are my favorite kind," David said.

"They make it easy," Avery agreed. He looked at Elise. "Aren't you still on medical leave?" He was working at his normal nonchalance, but during Elise's hospital stay he'd called her several times, and he'd even stopped by with flowers.

"I'm just kind of tagging along," Elise said.

"Well, we miss you." The words came grudgingly.

"So what do we have?" David asked.

"I just got here, but I'm guessing drug deal gone bad. Victim is a white male, sixteen years of age. Somebody in the wrong place, wrong time."

"ID?" David asked.

"Ran it. No previous arrests. Name is Edwin Kingfield."

"Of Kingfield Yachts?"

Avery shrugged. "Maybe."

"They're one of the wealthiest families in town," Elise said, searching her smartphone for more information.

"Slumming?" David asked.

"Thought I'd heard that name before." Elise scrolled down a page on her phone. "He's a local football hero. Was being wined and dined by some of the biggest franchises even though he still had two years of high school left."

"So maybe it was robbery, not drugs," Mason said, joining the group.

"I don't know," Elise said. "Some of these rich kids are getting deep into meth and coke."

John Casper, everybody's favorite medical examiner, straightened away from the body and motioned for them to step closer.

"You'll want to see this," he said. "At first we figured fish had gotten to him, but upon closer inspection—" He pointed, and all three of them pulled in a sharp breath.

"Damn," David muttered, while Elise thought the same thing.

In the center of the victim's chest was nothing but a gaping hole. It almost looked as if someone had reached into the chest cavity and ripped out the heart.

A familiar MO.

"We called the hospital right away," Avery said. "Just to be sure Tremain was still there. Just to be sure he was still in a coma."

"And?" David asked in a voice that didn't hide the stress they were all feeling.

"Vegging like a good vegetable. And anyway, this isn't quite the same MO. Similar, but not exactly."

"I'm thinking copycat," Mason said.

"Maybe." David continued to stare at the gaping hole. "Maybe not."

Looks were exchanged.

Everyone, from the FBI to the Georgia Bureau of Investigation, had agreed with the theory that the Organ Thief murders had been committed by Atticus Tremain in order to get Elise's attention. What do you give a homicide detective? Not flowers and candy, but dead bodies. And with those dead bodies, the trap had been set. But the evidence against Tremain for the murders hadn't been overwhelming, and most was circumstantial.

"What do you mean, maybe not?" Avery asked.

"Maybe we were wrong about Tremain," Elise said, taking up where David had left off. "Maybe Tremain was never the person removing body parts. Maybe Tremain never killed anybody. Maybe the kidnapping and the Organ Thief murders aren't connected in any way."

"Shit," Mason said with a drawl so heavy it came out more like *shee-it.*

Elise followed the direction of his glare to see a familiar white van with the local news logo on the side and a broadcast dish on the roof.

"The media is going to spin the hell out of this," David said under his breath. "And make a victim out of Tremain."

CHAPTER 11

"H ome sweet home," David said with fresh disapproval as he deposited a pizza box and Elise's black messenger bag on the kitchen table. They were back at the plantation, and dusk was coming on. All Elise wanted to do was go to bed. Instead, she crutched her way to the couch and lay down, all the while trying to move like someone who wasn't in extreme pain.

David picked up a pillow and tucked it behind her head. They'd already had another tedious argument about her staying at the plantation, and Elise convinced him that she had no plans to stroll around the pool again. But she did have other plans.

"I want to go to his house," Elise said, looking up at him.

"Whose house?" David's hands stopped fluffing another pillow, and his breath caught as he waited for her reply.

"You know who." Tremain's.

"Elise . . ."

"Is it still a crime scene?"

"I don't know. I doubt it."

"Find out."

David carefully lifted her leg and slid the pillow under her ankle. "This is a bad idea."

Elise started thinking maybe she could get used to being waited on by the one guy she spent her days bickering with. There was something extremely satisfying about it.

"What if you missed something?" Her ankle was killing her, but the soft pillow helped.

"I'll give it another pass. Just me."

"I'm coming too."

"Not with me you aren't."

"Then by myself."

"How?"

"I'll break in if I have to."

He knew she wasn't exaggerating. She'd do it. With or without his help. With his help, he could get a key. Get permission. Without his help, she could end up getting arrested and lose her job.

"I won't fall apart," she promised.

"Never said you would."

"But you're thinking it. Right? You're thinking it."

"You don't have to be tough. You don't have to always be strong."

She was thinking of a time long before they'd known each other when David hadn't been so strong. When he'd shattered. Yes, they couldn't always be strong.

"Clues," she said. "That's all I'm after. I'm not going back there to relive anything. I don't care about that. I'm past that," she lied. "I'm a detective looking for information. That's all. And I'm going to investigate with or without your help."

"I can't win here, can I?"

"No."

"You're in pain."

"I was trying to hide it, and I thought I was doing a pretty good job."

"The casual observer wouldn't have noticed."

He handed her a pill and a glass of water.

She didn't argue. She already knew pain interfered with healing, and she needed to heal.

While they ate the pizza they'd picked up from Vinnie Van Go-Go's, they discussed the newest murder. And Elise voiced her biggest concern, one she'd originally thought to keep to herself: "Maybe Tremain wasn't working alone."

David looked up from his seat on the other side of the wide coffee table, pizza forgotten.

"Which is why I want to visit Tremain's house," Elise said. "I doubt people were combing it very thoroughly back when we all thought the case was closed and Tremain wouldn't live."

"The Kingfield murder doesn't really fit Tremain's MO." David got to his feet and began cleaning up. With a gesture, he asked if she was done with her plate. She nodded, and he carried it to the sink and began running water. Earlier, he'd kicked off his shoes, untucked his white dress shirt, and rolled up his sleeves a few turns.

"There are a couple of tangelos in the refrigerator," Elise told him.

He looked and shook his head. "No tangelos."

"Yes, there are."

"No, there aren't." He shut the refrigerator door. "Tremain's a loner through and through," he said, getting back to the conversation.

"It's just weird." A lot of weird things going on lately.

David turned around, crossed his arms, and leaned against the counter. "My gut tells me there's no connection."

At one time, David had been one of the FBI's most promising profilers. Elise trusted his instinct and felt reassured by his take on the recent homicide. But she still wanted to go to Tremain's house.

CHAPTER 12

Using a crowbar, David pried the plywood from the front door while Elise stood watching, crutches under her arms. In the house next door, a curtain moved as a curious neighbor watched from the safety of her own home. How odd it must have been to find cops and detectives swarming the lot next to yours. Would you ever feel safe again? Would you ever look at your neighbors in the same way? Would each and every one be suspect?

It had happened to Elise. When you dealt with bad people all day long, pretty soon everybody was painted in dark colors. The world was painted in dark colors.

But today . . . today was lovely. It was another surprisingly cool day for November, and they were both dressed for the weather: David in his black coat, Elise in a pale vintage jacket with giant buttons she'd found in Anastasia's closet.

A breeze was blowing off a nearby marsh, and birds called overhead. The sky was so blue it hurt her heart, and the occasional cloud almost needed a happy face. The day was that perfect. All a stark contrast to what they would find once they entered the building.

David hefted the sheet of plywood aside and pulled a key from his pocket.

The house was one of those places you pass and wonder if anybody could possibly live there. An overgrown yard. Trash caught in dying shrubs, a tarp over one side of the building, a collapsing fence, and vines growing from wood so rotten water would seep out if you gave it a squeeze. It was a place you could smell from the street. Not a real smell, but an imagined one of rotten food and feral cats.

David shouldered open the door. Even though it was sunny outside, a black rectangle waited to swallow them.

Over the years, Elise had learned to shut off the emotional part of her brain when dealing with crime scenes. That skill was so second nature to her that she found herself looking at the house with the eyes of someone who'd never been there before.

David flicked the light switch. "No power." He pulled out a flashlight and moved inside. Elise followed, the act of stepping over the threshold bringing back the minutes that led up to her capture.

He'd trapped her. Atticus Tremain, the man who was now in a coma at Memorial Hospital, had lured her to his home and trapped her. So easily. Using Audrey as bait. Elise had gotten a call at work from Tremain, who'd posed as a parent. He'd told Elise that Audrey was at his house, and that she and his daughter had skipped school.

Elise drove there. She got in her car and drove there. To the address he'd given her. She'd marched up to the house, and she'd knocked on the door.

There was no Audrey. Audrey was safe at school, but Elise hadn't known that. Immediately assessing the situation, she'd realized something was very wrong.

"Watch your step." David panned the broad beam of light across the dirty vinyl floor. Nicotine-stained curtains hung over the windows above a sink stacked high with dirty dishes. Trash everywhere. Twisted clothes mixed with fast-food containers. She could smell mice and rats.

"I have to say, this doesn't look like the kind of place you'd walk into with no backup," David said.

"He said he had Audrey," Elise said. "The cop in me vanished. I was a mom trying to save her daughter, and yet I still can't believe I fell for it."

"It's different when it's our kids," David said. "It's easy to fall."

Using the tip of a crutch while trying to remain detached, she pushed a pile of trash aside. "I feel bad that I was so quick to believe she'd ditched school in the first place."

"Oh, come on. We both know Audrey. I love that kid, but I'm sure she's ditched school more than once."

Elise laughed. She couldn't believe she laughed. In this place. The sound was so strange, as if nobody had ever laughed here. But David was right about Audrey. She was a handful.

In the living room, the very blandness told a story, the space devoid of personality unless you considered the conditions a personality. The furniture matched. Dirty, stained, but it matched. Most likely purchased at one of those shops where a whole ugly room could be delivered.

She knew the specs on Tremain. Quiet. Kept to himself. Seemed nice, but when pressured neighbors finally admitted that he'd always given them the creeps. But Elise knew people were prone to those kinds of comments after a kidnapping. After someone did something horrific. In retrospect, every criminal was an oddity once people understood that the guy they said hi to on a daily basis was some murdering psychopath.

"Wanna talk about it?" David asked.

She remembered little of those last hours at Tremain's house. Maybe because she'd lost so much blood, maybe because she'd simply blocked it out. But she remembered David. Running his fingers down her face. Covering her, wrapping a blanket around her. Telling her everything would be okay. That she would be okay.

She'd asked him about Audrey, and he'd said she was fine. And she may have apologized for being so stupid, for walking into a trap. And he may have shushed her, telling her it was okay.

"Is he dead?"

That had been her next question.

And she remembered the hesitation in David's eyes. And his reluctant reply. "No."

She'd let out a sob because she couldn't stand the thought of that monster being alive. But if he ever came out of the coma, he'd go to trial. He'd go to prison. He might be put to death. Thank you, Georgia.

"You think that's why I wanted to come here?" Elise asked. "To talk about it?"

"The thought crossed my mind."

They moved down the hall. "You don't know how many times I've imagined visiting him in the hospital and finishing him off," she said, trying to keep her mind from returning to the days she'd spent here. She could allow herself to recall before and after, but not during. Not yet. "But then I think about Audrey. I think about going to prison for murdering him. He'd win if I did that."

David paused and turned to her. "I actually went to the hospital. I was going to remove his oxygen and smother the bastard."

"But you didn't."

"No. I didn't." There was regret and frustration in his voice.

The David she'd first met would have killed him. He was learning. He was practicing self-control.

"Once he had me . . . I didn't know," Elise said, getting back to the surface facts of being captured by Tremain. "I didn't actually know if Audrey was still alive. That's all I could think about. What he did to me didn't matter." She swung around. "Don't tell Audrey. I don't want her to know I came here looking for her."

"For what it's worth, I probably would have done the same thing. I would have lost my head. But you should have called me. Why didn't you call me?"

He was hurt. They were partners. Friends. And she really couldn't say why she hadn't called him. "I don't know. Maybe I was afraid that you'd be the voice of reason."

"That doesn't happen very often. Me and the voice of reason." He perused the room. "God, this place is a hole." And she suddenly had the idea that it was just as hard for him to be there as it was for her. "Sorry," he said, his voice catching. "I'm sorry you had to go through this."

"I'm alive."

He stood up straighter, and pulled in a deep breath. "Yeah."

They reached the bedroom, the lair, the place where Tremain had spent a lot of his time. Bookshelves lined one wall, and Elise leaned her crutches against a shelf and began pulling out hardcovers one at a time, turning pages, because books were a popular hiding place.

"You aren't the only one who thinks about quitting," David said, hands on his hips, coat hanging open as he stared at the disgusting mattress with no sheets. A double bed, two flat pillows, a nasty, stained blanket. "Sometimes I think about moving to one of those islands where you can live really cheaply. You know the ones I'm talking about? Just move there and lounge around in a hammock all day. Never wear shoes. Walk along the beach. Watch the sun come up and watch the sun go down."

"That sounds nice." She replaced a book and pulled out another. Tremain read a lot of philosophy. And a lot of self-help books. But there were also books about root doctors. Her hand paused, then she pulled out a familiar one, written about her father. "You'd get bored though. Don't you think?"

"I don't know. Maybe. Depends."

She glanced over her shoulder to see him lifting one of the pillows with two fingers before tossing it aside. "Depends on what?"

"Who was with me."

"You wouldn't be alone? I always imagine myself alone on that beach."

"Sometimes I'm alone, but not always."

She felt a little twinge of jealousy even though she knew she had no claim on him. But thinking of him with someone . . . It was something she wasn't really prepared for.

Turning the pages of the book, she said, "If I talked to anybody, it would be you." She'd seen the paperback before. She even owned a copy, although she kept it hidden in a drawer.

"I saw your report," David said. "It pretty much glosses over the three days you were here. I understand not wanting people to know. Particularly not wanting people in the department to know. But if you ever *do* want to talk about it . . ."

If he only knew how many times she'd thought about telling him what had happened, and how many times she'd thought about how she never, ever, ever wanted him to know. Or anybody to know. That was the only way she could get past it. If she told him, if he knew, then she'd see her humiliation reflected back at her every time she looked at him. If no one knew, she could push it away, cover it up.

Sometimes in her life, in dealing with her parents or other people who were simply acting in ways they shouldn't, she would briefly consider pretending. Pretending they were a normal family. And pretending that her father had been a good father, and her mother had been a good mother. And she would briefly put that pretending into motion, as if by the very pretense the pretending would eat into her life and suddenly the pretending would become real. It was the same self-delusion killers sometimes used. Where they twisted the plot in their heads, where they became the heroes of their own stories. Because the bad people were almost always the heroes of their own stories. How could it be otherwise? Most bad people didn't think of themselves as bad, no matter what Strata Luna said. *Evil doesn't need a reason to exist.*

That was true, but evil didn't recognize evil. Killers normally killed for two reasons. One was for personal gain, the other was for pleasure or fantasy. And sometimes those two things combined. When that happened, the killer became harder to predict. A n d the pretense? Did the whole world pretend? Did that make up most relationships, whether family or lovers? How much of it was people simply going through perceptions of what life should be like? And when those societal impressions were dropped? What was left? Killers? Murderers? Where was the line? And how real was that line? That artificial line? Fabricated morals?

There were days when her brain took this weird turn, and for a brief second the criminals made sense. *They made sense.* Like when you stare at the grass and suddenly you see this whole world down there that you couldn't see before. Houses and streets and families. If you made your eyes go funny, if you could somehow lift the veil, then this other code would make sense. And that scared her. What separated her from them? Just some synapses firing a certain way?

"Did he ever talk to you about root work?" David asked. "I mean, considering your background . . ."

"He asked me about my dad." She held up the book so he could see the cover. "This book is about him, about Jackson Sweet."

"That's an interesting bit of information." What he didn't add was that it was something she should have mentioned earlier.

"Anything specific you can recall?"

She didn't want to think about it. She wanted to look at this from the outside, not the inside. She wanted to look at it from the perspective of a detective, not a victim. But over the years she'd come to realize that putting yourself into the mind of the victim was often the way to figure out the criminal. The victim was often the secret. But even though she understood the process, she didn't want to go there.

"He . . . he wanted me to tell him about Sweet." She forced herself back to the place she didn't want to go. Back to that day, that moment, that conversation. But not beyond. She would isolate that one thing. It was enough; it was all she could handle for now. "He wanted to know what it felt like to be the daughter of a conjurer."

"What did you tell him?"

She thought about it a moment, trying to remember. "At first I told him I didn't know. That made him mad." And then he'd hit her. He'd done things to her.

She stared at David. At his hair. All soft and clean. She could feel it and smell it even though she wasn't touching him. "I told him what he wanted to hear. It was all a lie, but I told him."

"That's often the best thing to do in a hostage situation," David said. "We kept thinking he was obsessed with you, the cop. All the newspaper clippings, the news footage, the secret photos. But I don't think it had anything to do with Elise, the cop, Elise, the detective. I think it was all about Elise, the conjurer's daughter."

Now that she was looking at Tremain's books, and now that she'd found the one about her father, she had to agree.

Would she ever leave her past behind? Would it always haunt her? Here she'd taken up the most practical, the most pragmatic of occupations, yet the past wouldn't let her go. It seemed impossible to hate a person she'd never met, but she often found herself hating her father. It was bad enough to be abandoned by him, but the legacy he'd left . . . It had made her the target of many jokes, and her adoptive mother had turned against her because of it. And now . . . If what David was theorizing was right, then her legacy had drawn a madman to her. And she'd done nothing. Absolutely nothing in her life to earn such negative attention other than deny, deny, deny root magic and conjuring.

"I thought he was obsessed with me because we were closing in on the Organ Thief murders." That's what they'd all thought. But no . . .

Many times she'd fantasized about moving to another part of the country where nobody knew her history. Take up a new name. Create a new identity, an identity that had nothing to do with Jackson Sweet, the man who seemed forever tied to her.

But what about David?

He'd have a new partner. Or maybe he'd just work alone, with the help of Mason and Avery.

"I don't want to be thought of as a conjurer's daughter. It has absolutely nothing to do with me. Nothing to do with who I am." She could feel her mind shift from where it had been ever since her kidnapping, to this. And this was anger.

Over the years, she'd felt a slow-boiling anger directed at her father, an anger she felt was somewhat unjustified. Recently she'd begun to accept what he'd done, and had begun to come to terms with her heritage. But apparently she was fooling herself, because now, realizing that the kidnapping might have been due to her connection to Jackson Sweet, the man who'd abandoned her, the man who'd never seen her or called her or said one word to her . . . now she was once again filled with resentment and rage.

She was an adult. She had a teenage daughter. How could she still harbor these feelings toward a man she'd never known? A man who wasn't even alive any longer? And maybe that was part of the problem. He'd died. He'd slipped away before she could confront him. For years she'd imagined their encounter. She'd imagined finally meeting him face-to-face. And sometimes those meetings were tender. In those imaginings, her father had apologized. He'd explained the why of his actions, and he'd told her that he'd been young and foolish, and that he regretted the years he'd wasted not knowing her. And in other imaginings, she'd told him coldly and firmly that he was nothing to her. That he didn't deserve to speak to her, and he didn't deserve to meet his granddaughter.

Closure.

His death had robbed her of the closure she dreamed of having, no matter how positive or negative. Now there was nothing but the legacy he'd left, a sort of branding, a claim he had no right to claim. A claim she could do nothing about. It was almost as if her father had reached beyond the grave to stamp her as his own.

"Tremain was a clown," Elise said. "Just a clown." A clown who'd tricked her. A clown who'd tortured her, but in giving him a foolish identity, she was able to see him for what he was. A weakling. A psycho, who no longer had any power over her.

"I've always hated clowns," David said.

"Me too."

And maybe somewhere in her head her hatred of clowns got mixed up with her newly minted hatred of Jackson Sweet. Maybe somewhere in there she was able to make her father completely evil and completely bad, because that's what she needed to do.

Before coming here today she'd felt herself succumbing to fear and paranoia. She'd felt the strong Elise receding into the background, to be replaced by someone she didn't want to be. But sometimes the monster in the closet was really just a worthless clown in a coma.

"I don't think we're going to find anything," David said. He'd only come to humor her anyway, which was nice of him. "We went over it pretty thoroughly."

"Did you look through every copy on the shelf?"

"Um, no."

"Okay then." She turned her back and pulled out another book, this one appearing to be homemade, with a leather cover.

She opened the book, and grew silent. Then, slowly and carefully, she turned one page after the other.

"Find something?" David asked. She hadn't made a sound, but he must have picked up on her stillness.

"Yes." She turned another page, and another. Illustrations. In ink. Ornate drawings. Some beautiful, some not so beautiful.

David came closer, looking over her shoulder. So close she could feel the heat from his body. "These are amazing," she whispered, unable to take her eyes from the artwork in her hands.

"What is it?" he asked. "Some kind of sketchbook?"

"You could say that." She opened the book to one particularly lovely page. A drawing of an angel. She turned it around so David could see. He frowned, still unsure of what he was looking at.

"Remember the victims with the squares on their arms and back? Skin that had been removed? I think we've found another piece that will help convict Tremain if he ever wakes up. This book."

"Drawings? How will drawings help?"

"Not just drawings. A book of skin."

David stared. And when he finally comprehended, he said, "My God."

"He removed the tattoos from his victims. He cut them off and put them in this book."

David did a bit of a double take. They'd both seen a lot, but this was something new. "We need to get this tagged as evidence."

"And we—you—need to see if the victims' family members can ID any of these tattoos." She was betting on several matches.

David pulled out his cell phone. "I'm calling the ME." When John Casper answered, David asked if the newest victim had any patches of skin removed. Then he asked if the victim had any tattoos. He pocketed his phone and said, "Recent victim has tattoos, all still intact."

Which meant the newest murder was most likely a copycat, and copycat killers were usually easier to catch.

"I still don't get the book of skin," David said.

Elise thought about Tremain's obsessions. Her father, for one. Root work, for another. And Elise. She couldn't deny that she was one of Tremain's obsessions. And if not for that obsession, she'd be dead. Unlike his other victims, he'd been unable to kill her. But Tremain had another obsession. "He loves tattoos," she said. She knew that very well.

CHAPTER 13

You aren't endearing yourself to me by coming here and demanding to return to work."

"Sorry," Elise said, sitting across from Major Coretta Hoffman's desk in an office located on the third floor of the Savannah PD. "But I feel strongly about this, and I think I can bring something to the mix that others can't."

"No doubt. But you could also bring too much emotional instability. And between you and Gould . . ." She shook her head. "He's still on probation, isn't he?"

David had a bad habit of breaking the rules. "It ended a month ago."

Major Hoffman leaned forward, elbows on her desk, putting on her friend face. She had gorgeous dark skin, and Elise had often wondered about her heritage. Gullah?

She always wore the same red nail polish and the same perfume. If Elise were more of a girly girl, she'd probably know the name of the scent. Something flowery.

"Elise, are you ready to come back?"

Being careful not to annoy the major further, Elise said, "I couldn't be more ready."

"You'll need to see Dr. Kicklighter. She'll have to sign off on you before I can release your gun."

Elise wanted to make sure Major Hoffman understood her motivation for returning early. "I want in on the Tremain case as well and the Organ Thief case. I don't want to come back to find myself on desk duty. Plus, I should point out that I found important evidence at the Tremain house that everybody else overlooked. Evidence that links Tremain to the Organ Thief murders."

"A house you weren't supposed to even be at. You're pushing me. Don't push me. On top of that, I don't know what to do about my detectives. The position of head detective has been vacant for almost two years. Why? Because I have nobody to put there." She produced a bag of trail mix from a drawer, opened it, and offered the bag to Elise.

"No thanks."

"Then really," Major Hoffman continued, pouring trail mix into her palm, "it's basically you or Gould, and neither of you seem ready. Before all of this Tremain stuff, I'd pretty much decided to offer it to you, but now is certainly not the time. And Gould. How can I even consider him? With his background? His unpredictability? An ex-wife on death row? And Detectives Avery and Mason are out of the question, plus I doubt either of them would want it. They're clock-punchers. That leaves me to bring in someone from the outside, not anything I relish doing right now. So I'll let it ride. Another few weeks, but then I have to make a decision." She picked at the nuts and fruit in her hand, popping one at a time into her mouth. "Go ahead. Go talk to Dr. Kicklighter and we'll take it from there. I'm not promising you anything until I see a thorough psych evaluation. Until she tells me you're ready to be put back on the case."

"Thank you." Elise would make sure she was the sanest person in the room for that interview.

David was waiting for her in the hallway. "What'd she say?" he asked, keeping his arms crossed as he shouldered himself away from the wall.

"Have to see the shrink."

"Welcome to my world."

In fewer than twenty-four hours, Elise sat in Dr. Kicklighter's office. Dr. Kicklighter had been with the department for a few years, but Elise hadn't had any reason to visit her until now. David, on the other hand, was a regular. Mondays 4:00 to 5:00 p.m. He never talked about the sessions and Elise didn't pry, but she'd always imagined David lying on a couch, feet crossed at the ankles, just blabbing about whatever he wanted. But it wasn't like that. Dr. Kicklighter asked the questions. Very direct questions.

The doctor was one of those tall, gorgeous blonds who'd probably grown up in a wealthy, gated suburb. Georgia was full of women who looked like her. Elise had nothing against her type, but she knew it might take her longer to warm up to her. Unfair, but the truth.

There was no couch.

Elise was disappointed by that, but did anybody really lie down?

Dr. Kicklighter sat on the other side of a massive mahogany desk, an open file in front of her. "I want you to know that everything we talk about in this room is strictly confidential. No one inside or outside the department will hear what you decide to share. I'll file a report, but it will just contain my evaluation with no direct reason for that evaluation."

"I'm not really concerned about that."

"Just so you know."

Dr. Kicklighter's scallop-edged suit was red; her lips were red; her fingernails were red. Did she and Major Hoffman use the same nail color? It almost looked the same. Elise imagined the two of them having a girls' night and sharing polish.

"I was looking at the report that was filed about your capture." She turned pages, going back and forth. "It's kind of vague." Their initial conversation about the event had taken place in Elise's hospital room, and the doctor had gone easy on her due to Elise's injuries. But now that Elise was hoping to be reinstated, Kicklighter seemed prepared to get tough.

"There wasn't a lot to say."

The doctor moved papers around again, then looked at Elise. The desk between them was big enough to tap-dance on. Had David ever thought about that? She'd have to ask him.

"There's a lot of speculation within the department. About what happened there. And we know that he killed his previous victims immediately."

"If the killer is indeed Tremain," Elise reminded her.

"Yes. But anyway, three days. There's really nothing here about those three days." She closed the file and clasped her hands together. "Like I said, nothing leaves this room."

"There isn't much to say. He kept me tied up. He loosened my restraints, and I was able to break free and knock him out. That's it."

"Were most of your injuries sustained that last day? When you took him down?"

"Not all."

"How was he able to overpower you initially?"

"Taser."

Was she looking a little impatient? "Think of this as a conversation," Kicklighter said. "Your very reluctance to participate is indicative of a problem."

Elise had stepped into the office with the intention of coming across as friendly and levelheaded. Where had that plan gone?

Instead, she was struggling to keep her cool while remaining evasive. "No problem."

"What happened those three days? How did you keep from being killed?"

"I'm used to dealing with criminals. I know how they think, which means I know how to talk them out of things. Things like killing me."

"I'm sure you're very good at your job. And your knowledge of the criminal mind probably did save your life."

"Thanks."

"But you were there three days. Did you fear for your life that entire time?"

She wouldn't let go of the three days. "Yes."

Kicklighter nodded. "Did you ever have to compromise who you were, your core values, in order to stay alive?"

"Do you mean did I have to do things to him, with him, to stay alive?"

"That's exactly what I mean."

"Let's just say he did things to me, but I never reciprocated."

"Like what?"

"I don't feel the need to share that with you." This had turned into an interrogation. Elise wanted to get up and walk out, but she managed to restrain herself.

Kicklighter gave her a long, thoughtful stare that was probably meant to intimidate. "Let me ask you this. Do you worry about Atticus Tremain waking up?"

"No." Elise leaned back in her chair and returned Kicklighter's stare. "I'd like for that to happen."

Dr. Kicklighter jotted something down.

"You know what else?" Elise said. "It doesn't matter how I feel about this. It doesn't matter what Tremain did to me or didn't do to me. None of that matters. What matters is that I get put back on the case. The reason? Because I'm the best chance the city has of catching the killer. That's all there is to it."

"That's not my job. I'm here to evaluate your mental state."

"Do you have any kids, Dr. Kicklighter?"

"Two daughters."

Elise felt a little guilty turning the tables on the doctor, but there was too much at stake here for her to sit back and take this nonsense. She didn't like getting tough with a fellow PD employee, but she could do it if she had to.

"Wouldn't you sleep better at night knowing the person or persons trolling our fair city for seemingly random victims, removing their organs, dumping their bodies in public and private places . . . Wouldn't you sleep better knowing those people were behind bars and off the streets? It doesn't matter if I fall apart. It doesn't matter if I end up hiding in a closet chewing on my arm. What matters is catching this person. What matters is keeping your daughters safe, and my daughter safe."

Elise got to her feet.

"The hour isn't up."

"I've said everything I need to say. And I've told you everything you need to know about me." If they didn't put her back on the case, she'd work it on her own. Her little rant had underscored what really mattered here. Not her job. Not making head detective. Not her sanity. None of that mattered. What mattered was catching a maniac who was killing innocent people.

An hour later Elise was riding in a pedicab, heading down Abercorn toward her house to check on the progress of the construction. She'd never taken a bike taxi in her life, mainly because she felt sorry for the person pedaling. Her driver, with her beautiful lavender hair, was most likely a Savannah College of Art and Design student who couldn't have weighed a hundred pounds. Elise felt like a lazy bum even though she was still using crutches.

Her cell phone rang. Major Hoffman.

Elise hit "Answer." "Hello?"

"Congratulations," Major Hoffman said. "You've been reinstated. You can clock in starting tomorrow."

"On both cases?"

"Yes. I don't know what you said to Dr. Kicklighter, but I've never had a psych evaluation hit my inbox so fast. She gave you high marks in all areas."

Elise thanked her and disconnected, then she called David. "I'm back," she told him as soon as he picked up.

"What?" She heard the disbelief in his voice. "I've been going to Kicklighter for over a year, and she still won't remove some of the red flags from my file. How the hell did you swing that? Voodoo?"

"I put together a little don't-call-me-crazy spell."

"Maybe you can work one of those for me. So when will you be back?"

"Tomorrow."

After a long pause that indicated deep thought from David's end, he said in his serious voice, "Are you sure you're ready?"

"I'm sure. Oh, and you know I was kidding about the spell, right?"

"And you know I don't believe in that stuff, right? Where are you? I hear traffic."

"I'm heading to my house in a pedicab."

"You're kidding."

"I'm not."

"I've always wanted to ride in one of those."

"You should do it. It's a little rough, but kind of pleasant."

"So really, how'd you do it? How'd you get a good review from Kicklighter?"

The pedicab stopped in front of Elise's house. "I had to play the bitch card. I feel kind of bad about that, but it had to be done."

He laughed. She told him good-bye, then got out of the cab, wedged her crutches under her arms, and paid the driver, tipping what must have been more than the usual because the girl's eyes got big and she smiled and stammered. So Elise asked her if she'd mind waiting to take her back to the police station.

"No problem."

Elise's house was a narrow yellow Victorian, three stories tall, with a courtyard and porches on all three levels. She'd purchased it years ago for not much money because it was in need of a ton of work and was located in a bad area of town. The area had improved until her house was the only one on the block that looked like hell. Her initial plan had been to restore the entire thing herself, but she'd quickly lost interest once it was obvious Audrey hadn't wanted to spend much time there. But that had changed, and now Elise was anxious to create a cozy and safe place for them both to live.

Inside, it didn't look like the construction workers were making much progress, and there were only two people on site, one being the foreman.

"The asbestos removal is done," he said, slapping his leather gloves together and wiping his forehead on his sleeve. "But the house isn't livable. No electricity, and the plumbing isn't finished. Some walls are still stripped down to the studs. You had a lot of water damage from that leaking roof, and most of the drywall in the second-floor bedroom and the kitchen had to be replaced."

She wanted to tell him that if it hadn't taken him so long to get there the water damage wouldn't have been so bad, but she kept her mouth shut. She'd probably used up her quota of blunt talk for the day. "When will it be livable? Can you give me a projected date?"

"Four weeks, maybe?"

"How about Thanksgiving? Because I'd really like to be home by Thanksgiving." Audrey would be back, and Elise wanted her daughter to have a place to come home to.

"Thanksgiving?" He looked doubtful. "We'll try."

She wanted to tell him to try harder, but she figured that would just make him mad. Maybe cause him to suddenly find himself called to another site, another job. She could be pushy if the need arose, when it meant getting information out of a criminal or a victim, but she didn't dare piss off the guys working on her house.

Her phone rang. It was a woman from the evidence lot, calling to tell Elise that her car was being released and was no longer evidence. All in all, a day of good mojo.

CHAPTER 14

I t feels good to be back," Elise said from the passenger side of the unmarked car as she and David left the police department parking lot for a day of fieldwork. It not only felt good to be back, it felt good to be independent once again. Shortly after the visit to her house, Elise had picked up her yellow Saab and driven to the plantation with only a slight amount of difficulty. A left-foot injury was better than a right. And today she'd driven to Savannah.

"Doesn't anybody ever fill up before returning the car?" David pointed to the gas gauge. "I'll bet if we check the log book we'll see this was last driven by Mason and Avery." David's relationship with the other two detectives was better than it had been a year ago, but it was still rocky.

"Stop at Parker's and I'll put it on the department card," Elise said. After all she'd been through, the thought of doing something as commonplace as pumping gas gave her a thrill. Yesterday she'd gone grocery shopping, and she'd actually enjoyed it. Her life was getting back to normal.

"I would never return a car with an empty tank, would you?" David asked.

Maybe she was trying too hard to prove she was physically on the mend, but as soon as David pulled up to the pump and cut the engine, she hobbled out and swiped the card.

Before she could grab the nozzle David was there, pumping the gas. "I mean, it's like being married to those guys," he said. "If the car isn't on empty, it smells like some nasty fast-food place. Like greasy fries."

He was wound up, like a kid on a sugar high. Sometimes she missed the David who kept himself level with prescription cocktails. What was she thinking? That wasn't true. But this rattled David was hard to deal with. He just never shut up. Exhausting. But, come to think of it . . . "Are you on something?"

He blinked as if she'd flicked water in his face, and she instantly regretted her question. "Too much caffeine," he said. "I swear to God they add a few extra shots of espresso just to mess with me. Look at my hand." He held it out so she could see how he was trembling. Not that much, but noticeable.

She was going to apologize, but he moved on. That was one of the things she liked about David. He didn't take offense easily. He just kept moving. Unlike her, he didn't stop and stare and dwell.

"Do you think of *Easy Rider* whenever you put gas in the car?" he asked as the pump stopped pumping and the nozzle clicked. "Like right now?"

"What are you talking about?"

"The opening scene where Peter Fonda is putting gas in the motorcycle tank. And then he carefully removes the nozzle and wipes a drip. I always think of that. Always."

"I think of *The Birds*. The gas station scene where the vehicles blow up."

"Oh, that's a good one."

"If Mason and Avery had left the car with a full tank we wouldn't be having this conversation," she pointed out.

"True."

Elise liked days like this, where she and David drove around the city, following one lead after another, interviewing person after person. In the past, there had always been an air of excitement to these events, an air of expectation. One clue. One small clue could crack a case wide open.

In between, they talked. Usually about the case, but not always. Because sometimes the eureka moment came when your mind was distracted, when you suddenly found yourself focusing on something else, usually something mundane. And then, out of the blue, pieces would start to fit together.

But of course now they were gathering information on Atticus Tremain. She tried to distance herself from the reality of the situation, but it was impossible. She also knew if she reacted in an unprofessional way, if she allowed her face to reflect what she was feeling, she'd get yanked from the case. Sure, David would much rather partner with her than work with Mason and Avery, but he also felt a level of responsibility. And she knew he'd been instructed to keep a close eye on her.

"What are you thinking now?" David asked, as he drove down Broughton looking for a place to park. "Still feel this is a copycat or someone who worked with Tremain?"

"I'm feeling copycat, but copycat killers are so rare. If it's someone who worked with Tremain, then he didn't learn the ropes. It's all so sloppy. And Tremain is guilty. No doubt about that," Elise said with conviction. But did it matter? The man was in a coma, and he would most likely never wake up.

She wanted him to wake up. She wanted him to stand trial. She wanted to see him get the death sentence. But if he went to trial, she'd have to take the stand. She'd have to sit in that courtroom and look at him. And she'd have to tell the jury what he'd done to her. Worse, she'd probably have to *show* the jury what he'd done to her.

David glanced at her. "You okay?"

"Are you going to ask me that every day?"

"As long as I keep seeing that haunted look on your face, yes. I'll keep asking. And you'll keep brushing me off." He backed the car into a parallel parking spot, palm to the steering wheel as he looked over his shoulder. "And you know I'm no stranger to working while falling apart."

"I'm not falling apart."

"I didn't say you were."

"You did."

"I just meant if you were I would know how you feel. That's all."

With lattes from Sentient Bean, they ate lunch in Forsyth Park, sitting on a bench under a live oak draped in Spanish moss, the clomp of carriage horses and the splash of a Parisian fountain as a sound track.

Elise had packed her own veggie sandwich made with tomatoes and avocados and sprouts, and David had picked up a slice of quiche from Parker's Market. The weather was ideal. Kind of cool, but the sun was warm, and roses were blooming.

November was one of Elise's favorite times of the year. Summer was too hot. Spring was sometimes too stormy, but November . . . yes, sometimes cold, but most of the time . . . glorious. She wasn't a sun-worshipper. She didn't go to the beach. She preferred to stay fully clothed and enjoy the feeling of the sun on her face. And really, she could never wear a swimming suit again. But right now she wanted to enjoy being back in Savannah.

Visitors often said the city was too dark. Too sad, too dirty, too secretive, too creepy, but those were all things Elise loved about it. No, it wasn't all shiny and sunny and clean and bright like Hilton Head or Charleston. Being in Savannah was like landing on some alien planet where even the residents were visitors, living on the shoulders of a dark and brutal and beautiful past. The city felt organic. That's what it was. The buildings almost felt like a part of the soil, a part of nature.

They threw away their trash, and Elise stuffed her insulated bag inside her purse. Without looking at David, she said, "We should go see him."

He shot her a glance over the rim of his coffee cup. "Who?" But she could see he knew who, and he was hoping he was wrong.

"Tremain." It wasn't a strange thing to say. It made sense. "See if anybody has tried to visit him. See if there are any changes."

"They said they'd call."

"It's good to stay on the hospital's radar." And it was good to check in and make sure everything was being done that was supposed to be done, including an armed guard. *Especially* the armed guard. "I know you don't like hospitals," she said.

"I'm getting better. I was okay the other day."

True.

So they went.

"I think you should wait in the lobby," David said once they'd parked the car and were heading up the sidewalk toward Memorial Hospital.

"Would you quit treating me like some weak victim? I'm a cop. No matter what happened, I'm a cop. Treat me like a cop. Can you do that?"

"Quit slamming the door in my face," David said.

She was surprised by the hurt in his voice, but there was no damn way she was going to let him see her bleed. She wasn't like him. And why did he insist on shining a light on her weaknesses? Uncovering them? The only way she could function was by stepping back, closing that door, forgetting about Elise the victim, and instead focusing on being Elise the detective. Couldn't he see that? She needed to keep that door closed; otherwise, she might fall apart. Otherwise, she might not be able to continue.

Maybe someday she'd be able to talk about it, but not now. Now she had to be tough. Now she had to embrace her work persona, not her personal one. If David knew her the way he thought he knew her, he'd understand that. He wouldn't keep bringing it up. The last thing she needed was group therapy and a warm hug. Hugs led to breakdowns. She didn't want his soft eyes. She didn't want his compassion. None of that helped.

"Okay," he said quietly. "But you know I'm here for you. If you ever feel like talking. Day or night." He gave her a level stare. And in that moment, she was aware of the beauty that was David Gould. Forget about the rambling man at the gas station. Forget about his previous drug issues. Forget about how he sometimes acted without thinking. She was looking at his core.

David wasn't about being a tough cop. No, he was actually the opposite of that. He'd laugh if she said it aloud, but he was more about being a sensitive cop. He was like some spiritual guide who was able to connect with crooks and victims alike. He put up no walls. None.

"I need my walls," she said. And even that admission made her feel weaker, made her feel shaky inside, and shaky outside, and she hoped he couldn't see that shakiness, that weakness. But he did. She knew he did, but at least he pretended he didn't. She needed that. She needed for him to pretend.

He pressed his lips together, and he nodded. As if he'd been there. And he had. And then he looked into her eyes, deep, deep, while they stood there on the sidewalk. While people walked past them, brushing their shoulders.

Would she live until Christmas? she wondered. What a strange thought. What an odd thought. She remembered how David had come to her house last Christmas and they'd played Frisbee in the park. He'd baked pumpkin bread, and it had been delicious. Those were the things life was made of. Not memories of torture, of humiliation.

Together, they turned and walked toward the hospital, their shadows long as the fading sun chased them inside.

Maybe it was just the idea of coming face-to-face with the man who'd held her prisoner. Maybe it was the idea of coming face-to-face with a monster. Maybe that's why her head was in such a strange place, but she had to stay strong. And she had to see Tremain. She wanted to reassure herself that he was indeed harmless.

CHAPTER 15

Not that I'm in any way trying to minimize what this guy did to you, but he's long gone," David said, standing at the foot of Tremain's bed, hands buried in the pockets of his coat. "We might as well be looking at a potato. Or a carrot."

Elise wanted to believe him, but they'd both seen bodies that had been pronounced dead come back to life. And she'd read about people waking up from comas years later. "I wish we could just—" *smother him.*

David's eyebrows lifted, and he nodded his head toward a pillow in a nearby chair, his meaning unvoiced but clear.

The cramped space was way too bright and blinding. Elise was tempted to pull out her sunglasses. "No."

"I'll do it."

"I have no doubt of that, which is what worries me."

They both fell silent, staring at the comatose man. Was he in there? Elise wondered.

Tremain was tall, probably six feet. Dark hair that would have touched his shoulders if he'd been upright. And so odd that a beard was beginning to appear. His face had been clean shaven when she'd last seen him.

Oxygen tubes in his nose, his chest rising and falling as his body took shallow breaths. IV bag on a rack, urine bag on the side of the bed. He was ten years older than Elise, but he looked at least sixty now, his skin gray and dehydrated. He *looked* like a corpse.

"I've seen a lot of dead bodies in my life," David said. "You have too. And I've seen people die. I'm always struck by the absence, the *nothing* I sense once they are truly dead."

"And you don't feel anything in this room?"

"No."

"Look at his eyes."

"That's typical of coma patients. That rapid eye movement."

"And his fingers. One of them keeps twitching."

"Touch him."

She felt herself jerk. "What?" she said in disbelief.

"Like poking at something dead to reassure yourself nobody's home. Or draw on his face with a Sharpie. I don't know."

Now that he'd brought up the touching . . . She stretched her hand toward him. In her mind, she imagined making contact, imagined his fingers wrapping around her wrist, his eyes flying open. None of that happened. There was no response as she dragged her fingers down his arm, as she touched the back of his hand. The only response was from Elise herself as she pulled in a trembling breath.

"See?" David said. "Carrot." He grabbed the clipboard from the end of the bed and read the most recent report. Words like "persistent vegetative state" and "no change" were things she liked to hear.

"Let's go." He returned the clipboard to the hook.

But Elise couldn't tear herself away. She couldn't quit staring at the comatose man in the bed. Just a body. Just casing. But he felt every bit as alive, as present, as he had the days she'd spent with him.

She could feel him all over her. Touching her with his cold, smooth hands, breathing against her naked skin, his breath hot and poisonous. She could still feel and sense his unstable mind, a mind that had quickly washed her away. She could still feel the darkness in his head, his brain, a darkness that had pulled her under, smothered her.

She'd never understood how kidnap victims were so quickly brainwashed, so quickly overpowered. She'd thought they lacked fortitude. She'd thought them weak, with some kind of deficiency. But it was easy to succumb when locked in that world of madness. No food, no sleep. Just the room and the darkness of a sick mind. *It was so easy.*

If David hadn't been in the room right now, she feared she would have put her face next to Tremain's and inhaled his toxic scent, pulling him deep into her lungs. Repulsion intermingled with something she couldn't understand. A weird and twisted kind of attraction. Fascination. Obsession. And while she was horrified by her response to seeing him again, she found herself thinking that this would make her a better cop. She now had a personal understanding of victim mentality and what might be considered an offshoot of Stockholm syndrome. Warring with that obsession was an overwhelming desire to see this person dead. To know he would never get up and walk out of this room. She wanted him to leave the hospital via the morgue. She wanted to see him lying on a slab downstairs, not in this bed. Only then would he get out of her brain.

She tried to be the logical Elise. She tried to tell herself that the ordeal had made her more emotional, more fragile. Maybe she *had* come back to work too soon. Yes, she was sure of it. But she couldn't sit around doing nothing while a killer was still out there, whether he had a connection to Tremain or not.

"How long was I gone again?" she asked in a monotone voice.

"Three days and three nights."

"That's right." How could she have forgotten? Especially with Dr. Kicklighter on her about it. "It seemed so much longer. It seemed like weeks. Months."

"But not anymore, right? When you think about it? Does it still seem like weeks or months?"

She knew he wanted her to say no even though it would be a lie. She hadn't thought about how it must have been for him, looking for her, thinking she was dead.

"How did you find me again?" She felt like a kid, needing to hear the same story over and over. *How did you rescue me again, Daddy?*

"You called me."

"Oh, that's right."

David hadn't saved her. She'd saved herself. On one rare occasion, Tremain had untied her hands, she wasn't sure why. Maybe because they were blue. With her mouth gagged, with her hands numb, she'd managed to fight him, but he stomped on her ankle and she'd collapsed. Once she was down, he kicked her in the ribs and stomach. A knife appeared, the one he'd used to cut the ropes from her wrists, and when he stabbed her she didn't feel it. She remembered that part. Knowing she'd been stabbed but unable to feel any pain.

She grabbed his boot with hands so numb they felt like stubs, and she tugged. He flew backward, his skull cracking against the floor, his body sprawled in the bedroom doorway. She struggled to her feet and slammed the door against his head. How many times, she wasn't sure.

They didn't know which blow caused the most damage, the fall or the door. Probably the door. She dragged an unconscious Tremain into the closet where he'd kept her part of the time, locking him inside. With fumbling fingers, she untied the gag. Then she found her clothes, got dressed, and called David with the cell phone Tremain had left on the dresser.

She'd saved herself. Did that bother David? That he hadn't been able to find her? That he'd searched for days, all the while knowing in that detective heart of his that she was most likely dead? But Tremain had been obsessed with Elise. He was okay torturing her, but he wasn't ready to kill her even though she sometimes wished he would.

David's voice, when he'd answered his cell, had been abrupt, distracted. Imagine his surprise to find the cause of that distraction at the other end of the line.

"It's me," she told him.

She heard him gasp. That was followed by something that sounded like a sob. "Oh, Christ," he said. "Where are you?"

She couldn't remember. She had no idea.

She found a pile of mail. She found an address. She read it to David, and then she sat down to wait while the life drained out of her. That was when she recalled a chant, a spell, and found herself whispering it to herself as she waited for her partner to arrive.

"Let's go," David now said.

His words hardly sank in; she couldn't quit staring at Tremain.

"Come on." David touched her arm, and she jerked and let out a gasp. She pulled her gaze from the comatose man, her eyes tracking across the beige blanket. And there was David's coat with the black buttons. She could just make out a slight outline of his shoulder holster and gun. And there was his white collar, and the jaw that seemed to always need a shave. A mouth that always seemed to hint at the smart-ass or self-effacing comment. The eyes, with dark lashes under sharp, dark brows. Eyes that were saying too much again. Full of worry. And more.

Maybe Tremain had cracked her wide open. Broke her shell, removed her skin, made her feel, good or bad. Cops couldn't feel. Detectives couldn't feel.

"Let's go," he whispered.

Comatose or not, the man in the bed still had power over her. There was only one way she would ever be free. "Leave me alone with him for a minute," she said.

"No." He saw right through her.

"You just threatened to do the same thing," she said.

"This is different."

"How is it different?"

"I have nothing to lose."

Her brain faltered over that. Not what she'd expected to hear. And it broke her heart a little.

"You have Audrey," he said. "You have a job you're damn good at. People need you."

She wasn't convinced that Audrey needed her. There were glimpses of a mother-daughter relationship, but Audrey's step-mother was more of a mother to Audrey. Vivian was a soccer mom. Not the psycho kind, but the levelheaded, be-there-for-you kind. Elise adored her even though she was everything Elise could never be. And Elise knew Vivian loved Audrey.

"And people don't need you?" she asked.

"Not to get all violin, but no. The world would get along fine without me."

"I'm not talking about the world." No reason to elaborate. Why were they always treading so close to relationship territory? But for him to think she would get along fine without him—she wouldn't. *She wouldn't.*

"You got along just fine before I came here, and you'd get along just fine if I left."

That wasn't true. Not at all. She had gotten along fine before, but now . . . now she'd miss him.

"Let's go," he said.

For a second she thought he was going to take her by the hand and lead her from the room. But with a jerky start that quickly smoothed, she took the steps needed to get her out of there, to get away from the monster in the bed.

Her soft Southern drawl reached deep into the black pit where he'd been hiding, dwelling. It called to him. It comforted him. And then—physical contact.

Even now, after the voice and footsteps echoed away, his arm and hand tingled where she'd touched him with her fingers. Just lightly. A caress, really. Yes. That's what it had been. A caress.

He didn't know how he'd gotten where he was. He didn't know how much time had passed. He didn't know what had happened. All he knew was he and Elise Sandburg belonged together.

CHAPTER 16

From down the hall came a muffled pounding on the plantation house door, rousing Elise from a deep sleep. She tossed back the covers and grabbed her handgun from the bedside table.

"Elise! Open up!"

David. She put the gun away and shrugged into her black hooded sweatshirt, the hem of her cotton nightgown brushing her legs as she hurried down the hallway on her crutches.

She turned the dead bolt, and David burst inside like some crazy man, slamming and securing the door behind him. His hair was wild and his eyes were wild. His coat hung open, revealing his shoulder holster hastily tossed over a white V-neck T-shirt. "Get dressed. You're getting out of here."

Was he drunk? High? She felt bad for thinking that about him whenever he was out of control, but that's where her brain went. She'd tell him she was sorry if he was able to read her mind. "David—"

He charged down the hallway to her bedroom. She followed to watch him pull out her plaid suitcase, toss it on a footstool, and begin digging through the dresser, grabbing handfuls of her clothes.

"Stop. Just stop for a minute." She had an awful thought. "Is it Audrey? Oh, my God. Is that it? Is she okay? Please tell me she's okay."

"She's fine. Audrey's fine. It's Tremain."

"Tremain?" Her heart slammed. "Did he wake up?" She didn't understand what that had to do with David's behavior.

He straightened and rubbed his head, elbows high, then dropped his arms. His breathing was coming hard and fast, as if he'd run instead of driven there. "Yeah, he woke up."

The news jarred her, but she tried to remain calm. All along she'd had the strangest feeling, regardless of what the doctors had told them about Tremain's chances of regaining consciousness. "Now he can be convicted," she said in an attempt to see the positive in this new development. *This is good,* she told herself. Her worst fear had been that he'd wake up. Now it had happened, and now she could deal with it. He could be put away. Or put to death. This was good. Right? *Good.*

"He's gone," David said.

Gone? She didn't understand. "What do you mean, gone? As in dead?"

"No, gone. As in no longer there. The night-shift nurse went to check on him, and his bed was empty."

"What about the officer on guard?"

"Let go. Shortly after we were there today." He checked his watch. "Yesterday. The newest doctor's report said they didn't expect Tremain to wake up, so the department pulled the guard. Costing the city too much money. You know how everything has been about money lately."

Her brain struggled with a number of scenarios. "Maybe he's not awake. Maybe somebody just . . . maybe somebody took him." And then she had a disconcerting thought. "It wasn't you, was it?"

"What? No. God, no. After his bed was found empty, they checked the surveillance tape. He walked out on his own. A little unsteady, according to hospital security, but he walked out."

Escape, especially from hospitals, wasn't uncommon. And Ted Bundy had escaped from prison not once, but twice.

Elise dropped into a chair. She thought about their trip to the hospital. She'd *touched* Tremain. Had he felt her? Heard her? Had her visit woken him up? "Why are you packing my things?" she asked.

"He'll be coming for you. Maybe not tonight or tomorrow, but soon. Sometime. Even if your house wasn't under repair, you couldn't stay there either. No, you're coming to my place, at least for now. Got an APB out. Somebody is bound to spot him. How far can a man go who just woke up from a coma?"

She should have been terrified, yet she was the one being logical while David was in a blind panic. "He's still in a weakened condition," she said, trying to reason with him. "He'd have to go somewhere to recover. And because of his condition, I think there's a pretty good chance he'll be caught within a few days. But regardless, the plantation is probably the safest place for me. Think about it. He would have no way of knowing I'm here. There's nothing to connect me to this place."

"Elise, can't you just humor me?"

She could see she wasn't going to win, at least not right now. "It's late," she said. "Let's get a good night's sleep so we can deal with this in the morning. If he hasn't been caught by tomorrow evening, I'll get a hotel room. How's that?" She read his face, then recanted. "I'll stay at your place."

"I'm not going anywhere," David said.

"Suit yourself. There's a guest room down the hall. The sheets might be dusty."

"I'll sleep on the couch. It's centrally located, and I'll be able to keep a better eye on things."

"I don't think there'll be anything to keep an eye on." Logically she knew she was right, yet at the same time she was glad David was staying. He was halfway down the hall when she called his name. He stopped and turned. "Thanks," she said. And she meant thanks for tearing out there in the middle of the night, and thanks for acting crazy with worry, and thanks for caring about her.

"I wasn't there for you once," he said. "That will never happen again."

The next morning Elise made her way to the kitchen/living area using the crutches while testing her ankle by putting careful weight on it. Not much pain. Maybe she could graduate to a cane.

David looked like hell.

"The sun was coming up before I finally dropped off," he said, reading her silent appraisal of his condition. David, sitting on the couch, elbows on his knees, hands dangling, one sock half off his foot; bloodshot, puffy eyes; hair sticking out in every direction, looking like he'd been on a three-day binge.

"You could have slept in the guest room."

"It had nothing to do with the couch. I kept hearing stuff. These old houses . . ."

"Like what?"

"Like scratching and creaking."

"Voices? Music?"

"If I'd heard voices and music I would have torn the place down looking for the cause. Just rodent noises. And old building noises. Wind. Tree branches. I was on hyperalert, so every sound was like a bomb."

"What do you want for breakfast?" Resting one crutch against the counter while keeping the other under her arm, she opened the refrigerator. "I still have some orange juice. Wait. Did you drink it?"

"No."

"I could have sworn this was almost full." She shook a near-empty container.

"How's this for normal?" David asked, rubbing his face with his palms and looking up at her. "You and me, waking up in the same house. You, with a pillow crease on your face. Me, needing to shave. You, asking what I want for breakfast. Me, just wanting coffee. You, blaming me for drinking the orange juice. Me, wondering if you have a spare toothbrush."

With her fingers, she examined the crease on her face. "You always need to shave. And I'll bet you did drink the orange juice."

David's phone buzzed, and he checked a text. "Major Hoffman summoning you to her office. The media is rabid, and she wants to talk to you before the press conference. Let's hit the road. We can swing by a gas station for coffee."

Wow. He woke up fast.

CHAPTER 17

I don't know how you got past Dr. Kicklighter. I don't really care at this point, but I do know you're hiding something."

Elise was back in Major Hoffman's office, sitting across the desk from her.

"I was willing to let it slide when it didn't look like Tremain was going anywhere," Hoffman said, "but now that he's on the loose I want an hour-by-hour, minute-by-minute report of the days you spent with him. Even if he made you do the most degrading and perverted sexual acts, I want it in a report. All of it. Every single thing you can remember. And yes, Gould will see it. And yes, Avery and Mason will see it."

She picked up her cell phone, looked at the screen, and put it back down. "I know how you are with witnesses and victims," she said, continuing where she'd left off. "You'd get every last ounce of information from them. I expect you to play by the same rules."

Hoffman was right. Elise would never have let herself get away with silence. David should have been the one to extract a full report from her, but he'd been hurting too, feeling guilty and responsible for not finding her.

Major Hoffman reached into a brown paper bag, pulled out a handful of boiled peanuts, dropped them on her desk, then offered the bag to Elise. Did she eat regular meals? Or just snack all day? Elise shook her head.

"Sure? These are boiled by the guy on the corner of Oglethorpe and Habersham."

"Okay." Elise took a handful and passed the bag back. Best in the city.

Hoffman cracked a shell. "I'll make sure your report never reaches the media. If the media gets hold of it, heads will roll. And two people will be my prime suspects."

"Avery and Mason?"

Hoffman nodded. "Exactly." She swept empty shells into her hand, then tossed the shells into the trash can under her desk. "But those two aren't bad guys. They like you. They respect you. I don't think you have to worry."

"I wasn't really worried about the media." Elise leaned back, elbows on the arms of her chair. "The whole thing makes me look weak. Vulnerable. A victim. I'm supposed to be the person who solves crimes, who stops crimes."

"The hero?"

"Kind of. Certainly not someone who can be tricked, who can be caught and overpowered. You and I both know that most of a cop's strength lies in the perception of that strength. Even within the department. People won't look at me the same way. And I'm pretty sure I won't be considered for that head detective position even if I wanted it."

"I suspect people will see you as more human. Because, Elise, sometimes you come across a bit chilly."

"That's just who I am."

"Is it?"

Elise stared at Hoffman with exasperation. "If it makes you feel any better, I've never been a victim before. I never knew what it felt like. Now I do."

"I don't know if that's good or bad. I'm sorry you had to go through it, and I'm sorry the perp is loose. Regardless, I want a full report on my desk in two days. I want it to cover every second you can remember, from Tremain capturing you until you were in the hospital. Don't leave anything out. You, of all people, know how often the most insignificant detail can crack a case wide open."

"You'll get your report."

"What about somewhere to stay? I know your home is being worked on. I'm sorry that we can't put a cop on you."

"Budget, I know." And she didn't want anybody watching her every move. "I'll find a secure place."

"What about your daughter?"

"She's out of the country right now. Foreign exchange trip."

"That's one less thing to worry about."

"I'm staying at Detective Gould's tonight, but after that . . . I don't know."

"Maybe you should stay there the whole time. Until this is over. Until we have Tremain. But I'll understand if you don't. Gould, twenty-four hours a day." She made a face and Elise let out a nervous laugh at the major's inappropriate comment.

"Gould's a good partner," Elise said.

"He's easy on the eyes, that's for sure. He doesn't seem to have any interest in any of the women in the PD. A couple of them have asked him out and he's turned them down," she said a little too nonchalantly. "Is he in a relationship?"

"I don't think so . . ."

Hoffman smiled.

Oh, this could get awkward. Elise was pretty sure the major was divorced and single.

CHAPTER 18

The elevator in Mary of the Angels was unreliable and slow and rarely used by anyone sane, but due to Elise's condition she and David slipped inside the tight space. He closed the metal accordion gate and pushed a freakishly large red button. A couple of seconds later, things fired up and they began to groan and creak their way to the third floor.

"Here we are," David said as he unlocked and opened the door to his apartment. "Anything you need, just say. It'll be a little cramped, but I'll try to stay out of your way. You can have my bedroom, and I'll take the couch."

She'd been in his apartment a lot of times. She'd even slept over when they were working late, or when he was too messed up to be left alone. The place had a feeling to it, a sense of the past and present colliding. A sense of tragedy, but, like a cemetery, a sense of peace as well.

"I can sleep on the couch." Elise paused to take in the lack of change since she'd visited a month ago. Dark? Check. Tiny? Check. Cat skittering around the corner to dive into the bedroom? Check.

"I sleep on the couch half the time anyway," David said. "Not a big deal. I put clean sheets on the bed. Toilet paper the correct way, unrolling from the top, not the bottom. Dishes are done. I'll order something to eat, and we can work on the case. Or take the night off and watch TV."

He was acting a bit too excited about this. "Can we make s'mores?" she asked.

He blinked in surprise. "Sure. I'll have to get some marshmallows and chocolate bars—"

"I'm kidding."

"Oh, right."

"I have a report to write."

"Not a big deal. I have some stuff I need to work on too. You can have the kitchen counter, the couch, or you can take your laptop to bed. Whatever you want."

She thought about what Hoffman had said earlier. "Do I sometimes come off as cold?"

"I wouldn't say that. More like reserved. A bit distant, but not cold."

"I think maybe I've overcompensated."

"Because of being a woman in a typically man's field?"

"Because of the whole conjurer's daughter thing. When I first started in the department, I overheard people whispering about me, and I saw the nervous glances. I felt I had to be extra . . . I don't know, normal."

"Nobody wants normal."

"Sometimes I think it would be nice."

"Normal is just advertising. Normal is a sales pitch. Normal is fiction. It's not real. What do you think normal is?"

"Soccer moms. White SUVs. An ironed skirt and bare, tan legs. Manicured nails. Maybe church. A dog." She erased that, and went for what she really wanted: "People sitting around a dinner table, laughing, talking, passing bowls of food, sharing their lives with one another. Maybe music. Maybe wine."

"You can have that. You can be a conjurer's daughter, someone left on a grave as a baby, and you can also have the dinner table. And a dog."

She considered the dog. "I'm not really a dog person. Maybe a cat."

"Okay, a cat."

Just minutes ago he'd been bugging her with his nonstop chatter. But now . . . "You ground me," she told him. Here he was the one who seemed so scattered. But he wasn't. Not really. "You bring me back again and again."

And in that picture they were painting together, he was there. And once again she caught herself wondering how it would be. The two of them. Together.

"There you go again," he said.

"Sorry. I drifted," she said, trying to cover herself. "I thought everything was over when I went to the plantation to stay. I thought it would be a little vacation, a time to heal. And here I am. Not only has Tremain escaped, we have another killer on the loose."

"We can do this," David said.

"Yes." She nodded. But she wasn't sure.

CHAPTER 19

L ater, when she played it back, Elise wouldn't be able to recall just how it happened. She'd been sitting on the couch, typing up her report. She'd gotten to the part where Tremain had stripped off her clothes and tied her up, and her fingers stopped. They just hovered over the keyboard as she stared blankly at the wall.

David called her name. More than once. She was pretty sure it was more than once. With a jerky motion, her gaze tracked to the right, latching onto him. And maybe she was crying. Maybe she wasn't, but everything was a blur. He said something, but she couldn't hear the words.

He crossed the room. He closed her laptop and put it aside. He grabbed her by both arms. Maybe he was on one knee in front of her, or maybe he was just bent at the waist, but suddenly they were face-to-face.

"Don't write the report," he told her. Those words got through to her. "You don't have to."

She clenched and unclenched her hands. "I think it's too soon."

"It might always be too soon," he said, and the compassion in his face threatened to undo her.

"It didn't really matter what he did to me," she said in a rushed attempt to explain her emotions. "I could deal with that, but all

I kept thinking about was Audrey. I couldn't bear the thought of never seeing her again."

"I know."

"And not just Audrey. You too. I thought about you."

"Me?" He sounded surprised as he dropped beside her on the couch, one arm stretched across the back.

Above all else, she hated weakness. Not in others, but in herself. She wanted and needed to be strong, and she remembered what she'd told Dr. Kicklighter about nothing mattering but catching the Organ Thief. She couldn't lose track of that goal. "I can do it," she said, shaking it off and reaching for the laptop. "I can write the report."

"Don't."

Elise's viewpoint tunneled out, expanding beyond David's blue eyes, his gray T-shirt, his jeans, the couch upon which they sat— close but not too close—his cat, Isobel, on the windowsill staring at something on the street below. The dark apartment was cozy and comforting; how could she have ever thought it otherwise?

"I'll tell Hoffman you aren't going to write it," David said.

"She's demanding a full report."

"She can go to hell."

Elise laughed. Mainly because his reaction was so typically David. Screw authority. "I'll write it," she said, her voice firm.

He stared at her, as if trying to gauge her mental state. *Could* she take going back there in her head? Maybe. Maybe not.

"You have the weirdest eyes," he said out of nowhere. "So many colors."

She didn't tell him Tremain had commented on her eyes too. He'd been particularly fascinated by them. "I'd like to cut them out and put them in a jar," he'd told her. She didn't tell David that either.

"I'm glad Audrey is out of the country," Elise said.

David immediately got what she meant. "Where she'll be safe." Her daughter couldn't replace the son David lost, but he loved Audrey. Elise knew that.

He was still staring at her with concern. And something else. Attraction? Maybe? Her typical response would have been to ignore the sudden sexual tension. But she didn't. For some strange, inexplicable reason, she didn't. Instead, she leaned close and placed a palm against the side of his face, barely making contact. He inhaled sharply.

With one finger, she touched his mouth. She'd known David for so long, and she'd never touched his mouth this way. How strange.

He inhaled again, and he grabbed her hand. And he kissed it. Seemingly embarrassed by the sweetness of the act, he followed the kiss with a smile. And then he said something completely David. "Are you on something? A double dose of pain medication, topped off by a drink?"

"Not even a Tylenol."

"Okay then."

They both laughed like two kids.

Maybe it was because she'd almost died. Whatever the reason, David had filled a large part of her brain since her abduction. All of the what-ifs. All of the wondering. Would she regret never taking that step, no matter the consequences?

Yes.

She would regret it. She had no doubt of that. But really, she had to admit that she was tired of the Elise who did the right thing. Who played by the rules.

Somewhere in the back of her mind she'd always thought she'd become her truer self later on. Once Audrey was through with high school. And during that exploratory period, she'd maybe take a dance class, or a glassblowing class, or a candlemaking class. And writing. She thought about writing, but writing took a certain level of navel-gazing, whether it was fiction or nonfiction. She wasn't sure she'd ever be ready for that depth of introspection.

But the unexamined life wasn't a life worth living.

Who'd said that? Socrates. Yes, Socrates. Smart guy.

Right now she could choose to simply curl up in one corner of the couch while David took the other. Sitting opposite each other, they'd work on their reports. And that would be okay. That would be sweet and tender and cause an ache deep inside because of the restraint, because of what she knew lay beneath the surface. The what-could-have-been. These were the pivotal choices people made. Even criminals. Especially criminals.

"How many times have you almost died?" Elise asked.

He relaxed, and it was odd to think that talking about dying relaxed him more than the unnamed thing between them. "Not that many," he said. "There was that one time when you thought I was dead. And I thought I was dead. But I've probably come closer to killing myself than I've come to losing my life on the job."

"After Christian?"

"Yeah. But you pretty much know about that. What a mess I was when I was transferred here."

She nodded. "And you're better? Now?"

She always had the feeling if David ever admitted to hurting, the façade he'd worked so hard to build would come crashing down, leaving him defenseless and exposed. "I'm better. I'm a lot better."

"That's good."

"But *you* aren't, are you?"

"No." She would admit at least that much.

"And you don't want to talk about it?"

"No."

"A lot of times talking makes it worse. It just makes it worse." He took both of her hands and looked into her eyes with a seriousness that didn't seem like David. And for a weird moment, she felt as if she was in a room with a stranger. "But I want you to know that when you fall apart I'll be strong," he said.

Her life was broken up by cases, and she always thought that once this case was over, and this case, and this case, then she could focus on herself.

But the murders kept happening.

The cases never stopped.

Work would always be there.

Murderers would always be there.

He was reading her mind. He understood what she was thinking, what she was finally, finally considering in a way she'd never allowed herself to consider before. He shook his head, but she could see his heart wasn't in the protest. And she could see the second his mind shifted and came over to her side. She could see the second she no longer had to convince him of anything. She almost laughed as she imagined him hitting a magical switch that caused the lights to dim and a fireplace to appear.

She stood up, and he did the same. He pulled her close before she had a chance to change her mind, and she dug her fingers into his belt, behind his belt buckle. "This can't interfere with work." As she spoke, a voice in her head told her she was behaving uncharacteristically. A voice—her voice—was telling her to stop, to think about what she was doing.

His lips brushed her brow, and she closed her eyes, inhaling the scent of him, skin and cotton and soft hair. "No. It will be business as usual at work."

Ignoring her crutches, Elise gripped David for support as they hurried to the bedroom.

Stripping off clothes. Skin against skin.

It all came back to her even though it had been a long time. Like riding a bike. Like swimming. Buckles undone, zippers down. Blouse unbuttoned and removed. Falling over tangled clothes. Laughing. A lot of laughing. Tumbling into bed.

This was David.

She couldn't believe it was happening. She knew she should stop it.

But why? Why stop?

The bigger question, why had she fought it for so long? Why had she fought it at all?

He felt so good. He smelled so good. And the way he touched her. With this kind of trembling reverence. Had anybody ever touched her this way? She didn't think so. With breathing coming in short bursts. With hesitance? Sweet hesitance, and maybe some disbelief. All shaky and out of breath, and they'd only kissed, only embraced and clung to each other. He was waiting for her to stop him. His breath would catch as if he listened for a protest. Waited to be pushed away.

She did neither.

Instead, she grabbed him by the shoulders and pulled him down on the bed. He was careful not to crush her, thinking of her injuries, thinking of her bruised ribs. It hurt, but she didn't care. "It's okay," she whispered, letting him know that he couldn't hurt her, and shouldn't worry about hurting her.

She'd often wondered what kind of lover he would be. Wild? Passionate? Out of control? Now she understood. He'd be playful. He'd be innocent.

Her head hit the pillow, and he eased himself half beside her, half on top of her, careful of her ribs even though she didn't care. Her hair fanned out, and the pillow sank, and a scent wafted around her, and over her, and through her.

A familiar scent.

Old. From years ago. From the days when she was taught a few simple spells by the old woman down the road.

Elise rode her bike to the woman's house after school, and the elderly practitioner would spread the herbs on the table, along with essential oils. Elise made a love-me-or-die spell for a boy at school. The boy had never noticed her until the day she stuck the bag of herbs in his locker. But by the next day . . . he was infatuated. And later, that boy married her . . .

Elise shoved herself up on her elbows. In the dark, in the sliver of light cutting in from the living room, she reached under the pillow, her fingers coming in contact with something small and soft. A velvet pouch with a drawstring. She pulled it out and stared at the object in her hand. Then she groped around, found a lamp, and turned on the light.

"What the hell is this?" Without waiting for David to answer, she shoved him away and sat up. She opened the pouch and shook the contents onto the rumpled white sheet. Herbs, and a piece of rolled paper soaked in scented oil.

She unrolled the paper, and there was her name, written over and over. "What the hell?" she repeated, jumping from the bed, unheedful of her ankle. She was only slightly aware of standing there in her bra and panties, too mad to care. But she could still smell his skin, still feel his ribs under her fingertips. Because that was the way of these things. Spells. And relationships. Men and women. Once it started . . .

"This explains everything," she said, speaking as much to herself as to Gould. Now he was Gould and no longer David. Half shouting, her tone accusatory. And how could it be otherwise? "All of these things I've been feeling ever since I got out of the hospital." The confusion about him. How she couldn't get him out of her brain. How being around him was this heady thing where she almost felt drunk. The daydreams. The sensations of him touching her. The way, if she turned her head quickly, she swore she could smell him. In her hair. On her skin.

"None of it was real. Here I was thinking I was going crazy. And it was you. You and this stupid mojo." She gathered up the herbs and the bag and tossed them at him. Lying there in bed, shirtless, belt undone, jeans unbuttoned, unzipped.

"Elise, no. It's nothing."

"Where did you get this?"

"Strata Luna. She—"

"Strata Luna? Are you kidding me? This might be a joke to you, but mojos aren't anything to mess with. And one made by Strata Luna? You might think she's just a crazy, eccentric woman, but she's powerful."

"Spells aren't real. I can't believe you think they are."

"Did you forget who you're talking to? Daughter of a conjurer?"

"That's like believing in unicorns."

"*You* are dangerous." She pointed. "*This* is dangerous." Just in case he decided to try to put it back together, she swept up the bag and the herbs and the name paper, bunching everything in her hand. And as the scent swirled around her, she felt the remnants of the mojo's power. She still wanted him. "Did you think this was real? What just happened between us?"

"Yes, I think it was real. It *is* real. You're in denial, Elise. You don't want to feel an attraction to me, so you blame it on some oil and paper and words. Yours is a belief of denial. I don't under-stand you. Normally so practical. I think it's this town. The way it embraces the weird. Almost a religion. And I think it's your heri-tage. Who you are is something you hang on to because you have nothing else. You say you hate where you come from, you hate your history, but you know what I think? I think you're secretly proud of it. I think it makes you different from most of the people in the country."

"Don't try to tell me what I think. You don't know what I think. You don't really know anything about me."

"I know a lot about you. Enough."

"Don't say any more. This—" She gestured with the bag again. "This is no more than a date-rape drug."

"Oh, my God." He tumbled backward in bed, an arm covering his eyes. "Oh, my God." He lay there for several heartbeats, then rolled to his side, elbow to the bed, so he could see her. "Those weeds you're holding in your hand? They *have no power.*"

She turned her back to him and reached for her top. From behind, came a gasp, followed by silence.

CHAPTER 20

David stared at Elise's back. Her dark, straight hair, falling past her shoulders. The curve of her spine. The straps of her bra. Her bikini panties, both undergarments red. That was a surprise. He figured her for white. White all the way. But the biggest surprise was her back. Or rather, what covered her back.

A tattoo. And not just any discreet tattoo. Not the kind of tattoo someone got when dealing with a midlife crisis or wanting to experience a tattoo. It wasn't one of those uncommitted tattoos. This one started just below her neck and covered most of her back, with pieces disappearing into her panties. Black and gray, no color.

"How long have you had that?"

She stood up straighter but didn't turn around. "Awhile."

"It's beautiful." He didn't know much about tattoos, but the one on Elise's back was amazing. The image looked like something from a lithograph, or a turn-of-the-century painting. Across her shoulders was a massive tree with Spanish moss hanging from its branches.

The room was semidark, but it looked as if the landscape moved toward a river, or a lake. And there was a moon, a reflection. And maybe a cemetery stone. He wanted a closer look; he wanted to turn on a brighter light, but he didn't move closer, and he didn't turn on a brighter light.

He frowned, puzzled. "You don't really seem like a tattoo person." Or a red underwear person. Maybe she was right. Maybe he didn't know her at all. And that area above her right buttock. Teflon body art he'd seen on someone who was now dead. He knew how the art was done, and it couldn't have been a whim, not an easy, painless procedure. An incision was made in the skin and the carved Teflon was slipped inside. Elise's was about the size of a silver dollar.

"Black Tupelo," he whispered.

She looked over her shoulder, down at the raised tree design. "Oh, that. Strata Luna begged me to get it, and I finally agreed."

It was a design used by Strata Luna's prostitutes.

Elise laughed, reading his mind. "No, I never worked for Strata Luna. She thought it might protect me. That's what it's really for. Protection."

"It didn't do a very good job." He thought about her being captured.

"Maybe it did." She slipped her arms into her blouse. And now that she was facing him, he saw that her body was covered in healing cuts and red, raised areas, courtesy of Tremain.

"I think without the implant I might have been killed. And as far as not being a tattoo person? I guess that just proves how little you really know me."

How had this happened? How had the evening fallen apart like this? He'd closed her laptop. Just closed her laptop. Damn Strata Luna and her mojo.

He watched as Elise began buttoning her black blouse. He wanted to button it for her. What a crazy thought.

Once the top was fastened, she searched the darkened room for her pants and pulled them on. That's when he realized there'd been a change of plans. He zipped his jeans and buckled his belt.

"Yes, I'm leaving," she said. "I don't need your"—she made air quotes—"'*protection.*'" He hated air quotes, but he supposed they were appropriate here. Deserved.

"Where are you going?" he asked.

"I'll sleep in the office. I doubt Tremain will come looking for me at the Savannah PD. I should have gone there to begin with."

"You don't need to leave. I'll leave. I'll sleep in the parking lot. In my car."

Dressed, she slipped on her shoulder holster, then let out a deep sigh, as if she'd come to a conclusion she didn't care for. "You need to grow up."

"Me? I'm not the one flipping out about a bag of weeds." He hated like hell to see this happen. Their relationship was being set back to zero, and now the old Elise was standing in front of him. The one who'd disapproved of him, the one who'd treated him like a giant pain in the ass. But over time, she'd softened. Over time, she'd come to trust him.

All of that—blown to hell. All because of a stinky bag tucked under his pillow.

"I'm a good cop," he said.

She tugged on her boots. "You weren't good enough to find me."

Ouch.

So there it was. Her resentment. His regret. *I tried, but I was out of my mind.* "Okay, go. But text me when you get to the office. If I don't hear from you, I'll come looking."

"I will."

And then she left, messenger bag slung over her shoulder.

Once Elise was gone, David was tempted to call Strata Luna to tell her just how well her little love charm had worked. But that would be childish of him.

Elise had lied about going to the office. When people were hurting, they went home. Good people and bad people. They all went home. That's what she did. It took ten minutes to get from Gould's apartment to her house. She pulled up next to the curb and saw the machinery, piles of dirt, and no lights, said to hell with it, and drove back to the plantation. It was as close to a home as she was going to get right now.

CHAPTER 21

He stood outside windows edged in blue and watched her as he'd watched her so many times over the years. With distance. With control. With an obsession and a sense of guilt. He could no longer count the number of times he'd stood outside her place in the Garden District, watching her get in and out of her car with her daughter. Watching mother and daughter laughing together as they entered the house. The lights would come on, one room after the other. Was that her bedroom? Upstairs? Yes, he was sure of it, because the light often burned late into the night.

Over the years, he'd collected newspaper clippings. He'd cut out photographs and articles, tucking them away in an envelope that grew fatter.

And those times the two of them had come face-to-face? Hadn't that been something? When she'd been so close he could have touched her? And one time he'd even nodded his head and said hello. Just to see what it felt like. Just to see if she'd notice him.

But she never noticed him.

He'd learned to blend. When he was younger, people said his mere proximity had been imposing. But he'd learned to disappear into shadows and into crowds. So why, after all these years, had he been unable to forget about her? Why couldn't he simply move on?

She haunted him.

And the older he got, the more she haunted him.

He wanted to know her. Everything. And when he saw her with other men, laughing and talking, he was jealous. Because he wanted to be the person she laughed with and shared stories with. He wanted her to see him. To acknowledge him.

So now, as he stood on the porch of the decaying plantation house, his hand shook as he reached for the doorknob. Entering would mean stepping through the blue rectangle. Could he do it? Would the spirits allow him to pass? Or was he unworthy? What kind of spell had been cast by the owner? Something to keep out all of the bad, living and dead? Or just spirits? Because there was no doubt in his mind that he was a bad man. A very bad man. In his lifetime, he'd hurt many people, and he'd even killed a few. But they'd deserved it. Some people didn't deserve to live, and he had no qualms about taking a life if it needed taking. And he had no qualms about torturing someone to get what he wanted out of them.

But this woman . . .

Elise.

She was special to him. He couldn't shake her. And when he thought about her, all resolve vanished and he became weak. He lost his self-control. Sometimes he could almost convince himself that he hated her simply because no matter how much he tried he couldn't shake her. He couldn't shake his obsession.

Through the cloudy glass with its cobwebs that clung to corners and cobwebs that had long ago been abandoned, now just veins that crept across the surface of the window, he saw her sitting at the table, her shoulders shaking, a hand pressed to her mouth.

In all the years he'd watched her he'd never seen her cry. He'd seen her horrified and worried and hurt, but he'd never seen her broken.

And he wondered what had broken her. *Who* had broken her.

The knob made a small click, but she was too wrapped up in her own grief to notice it. In the past, he'd turned a lot of doorknobs knowing she was on the other side. But in the past, all of the doors had remained locked. In the past it had always been the rush of anticipation and not the actual act that drove him.

To his surprise, and maybe a little to his dismay, this door was different. Another click and it creaked open. There was a slight catch of his breath as he took in the surprise of the moment, and then he was following the swinging door; he was stepping through the rectangle of blue.

Elise heard a sound and recognized it as the soft scrape of a shoe across a wooden floor. That was followed by the sounds of the night, and a slight breeze that brought with it the scent of the nearby marsh. A sob stuck in her throat, and through a glitter of tears, she looked up to see a man filling the doorway. Her mind, the mind of a detective, filed and calculated everything about him in barely more than a second. His canvas jacket, the creases that fanned out from intense eyes. Gray hair that was wild where it had escaped the band at the back of his neck. Skin that was tan and weathered, jeans that were faded and patched, boots that were leather, worn by the same feet for years and years. She pegged him as homeless. Not a victim of circumstance, but homeless by choice. There was a difference. This one gave off an aura of pride and independence, not shame and despondence.

At first Elise thought maybe he was one of her aunt's old friends. Someone who'd stayed at the plantation years ago. But then she noticed the way he was staring at her. As if he knew her. And she quickly understood that he had nothing to do with Anastasia.

"Elise."

He spoke her name, and that sealed it. He seemed familiar, and yet not familiar. Was he someone she'd arrested at some point in her career? Was he someone she'd investigated?

The door. In her rush to get away from Gould, she'd left the door unlocked. Foolish, foolish her. And now she would pay the price for that foolishness.

"Who are you?" she asked, playing for time, hoping to engage him in any way she could.

"Don't you know me?" he asked.

"I don't think so. Have we met?"

"Not really."

"What are you doing here?" She wiped at her eyes, clearing her vision. "What do you want?"

"I came to see you."

Moving quickly, she unsnapped her shoulder holster, pulled out her handgun, and pointed it at him. "Don't step any closer."

He held up both hands.

"Let's start over. Who the hell are you?"

"I'm Jackson Sweet."

CHAPTER 22

The hell you are." What was it about Jackson Sweet? Elise couldn't get away from him.

"I am."

How had he gotten there? She hadn't heard a car. By boat? On foot?

"And I'm Luke Skywalker," she said. He didn't get it. "Luke, I'm your father." Still didn't get it. "Never mind." She didn't lower the gun.

He glanced at the chair opposite hers, as if tempted to sit down, as if waiting for an invitation. Right. Like that was going to happen.

"You don't look anything like Jackson Sweet," she said, "so you might as well drop that line. Who are you, and what are you doing here?" He was just another fruitcake or opportunist. It wasn't the first time someone had claimed to be Jackson Sweet. The last one contacted the local news station, and they'd done a piece on him. There was never a good time to deal with a nut job, but this was particularly bad timing. And more disturbing, he'd figured out where she was staying.

"I really am your father."

"My father. Wait. Correct that. The man who deserted my mother and me . . . that man is dead. And anyway, you look nothing like him." And even if the guy standing in the kitchen was Jackson Sweet, which he wasn't, it wouldn't change anything.

"What does Jackson Sweet look like?" he asked.

"He's taller, for one thing. And thinner. And . . . I never met him, but I always heard he filled a room with his presence. That he had this kind of . . . power. But you . . . you're just a man. And like I said, Jackson Sweet is dead. You should have chosen someone else to impersonate. Someone alive."

"I always felt bad about it all. About leaving. I thought your mother would take care of you."

"We know how that turned out." What was she doing? Talking to him as if he was Jackson Sweet.

"I left because there was a price on my head. A lot of people wanted me dead. I thought the best thing to do was vanish. And the best way to vanish is to die." His voice was deep, and his accent was indisputably Georgia Lowcountry. *Tupelo honey*, as Gould said.

She decided to play along. "So why are you back?"

"You're in danger."

"I think that's been pretty well established. Sitting in some dive watching the local news would tell you that."

"I left for you," he said, steering the conversation back to his absence in her life.

"Bullshit." She lowered her weapon, but didn't put it away.

"It's true."

"Who are you?"

"Your father."

"DNA wouldn't even convince me of that."

He shrugged. "Do you mind if I sit down?"

"Good idea."

He sat down and she stood up, giving her a physical advantage.

He smiled and shook his head. *That kid. That crazy kid.*

"What can you tell me about Atticus Tremain?" she asked, hoping to trip him up.

"He's a bad man."

"Tell me something I don't already know."

"I've kept an eye on you for years."

"Like watching over me?" She blew out a breath and may have even rolled her eyes.

"Something like that."

"You've done a damn poor job of it, if that's what you're claiming. Where were you when I was being tortured by Atticus Tremain? Where were you when I was being treated like a pariah by my adoptive family?"

"I messed up."

He smelled like marsh and salt air, and a little like a campfire, leading her to believe her homeless theory was on target. Maybe she'd even passed him more than once in downtown Savannah. The thought was unnerving. "For the sake of argument, let's say you are Jackson Sweet," she said. "And you're telling me you see yourself as some kind of superhero? Some noble guy who vanished in order to protect his daughter? I'm not buying it. You were nothing but a deadbeat dad."

"I made a lot of mistakes in my life."

"No kidding. And I'm not a forgiving person."

"I'm not looking for forgiveness."

"Then why are you here?"

Hesitation, then, "For one thing, I wanted to see you. I followed it all on the news. About you being captured. I know you almost died." He looked down at his hands, then back up at her. "I wanted to see you."

"You can't make up for a lifetime of absence."

"I know. Like I said, I'm not asking for forgiveness. But I could help."

"How?"

"I could teach you things."

"Things? Like root work?" The last words were practically spit out.

He blinked, taken aback by her response. "Yes."

"You think I would want to learn anything about root work? My whole life has been an attempt to get as far away from that as possible. Everything negative that's happened to me has happened because of my connection to you, because of my connection to root work. Even now."

She slipped the gun back into the holster. "That crazy bastard who kidnapped me? You know why he held me and tortured me and cut me and raped me? Because of who I am. Because of you." She gestured toward him, angry. "Because I'm the daughter of a conjurer. So no, you left me with all the negative but none of the positive. And if you're a superhero, then so is he. So is that man who abducted me and held me prisoner."

"I'll kill him for you." His voice was monotone and icy and determined.

"Oh, my God! Listen to yourself. I don't want you to kill him. We'll catch him, and he'll stand trial. And I hope he's put to death."

"I want to kill him. Because of what he did to you."

"It's a little late to start feeling paternal concern. You should have threatened to kill Clyde Wilkinson when I was in third grade and he pulled down my pants in front of the whole class. You should have threatened to kill Curtis Fry in high school when he wrote voodoo queen on my locker in bloody-looking letters."

"I don't think that's a reason to kill someone, but I could have cast a good spell on him."

"I'm not serious! I'm just trying to point out the ludicrousness of this conversation! And the ludicrousness of what and who you are claiming to be."

"What about Strata Luna?"

"What about her?"

"She knew me. Years ago. She can vouch for me. She can tell you that I'm Jackson Sweet."

"This is ridiculous."

"Let's go see her. Let's go see Strata Luna."

"If you were really Jackson Sweet you would have been gone for years. You wouldn't look anything the same."

"Actually . . . it hasn't been that long since I saw her." In answer to the prodding in Elise's eyes, he continued, "Do you still have the blue glasses she gave you last year? The ones that used to be mine?"

Elise stared at him. The shabby man in front of her. Too short. Too stocky. Too old. Too nondescript. "She said Jackson Sweet left them with her years ago."

"I asked her to tell you that. But I brought those to her the day before she gave them to you. I was passing the mantle."

She experienced a cascading sensation, as if someone were running fingernails down her scalp. "Jackson Sweet is taller," she said numbly, mouthing words that made no sense as her brain struggled to acknowledge that this man in front of her was truly Jackson Sweet. "And Jackson Sweet is better looking. And Jackson Sweet is a force of nature. You . . . you are none of those things."

"Death can make a person more than he really is. I'm just a man."

Elise had left her phone on the table, and now it buzzed and danced around a little, indicating a message.

"You want to check that?" the man who claimed to be her father said.

"No." Now feeling annoyed by two men, she asked, "Does anybody else know about you?"

"Strata Luna is the only person who knew I wasn't really dead. She helped me disappear."

That part made sense. That part she could believe. Oh, my God. This was so confusing. Was this guy really Sweet? The one person she wanted to tell, to talk to about this whole crazy thing, was Gould. And she was mad at him. He'd betrayed her. But now, in light of this new development, his level of betrayal seemed not so much a betrayal but just childish stupidity.

And Audrey. This man sitting at the table might be Audrey's grandfather. Would she tell Audrey about him? No. Not now. Maybe someday, but not now.

Elise still didn't fully understand what he was up to, and why he'd chosen this moment to make an appearance. His story kind of made sense, but she knew how messed up people could be.

Her job hinged on just how well she knew and understood motivations. He was after something. What, she didn't know. But there was more to it than what he'd told her. Of that she was certain. A guy didn't vanish for decades and reappear because his daughter had almost died. She'd been in danger before. She'd been injured before.

Her phone continued to buzz, indicating more messages, and she continued to ignore it. "So," she said. "What now?"

"I don't know about you, but I'm hungry," he said. "How about I make us some pancakes?"

"Shaped like Mickey Mouse?"

He gave that some thought. "I guess I could try."

"I'm being sarcastic. You were never in my life, and now you want to suddenly make pancakes. And when Audrey—Audrey is my daughter, by the way—when she was little, I always made her pancakes that were shaped like Mickey Mouse."

"I know who Audrey is."

The sensation of fingers moving down her scalp increased. His eyes were a brittle gray, and she felt herself falling into them. A moment ago he'd seemed like just some nondescript man with not much personality. But with what seemed like a flip of a switch, she saw that wasn't the case. She could see it was all a façade.

She'd known murderers with the ability to camouflage themselves. They were adept at wearing a public mask so no one could see the monster underneath. Some of the biggest and most well-known serial killers in the world had been well liked and had seemed charming and maybe even a bit boring and often nondescript. Because from an early age they learned to hide their true identity from everyone they came across. Everyone, that is, other than the people they killed.

Maybe he'd lied to her about Strata Luna and the glasses. That wasn't proof of who he was. And for a few minutes she'd fallen for it.

She pulled out the gun again, and she pointed it at him. "Get out. And if you ever come around my daughter, I'll kill you."

He pushed himself away from the table and got to his feet. Then he began backing toward the door, never taking his eyes off her or the gun, keeping his hands, while not raised, at least visible and in front of him.

"You said I was never around," he said. "That's true, and it's not true. You said I was never there for you. True, and not true."

"You're getting a little too wordy again." And she was thinking about the blue paint. Like that had been any help.

"You used to come here when you were little. You spent summers here."

"So?" Whoever he was, he could have found that out. From somebody. It wasn't a secret.

"I came here once too."

"You are so full of it."

"No, I did. I found out you spent summers at the plantation, and you know how your aunt was. She pretty much welcomed anybody. Any starving out-of-work artist was taken in. I stayed here for a month. I helped build a new deck on the river. You used to go down there and swim during the day."

"That's creepy." Maybe she'd been around David too much, but she found herself being blunt and pulling up a lot of unprofessional terms. But this wasn't work. This was her life. "I don't remember you."

"I didn't call myself Jackson Sweet. I was Sam. Just Sam."

"Sam Nobody," she said, remembering.

"That's right. You asked me what my last name was, and I said Nobody. And you laughed. You thought that was funny."

Was he the same person? She'd liked Sam. He'd taught her how to roll onto her back and float—in case she ever found herself in a drowning situation in the middle of a river or in the middle of a lake. And a bike . . . something about a bike. He'd helped her ride her aunt's bike. It had been too big, and he'd lowered the seat.

But that didn't mean he was her father. On the contrary, it explained how he knew so much about her. He'd been some drifter who'd stopped at the plantation, who'd taken advantage of Anastasia's hospitality.

"One last thing," he said. "I want to tell you one last thing."

"Say it."

"If I find Tremain I'll kill him."

"If you do anything to impede this investigation I'll have you arrested for obstruction of justice."

Unruffled by her threat, he said, "Can I give you a hug?"

What? "Hell no!" She underscored those words with a move-along motion of her gun.

He held up his hands in more of an I-give-up than an under-arrest gesture. "Okay. I understand. It was good to see you, Elise." And then he left. Spinning around on the heel of his worn leather boot, he turned, opened the door, and jumped off into the darkness.

Once he was gone, Elise felt the presence he left behind. Strong. Powerful. As if the body had been his mask, just the form and shadow he dwelled inside.

She lunged forward, locked the door, and secured the dead bolt. But the solid sound, combined with the visual of metal sliding into place, didn't make her feel any safer.

CHAPTER 23

Elise picked up her phone and began going through Gould's texts.

Call me.

Call me.

Call me.

Did you make it to the office?

Then, *Are you okay? Just text me so I know you're okay.*

And finally: *If I don't hear back, I'm coming to look for you. Just let me know you're okay.*

Her phone was displaying one bar, and she wondered if he'd tried to call and been unable to get through. That would be a give-away as to where she was. She typed on her iPhone screen: *I'm fine. I'm at the office.*

Elise detested lies, and lying to her partner bordered on a mortal sin in her book, but if she told Gould where she was he'd be in his car heading toward the plantation before the text finished sending. She couldn't deal with him now. She needed distance.

He responded immediately: *Okay. Let's talk tomorrow.*

An assumption that she'd want to talk to him. She typed: *Let's don't.*

He didn't text back.

Good.

She scrolled through her contacts, checked the clock on the wall to make sure it wasn't too late, then, with one crutch, she walked carefully down the hall to the bedroom to use the landline phone. Before punching in the numbers, she removed her shoulder holster and placed it on the end table next to the bed. She zipped off her short leather boots, easing out of her left one, careful of her wrapped ankle, then she fluffed a pillow and leaned back against the headboard. Another pillow went under her foot to elevate it.

Strata Luna answered her call with her straightforward, no-nonsense voice.

"I just had a visit from someone interesting," Elise told her.

"How you doing, baby?" Strata Luna said.

Everyone in the police department might have lived in fear of crossing the woman, but for some reason, probably because of Elise's connection to Jackson Sweet, Strata Luna had taken a particular liking to Elise.

"I'm doing okay." But Strata Luna's concern made Elise's throat tighten for a second before she got control of herself. She needed to quit being a crybaby.

"You can call me anytime. And if you need anything, Strata Luna is here for you. You know that, don't you? I been thinking about you. Worrying about you."

"I'm sorry I didn't call earlier."

"Did you get my card? I woulda sent flowers, but I wasn't sure if you were home. Drove by your house and saw all the construction trucks there and the plastic over everything."

"I'm staying out of town for a while. And thanks for the card." Elise readjusted her position in the bed, sitting up a little higher. "I'm calling because I had a visitor. A man."

"That can be good or bad. But usually bad." Strata Luna chuckled.

And God it was good to hear her voice and hear that laugh. Why hadn't Elise called her earlier? And now she felt bad that she was calling, not to talk, but calling because she needed something. But she and Strata Luna were from different worlds, worlds that shouldn't cross. Elise had long ago chosen to look the other way when it came to Strata Luna and her "girls" and her business of sex at Black Tupelo. But to be friends with Strata Luna, a madam . . . They both understood that it wouldn't work.

"Not that kind of man," Elise said. She thought about Gould. She thought about the ridiculous spell. Maybe she was being too hard on him. If she didn't have this Jackson Sweet thing on her mind she'd talk to Strata Luna about Gould. She needed to talk to someone about him. "I'm staying out of town at my aunt's old plantation, and I had a visitor tonight. Someone who said his name was Jackson Sweet."

Through the phone, Elise heard Strata Luna gasp. That was followed by silence, and Elise could just imagine the older woman biting her lip, wondering how much she should say.

"Jackson Sweet . . . That can't be, honey. You and I both know that can't be."

Strata Luna was all about smoke and mirrors, and she was not beyond lying if it served her purpose. Her life had been built on lies and deception, even when it came to the people she cared about. Elise knew Strata Luna cared about her, but if she had to choose between Elise and Jackson Sweet, Strata Luna would choose Sweet. Even though Strata Luna claimed to need no man, Elise had long suspected the root doctor was the love of the Gullah woman's life.

"He told me you could confirm that he was still alive," Elise said. "And he told me he gave you the blue glasses to pass to me."

"Oh, darlin'." The woman was speechless, and that didn't happen to Strata Luna very often. "I don't know what to say. Jackson Sweet. Alive."

Her loyalty was with Sweet. Even if she knew he was alive, she wouldn't say so. Not without his permission. That was something Elise had always admired about Strata Luna. Her sense of loyalty, even if it was the loyalty of thieves. "Why don't you think about it," Elise said. "Sleep on it. I don't want to put you in a bad position."

"Dear, I can't help you. Strata Luna can't help you. You saw his grave. I took you there."

"An unmarked grave." Really, just an indentation in the ground.

"A root doctor like Jackson must be buried in a secret place, otherwise there'd be nothin' left of the corpse or the dirt. You know that."

She was talking about conjurers using his body and the dirt he'd been covered with for spells. Goofer dust, or dirt from a conjurer's grave, was supposed to be some of the most potent hoodoo around.

What surprised Elise was the fear in Strata Luna's voice. And she thought about the veil that had seemed to lift briefly from the man who'd sat across the table from her. And she thought about the chill that had crept into the room. Strata Luna feared no man, but she obviously feared Jackson Sweet, love or no love, dead or not dead. "That's okay," Elise said. "Don't worry about it. Please. It was just good to talk to you."

"Oh, you too, my darlin' girl. You too." The relief in the woman's voice was telling. "You should stop by ol' Strata Luna's one of these days. We can have sweet tea in the backyard. I got my girls to talk to, but a lot of them are just too damn flighty for me. Head in the clouds. Come by. I could read you too if you like. Because I'm sensing some confusion. Maybe I can help."

"I'd like that. Well, the tea and conversation. Not sure about a reading. I'm trying to stay away from that stuff."

Strata Luna laughed and made a *tsk, tsk* sound. She was back to her old self. "You ain't never gonna get away from that, darlin'. You might as well give up. You might as well quit fightin' it. Hey, how about a man? How about I send you over a man? I have the perfect man for you. He'll make you a nice dinner, and bake you a nice pie, and he'll draw you a bath with candles everywhere, and he'll rub your back and shoulders, and put on soft music and make the sweetest love to you. And like any good man, he'll leave when he's done."

Elise laughed. "No, thanks. I'll pass." Although she'd painted a lovely picture.

"Well, you know who to call if you change your mind. No charge either."

Elise told her good-bye, and they both disconnected.

CHAPTER 24

Noises that came in the middle of a deep sleep were confusing. Internal or external? So hard to know. Elise lay in Anastasia's room, trying to figure out if the sound had come from somewhere in the house, or if it had been part of a dream. She checked the clock next to the bed. A little after three. She'd intended to stay awake all night, just to be sure the man claiming to be her father didn't make another appearance, and she'd been doing okay until around two.

She was ready to file the noise away as a dream when she heard a dull thud, not from the pool area and not from the kitchen, but from somewhere above her head.

She was still dressed, still wearing the clothes Gould had helped her remove hours earlier. Silently she tugged on boots, then eased into her shoulder holster. Using her phone's flashlight app and silently cursing herself for leaving her regulation Maglite at home, she slipped from the room. Forgoing the crutches, she made her way down the hall, opened the door at the end, and took a narrow flight of stairs to the second story, all the while favoring her good foot. On the second floor, she examined the rooms one at a time, mentally checking them off as she went.

Like so many old Southern mansions, the plantation house was a maze, with narrow stairs and passageways that led to servants' quarters. Children had once played chase in the hallways, and perhaps a child had taken his last breath in some sad bedroom that overlooked a well-kept lawn. Wings had gone unfinished, halted by war and boarded up to eventually rot and collapse. A tunnel that had once led to the river, maybe for rumrunners during Prohibition, had long ago been forgotten. Whatever the house had been and whatever history it had experienced had been lost over time, and now it was simply a beautiful and decaying space of secrets and mysteries.

As a child, Elise was told to stay out of the tunnel, that it was unsafe. And now, as an adult, she understood that rumrunners were known to have booby-trapped hidden rooms for unsuspecting police.

She passed storage areas where heavy plastic had been hung over gaping holes that may or may not have been doorways at one time. The plastic snapped and popped as air from somewhere moved in and out. Time seemed to shift, and Elise had a memory of sleeping upstairs in the little room her aunt had decorated just for her. In there, she'd stayed up much too late reading Anastasia's old Nancy Drew books. Nancy herself had probably been in just such a house, and gone up just such a set of stairs. And maybe that's where Elise's interest in detective work had begun. Those nights tucked safe in her bed on the second story, the sound of Anastasia and her bohemian friends echoing through the floorboards from the dining room.

This place.

The smell was so familiar, and it brought with it such nostalgia.

Time was moving too fast, Elise realized with dismay. It seemed just a short while ago that Audrey was heading off to school for the first time, and now she would be graduating and going off to college in three years. Old people were always saying, "Where has the time gone?" Now Elise understood the bafflement in their voices, and the confusion in their gaze as they tried to attach the present to a past that still seemed so tangible.

Once she was sure the second story was clear, she headed up to the third floor, climbing a set of wooden stairs that had most likely been hewn by slaves from a forest that hadn't existed in decades, every step haunted by a memory she couldn't quite catch. Something that made her stomach clench in fear, something that was a wisp that shifted when she tried to see it.

Shouting.

And violence.

And something else.

Elise paused with her hand on the railing. The wood was uneven, cut with a knife blade, then worn away by many hands. Hands of men, hands of women, hands of children.

And Jackson Sweet.

Had a man named Jackson Sweet been here?

She tried to put him in that timeline she pulled up in her brain. Her birth. The house on Davern Street where she'd lived with her adoptive family. Her visits here, to the plantation, where she'd felt loved by Anastasia.

She reached the third story—and spotted the glow of a dim light falling across the hallway floor, coming from a small room. Elise pulled out her handgun and slowly approached the open doorway, flinching with each footstep and each creak of old floorboards. With a well-practiced move, she swung smoothly into the room, gun raised and steadied with a hand on her arm as she did an assessment of her surroundings.

The cramped room was drenched in darkness, faintly illuminated by a single floor lamp, a red scarf draped over the shade to mute the bulb. The base of the brass lamp was ornate, the clawed feet and nails something Elise recognized from childhood. Curled, brown-edged wallpaper in a fleur-de-lis design crumbled from walls to reveal dark wooden slats beneath. In one corner of the room was a narrow bed with purple sheets that tumbled to the floor. Hardcover books littered dressers and end tables, along with empty bottles of booze and dirty plates of half-eaten food.

Tangelo peels.

Somebody was living here. It explained the missing food, the weird sounds. The question was, who? Melinda? The guy who claimed to be Jackson Sweet?

She continued the visual sweep of the small space, relieved to note the lack of hiding places. She checked beneath the bed. Nothing but a plate and an apple core.

Assured that the space was empty, she stepped into a smaller room directly across the hall. On one side, as was often the case in old houses, the ceiling slanted to the floor. That tight space was filled with storage clutter that had accumulated over the years. Cardboard boxes, an ironing board, plastic bags, piles of fabric, some old curtains. In the middle of the mess was a large wooden steamer trunk.

Big enough for someone to hide in.

She gripped her gun a little tighter and set the phone aside, leaning it upright on a cardboard box so the light was directed at the trunk.

The latches weren't latched.

With a swift movement, Elise threw the lid open and jumped back, bracing her gun arm with her hand while keeping the weapon trained on the trunk.

In the semidarkness, she was able to make out the shape of a body.

"Come out of there," she said.

No response.

"Now!"

No response.

She grabbed the light and focused it on the deeper recesses of the trunk, chasing away the shadows. It didn't take a detective to figure out what she was looking at: a body curled on its side in a fetal position. A very old body, as in a body that had been in the container a long, long time.

Elise leaned closer, panning the light across the clothing. The style was late seventies, the shirt yellow-and-black-checked flannel. She took note of blond hair and a mustache. Jeans. Brown belt. The man's forehead had a dent in it, probably caused by a fatal blow or a fall.

Footsteps behind her caused Elise to straighten. Turning, she brought the gun around with her, fully expecting to see the man who claimed to be Jackson Sweet standing there. But this was a woman, the same woman Elise was pretty sure she'd seen in the pool the night she'd almost drowned. Not Melinda. No, the woman standing in front of her, gray hair curling wildly around her face, her dark eyebrows above even darker eyes, was without a doubt Aunt Anastasia.

"Oh, dear," Anastasia said in a fretful voice. "I wish you hadn't looked in there."

Smells collided, some good, some bad, the base scent being ancient wood that hadn't seen sunlight in a hundred years. Over the top of that was Anastasia's signature perfume that she made herself from vanilla and lavender. And then there was the odor of old wine and hard liquor that seemed to permeate everything. Along with that was the nasty tang of an unwashed body.

Anastasia had been hiding in her own house.

Elise lowered her weapon and asked a question that had been dogging her for far too long. "Doesn't anybody stay dead around here?"

CHAPTER 25

Y ou *live* up here?" Elise pulled closed the lid on the trunk, put away her gun, and grabbed her phone. It might not have been logical, but things finally made sense. She wasn't crazy. This was a good thing. And the house wasn't haunted—another good thing.

"I didn't have much of a choice, now did I? It's not like this is where I normally spend my time." With a flourish, Anastasia motioned for Elise to follow her back to the room across the hall. There her aunt dropped into a wooden library chair with a whirl of her hippie skirt. Her feet were bare, her toenails painted red. A single thick gray braid hung over one shoulder, and tendrils of escaped hair made a wild halo around her head. This was the wrinkled face Elise had seen in the pool room. These were the eyes that had watched her through chlorine and blue water.

"I wasn't staying up here until you decided to visit," Anastasia said. "I figured you'd come for a few days, and then you'd be gone." Her face softened and got a faraway look. "And I always liked you, Elise. And look." She motioned, pointing from Elise to herself. "Here we are. Just the two of us. And you know what? I'm actually glad you found me out. Now we can talk." Her face registered a new thought. "Now I can take a shower." She let out a luxurious sigh. "I can sleep in a comfortable bed. I can go for my swims without interruption."

"Anastasia, what's going on?"

Her aunt launched into an immediate explanation. "I didn't want to lose the plantation. It's my life, my identity. I haven't been able to pay the property tax for years, and I could no longer pay the equity loan. You know how it's been with the economy. But I couldn't let this place go. So I made Melinda the beneficiary of my life insurance policy, faked my own death with the help of an old friend in the funeral business, and there you go." She sat up straighter, quite proud of herself. "We were able to take that money and save the place."

An explanation in less than a minute. This was proving to be the fastest interrogation Elise had ever been a part of. "And to what end? Do you plan to hide here forever?"

"I hadn't really thought that far ahead. I was desperate."

"You know I'm a cop, right?"

"And I'm so proud of you!"

Elise let out a sigh and eased herself down in a plush, red velvet chair that smelled like the dust of an old antique shop.

"I'll make you some tea!" Like a good hostess, Anastasia jumped to her feet, bustled over to an electric teapot, turned it on, and began lifting one cup after the other, searching for a clean one. "I can't do dishes up here, I haven't taken a shower in a week, and I have to go outside to use the toilet or sneak down to the bathroom on the second floor. It still works, but I couldn't flush it if you were in the house. Really, Elise, this has been terribly hard on me."

"So it was really you in the pool."

"I'm sorry about that. I missed my nightly swim. You know how much I like to swim. And you were on pain medication. I heard you talking about it and saw your prescription bottles. I thought you'd sleep through it."

An hour ago, Elise hardly had any relatives left in her life. Now she had two, both of whom were supposed to be dead. And speaking of dead . . .

She looked back in the direction of the other room. "Who's in the box?"

Anastasia spun around in a whirl of India-dyed fabric, a tea bag in her hand, her mouth an O of surprise. "You don't remember?"

"Should I?"

"Why . . . yes." Her aunt frowned. "You really don't?"

"No."

The teapot began to make noise, and steam floated from the spout. "I don't know if I should tell you then," Anastasia said. "Some things are better off forgotten, and this would definitely be one of them."

Anastasia handed Elise her tea in a delicate floral cup and saucer. Elise tried to ignore the lipstick stain. "It's lemon ginger," Anastasia announced. "Good for digestion." She sat down on the bed with her own cup, crossing her legs like someone forty years younger.

"Tell me," Elise said.

Anastasia stared into her teacup, then looked up at Elise. "Do you remember the last time you visited here? I think you were about eleven."

"I loved that summer."

Anastasia nodded. "It was a wonderful time. Until . . ." She glanced in the direction of the box, then took a distracted sip of tea. "He just showed up one day, like so many people showed up here. He seemed like a nice enough person. Young. Funny. His name, if it really was his name, was Scott. We all got drunk and stoned one night . . . the way we often did. I don't know. It was late. You were sleepy . . . Does any of this ring a bell?"

Elise frowned. The name Scott . . . "Maybe . . . Tell me more."

"Oh, my God, Elise, let's don't go there. Please. Let's just drink our tea and maybe go for a swim. Wouldn't that be nice?"

Anastasia had always been about creating peace and harmony. But it was hard to ignore the dead body just a few feet away. "I'm not feeling like a swim," Elise said. She took a sip of tea and tried not to make a face. It was bitter as hell.

"I'll go for a swim and you can dangle your feet in the water." Anastasia looked quite pleased with that idea.

This was the woman from Elise's childhood, and it wasn't. But Elise supposed her memories of her aunt weren't accurate, painted with a child's view of the world. Back then her aunt had seemed so powerful and so right. As if she could do or say no wrong. Elise had worshipped her. Now she seemed bizarre and flamboyant and perhaps a bit unstable.

"Let's forget about that." Her aunt motioned toward the room across the hall. "The past is the past."

"Anastasia . . ."

She sighed. "It's lovely seeing you, but your being here is such an inconvenience."

Elise laughed. She couldn't help it. And she certainly couldn't deny that she was glad and relieved to find that her aunt was very much alive. Just days ago she'd been sad to think they'd never reconnected. And now, here she was.

But then she thought about the reason she was sitting across from a woman who was supposed to be dead. "Did you call my mother?"

"Oh, Grace." Anastasia's voice dropped in disgust, and she waved her hand as if to erase the woman from her mind as well as from the empty space in front of her. "What a vapid woman. It's hard when your own sister is just so boring, so dreadfully bland.

She had nothing to do with me while I was alive. You know what I mean. And now she's sticking her nose in my business."

"But you called her, right?" Elise repeated. Would she have to point out that Anastasia had started this? That Elise wouldn't even be here right now if Anastasia hadn't made that phone call?

Anastasia frowned in annoyance. "I might have. Maybe one night when I'd had a little too much wine and was feeling alone and sentimental."

Elise looked at the empty bottles that littered the room. *A little?* At least three were empty fifths of vodka. Which meant Anastasia had put away a lot of booze in a matter of days.

"Your aunt is a lush," Elise's mother had said years ago after Elise had come home from her last and final visit. "You can't stay at the plantation anymore."

"It's hard to be dead, sweetie," Anastasia said. "Harder than I thought. I can't go anywhere. I can't do anything, or see my friends. It's awful."

"I'm sure it is." Elise tried to sound sympathetic. "But you aren't really dead," she felt compelled to point out. Was there more going on here than simple eccentricity? Had her aunt lost her freakin' mind? Because that's what it seemed like. She thought about Gould's words when he spotted the crumbling mansion. "Why are the windows painted blue?" Elise asked.

"Well you know, Elise, it's never a bad idea to paint your windows and doors a haint blue. Nothing wrong with being proactive. But in all honesty, I did it to scare people away. I figured if anybody came snooping around here, they'd be afraid to come inside if they saw that fresh coat of haint-blue paint. And, darlin', I hate to say this, but I was hoping it would keep you away. With your background and all . . ."

It didn't matter. What mattered was the body in the box.

Elise gulped down the rest of her tea, fast, to get it over with, and then she reached into her pocket for her cell phone, thinking she'd text Gould, briefly forgetting that it was the middle of the night.

When her aunt saw what she was about, she said, "Elise, please don't contact the police about this. It happened so many years ago. Nobody ever came looking for him. Nobody ever reported him missing. Just let it go." Her mind jumped again. "I have an idea. Why don't you move in here? With me? Forget about the world out there. We'll have our own world here."

"I have a daughter."

"Bring her!"

"She's in high school." Elise slipped her phone back into her pocket. The body wasn't going anywhere.

"Take her out of school. Homeschool her."

For a moment Elise imagined puttering around the grounds with Anastasia; feeding hundreds of stray cats; drinking tea, good tea; and going for swims in the river. Maybe setting up easels under the shade of a live oak, painting peaceful landscapes of tranquil water and curtains of Spanish moss. And heaven help her, it seemed appealing. *Appealing.*

Just days ago, Elise had been internally bemoaning her life. She wanted a change. Anastasia was offering it.

Step into this safe, insular world I've created. Join me here. Forget about everything else beyond the gates. Forget about Atticus Tremain. Forget about what he did to you. Forget about the Organ Thief. And maybe even forget about David Gould.

Elise shoved a stack of books aside, clearing a small space, and put her teacup and saucer down on a black, doily-shrouded dresser. "Let's get back to the man in the box," she said, hoping her aunt wasn't astute enough to have picked up on those seconds that Elise had found herself actually contemplating her aunt's suggestion.

"Oh, Elise." This was spoken sadly, as if Anastasia thought her very disappointment would be enough to convince her niece to drop the unpleasant subject. It would have worked years ago. Years ago, Elise would have bowed her head in shame.

"What about the body?" Elise asked. "How did it happen?"

"You don't want to know. You truly don't. All you need to know is that he was an evil man, and he got what he deserved."

That must have been how her aunt justified hiding him for so long. "I need to know."

Anastasia's shoulders sagged, and Elise almost felt bad. She doubted those shoulders had done much sagging in their sixty years.

Her aunt put her teacup aside and unfolded herself from the bed to stand tall. And then she crossed the room and lit some incense, shook out the match, and tossed it in an ashtray.

"I know that smell," Elise said.

"I used to burn it all the time. Kind of triggers my asthma nowadays, but I thought it might help you remember. You know how it is with smells." Then she circled the room to stand behind Elise's chair. "Close your eyes," she said in a soft voice. "That might help too."

Elise complied, and let her head fall back against the softness of the chair.

Anastasia ran her fingers across Elise's scalp, then she rubbed Elise's temples with her thumbs, bracelets jingling, and whispered, "You've been in this room before."

"No, I don't think so."

"Yes, you have. Just believe me and let your memory take you there. Smells and sounds . . . They can bring it all back . . . if you want it."

The mysterious scent of the incense, burned nightly years ago; the scent of her aunt's perfume; the stale, sweet, organic odor that permeated the room, smells of alcohol and wood that had housed a million worms and a hundred years of sun followed by a hundred years of darkness—all blended into a cocktail that could have been bottled and sold.

The scent carried with it a whisper of the past. Elise felt the air shift, and she heard the soft whisper of her aunt's bare feet on the floor. A pause, followed by the sound of a record falling, and the *tck, tck, tck,* of a needle on scratched vinyl. A song she used to hear in her aunt's living room, a folksy, bluesy number recorded at the plantation.

Memories fired in her brain like snapshots. Things just out of reach, just around the corner. *Almost . . . she could almost see it . . .*

Elise got to her feet, pulled out her phone light, walked across the hall to the trunk, lifted the lid, and let it drop against the wall. Yellow-and-black flannel shirt. So familiar . . .

She reached inside and fingered the fabric of the untucked tail. So familiar . . . Suddenly she imagined the touch of the fabric against her skin, and she could hear a man's labored breathing, and she could feel a man's arms around her . . .

CHAPTER 26

Evenings at the plantation were pretty much the same. Magical. Full of talking and laughing and happy people. Good food. And sometimes her aunt would even let Elise take a sip of wine.

"Just a little," Anastasia would say, and then she'd laugh.

After dinner, the adults took candles and lanterns down to the dock so they could swim in the black river. Never flashlights. Flashlights weren't allowed. "They spoil the mood," Anastasia said.

"Gators in there," a man named Joe told Elise as he leaned his back against the trunk of a tree and took a deep drag from his cigarette. "Don't go in that water."

Elise remembered that.

"Sit down here by me and let's just watch the stars," he said.

She sat beside the man until Anastasia broke in: "That baby's sleepy. Somebody take her up and put her to bed."

Elise remembered that.

She wanted Anastasia to take her, or maybe one of the women who all seemed the same, who followed on the men's heels and cooked their meals and smoked a lot of marijuana—something she couldn't tell her mother once she went back home. She understood that this was a secret. This was a part of Anastasia's world, and if she told her mother what went on here, she might never be allowed to return.

"I'll take her."

The words came from someone named Scott. A guy who made Elise's heart race. A guy she couldn't quit thinking about. He was handsome and had a nice smile, and he played guitar while Anastasia sang. He said he'd written two albums' worth of songs, and if he could record them he might be able to find a label.

"I'll take her," Scott repeated.

The man who'd warned her about the alligators made some sound of protest, but not much.

"Where're your shoes, honey?" Scott asked.

Elise mumbled something, some sleepy apology about forgetting them in the house.

"And you walked down here barefoot?"

She nodded while all the adults stared at her.

Then Anastasia forgot about Elise. Her aunt tugged off her clothes and ran to the end of the dock, jumping in the water with a big splash. She was followed by several others, and the laughter seemed to bounce off the moon that hung low in the sky.

The man swung Elise up into his arms, and, as she watched the tree branches move against the clouds, she was aware of her nightgown and her body pressed against the man's chest. She felt his hands, and she smelled the cigarettes and the beer on his hot breath against her cheek.

"I can walk," she said.

"That's okay, kid. I gotcha."

His breathing became labored as he carried her up the stone steps set in the hillside, then through the back door, the screen slamming behind them. And then they were winding their way upstairs. She thought he would finally put her down when they reached the second story. Instead, he kept going, up another flight of stairs.

"My room's on the second floor," she said, her heart beginning to pound. She was afraid, but she didn't know why.

He didn't say anything. He just kept going, up to an area of the house where she'd been forbidden to go.

"It's not safe," Anastasia had said. "It's full of bats and mice and spiders and who knows what. You just stay down here where there are no secrets."

"Auntie A says I can't come up here," Elise told the man.

He didn't answer.

Her adoptive father was just a stranger who came home in the evening and ate dinner at the table before Elise went to bed, so she didn't know much about men, and she was a little intrigued by them and also scared of them because they were mysterious.

There was a wrong feeling to everything right now, a feeling she didn't like, but she was afraid of making the man mad if she spoke up. After all, he'd offered to take her inside. That was nice of him, wasn't it?

But when he put her down on a stack of mattresses, when he reached under her nightgown and pressed a hand to her mouth so she couldn't scream, that's when she knew he was bad.

She kicked and tried to twist away, but he was big and he was strong, and an eleven-year-old child didn't stand a chance against a man like him. She kind of knew about sex, and she'd heard people whispering about rape, and when she heard the sound of his belt buckle she knew what was going to happen to her.

She wondered if it would hurt.

She guessed it would hurt.

And then she stopped wondering, because she couldn't breathe. She flailed, slapping and tugging at his arms while she whimpered beneath his sweaty palm.

And then, just as suddenly as it started, he was gone. In the dark she heard sounds of scuffling, of glass breaking, and she heard cussing and pounding. And then silence . . .

Elise stared at the dried-up corpse inside the box. Someone had killed this man because of her.

"We were all swimming in the river," Anastasia said from the doorway. "And Scott took you inside. I heard shouting from upstairs, and the sound of breaking glass. I told the others to stay where they were, and I tossed on a shirt and hurried to the house. There was no electricity up here then, so I brought a lantern with me. And when I got here—" She pressed a hand to her mouth. "Oh, my God, Elise. I blame myself. I blame myself for all of it. There you were, on that filthy mattress, your nightgown pushed up to your armpits, and . . . and . . ." She covered her face.

Elise finished for her. "And Scott dead on the floor."

"Yes." Anastasia let out an anguished sob. "Yes. I took you downstairs, and I tucked you in my bed, and I gave you a sleeping pill. I just wanted you to stop thinking about it. I wanted it to go away for you. And you slept like death until the next evening. I think I gave you too much. But when you woke up, you never said anything about the previous night. You just acted like it hadn't happened, so I didn't say anything either."

"I don't understand. Why didn't you report it?"

"I was scared, and cops didn't much like what was going on out here anyway. One of the men helped me, because, let me tell you, a dead man is really heavy. We lined the trunk with plastic and we put the body inside. We were going to carry it downstairs and bury him, but then I got the idea to just leave him here. To fill the box with lime and sawdust and kind of mummify him. It was just supposed to be temporary, until everybody left, or until the police quit looking for him. But the police never came. For a while people talked about the dead rat smell, but I kept adding more lime, and burning more incense, and it finally stopped. And then I just quit coming up here. Until now."

Elise got to her feet. "And you never found out who killed him?"

"Oh, honey. I was drunk and high. I'd even dropped a little acid that night. I can't be a hundred percent sure about anything."

Elise had experienced cases of selective amnesia, or trauma-based amnesia, but she'd never been completely convinced it was real. Now she knew. "If it makes you feel any better, I don't think he did anything to me. I mean, I think whoever killed him got there before he could hurt me."

"Oh, thank God."

"What about the man who helped with the body? Was it someone named Joe? Or maybe Sam?"

"I don't remember. You have to realize it was a different time back then. People came and went, and after he left I never saw him or heard from him again. And I was relieved about that, because he would have been a reminder. But I'm glad he was here, whoever he was. I consider him your guardian angel."

Had the man who saved her been Jackson Sweet?

"You can't tell anybody, Elise. Not about this body, and not about me."

She could see Elise wasn't biting.

"I did it for you, darling. I did it to protect you."

"Auntie, you did it for you."

Anastasia put a hand to her chest and let out a gasp of matronly protest. "How can you say that? I love you, Elise. I was protecting you."

"And who are you protecting now? With your fake death?"

"Why, I'm protecting the plantation. I'm protecting my way of life. I'm not some amoral, soulless bitch, Elise. I live by my own rules, but I do what's right."

She'd denied Elise's assault, and she'd denied the murder, and now she was in denial about the plantation.

Anastasia made an obvious attempt to redirect the conversation. "Who is that man who's been here a few times?" She fanned herself with her hand, and rolled her eyes. "I watched him leave from the window in the turret, and my, my, my."

"He's nice enough to look at, but you don't have to deal with him on a daily basis." Oh, that was mean. And not true. But no way would she tell her aunt what had happened between the two of them.

"I could deal with a lot if he looked that fine."

Anastasia would say go for it. Not the advice Elise was seeking. *Jump, Elise.* "You have to turn yourself in," Elise told her.

"Come on, Elise." Her tone was begging, cajoling. "Tell you what. Let's have a girls' day. You and your daughter, and me and Melinda. We'll do our nails and do our hair, and talk and gossip." She gave Elise an appraising look. "Your hair is beautiful. So sleek and shiny, but we could put a streak of red in there. How about a streak of red?"

"This girls' day sounds appealing, but you forgot one thing. You're supposed to be dead. And you forgot about the body."

"Your daughter doesn't need to know what I've done. Just tell her there was a misunderstanding. And like Mark Twain said, 'Reports of my death have been greatly exaggerated.'"

Elise said nothing.

"Let's have our day, our family day. Because we *are* family. Then I'll turn myself in. What difference will it make if we wait? Whoever this is in the box—he's been here for over twenty years. What will another few days, even a few weeks, matter? Let's have some fun, Elise. Let's get to know each other again. You can rest up. I'll take care of you. And once you're all well, once you're all healed, I'll step forward. I'll tell the police everything."

Elise thought about it awhile. She knew her aunt was playing her. But at the same time, what did it matter if they waited a week or even longer? What difference would it make? Elise's plate was full right now with Tremain on the loose.

"Look at you. All in black. That's depressing. I'm sure you have to wear black for work, but you don't need to wear it here."

Elise looked down at her black slacks and black shirt. "I like black."

"I'll make you some colorful skirts. I have the most beautiful fabric I bought in a little boutique in New Orleans. Lovely red-and-purple velvet. I've been saving it for something special."

Elise tried to imagine herself in a colorful skirt. It couldn't be done. Why did all the women in her life want to change her? "No, really, that's okay."

"Skirts are so easy. I can make one in two hours."

"I don't need a skirt."

"You need someone to take care of you, that's what you need. I can cook meals, and I can bring you a glass of water and a pain pill. I can rub your back and make you tea."

"Why does everybody seem to think I need to be taken care of?"

"Why, look at you." She gestured at Elise, at the way she was holding herself up against a wall, her bad foot barely on the floor. "All broken."

"I'm not broken." A weak protest. She *was* broken. Inside and out.

Anastasia might not have been the Anastasia of Elise's child-hood, but her knack for rudely exposing a person's weaknesses hadn't changed, and for a split second Elise experienced the childish need to please the woman in front of her. Wear her colorful skirts, and be unbroken for her.

"Do you know that a person heals faster when not stressed and not in pain?" Anastasia asked. "Think of this as a trip to a spa."

That was amazingly close to the pipe dream Elise had concocted when she'd first decided to come to the plantation.

Here Elise had built this mental shrine to her aunt. She'd placed her in this lofty place, far above other mortals, only to find she was really your garden-variety crazy cat lady, *sans* the cats. That got Elise thinking about her other childhood memories, and the accuracy or inaccuracy of them. Had her mother really been as mean and as remote as she remembered? Her father so cold? Or had Elise misread them? God knew, her own daughter rolled her eyes at Elise and thought her about as uncool as a mother could be. And really, how had that happened? Elise was a cop. Elise carried a gun. Elise caught bad guys. That was like being a superhero, right?

"Do you like cats?" Elise asked.

Anastasia looked surprised, then wrinkled her nose. "I really don't care for cats. I'm more of a dog person." Then she laughed at a thought in her own head. "I'm really more of a man person. Bring that man of yours around here and I'll entertain him."

"Auntie!"

Anastasia laughed. "Let's go downstairs and I'll dig out a cane I picked up at an antique shop on Wright Square. You'd look good with a cane. And while we're down there, I'll go for a swim and you can cheer me on."

This was the Anastasia Elise remembered. The most important person in the room.

CHAPTER 27

The next morning Elise left the plantation for downtown Savannah, her plan being to beat Gould to work. She didn't want to deal with being chewed out for not staying the night at the police station. Not really his business anyway. But there was an accident on Interstate 16, and traffic was backed up. When she pulled into the parking lot, she spotted Gould's black Civic. Damn.

Once inside the office, his reaction to her little deceit was almost what she expected, except that he seemed distracted. Even more distracted than usual.

"Where'd you really stay last night?" he asked. He was sitting at his desk in his white shirt, sleeves rolled up a few turns, tie askew, hair even wilder than usual.

Seeing him brought the previous evening rushing back in a way that seemed more than just a memory. She felt his hot skin under her fingers, and she could smell his hair against her face.

In all the excitement of finding the corpse last night, and meeting the man who might or might not be her father, and finding out Anastasia wasn't dead, Elise hadn't gotten around to destroying the mojo. And you couldn't just throw a mojo away. That was dangerous. It had to be disposed of according to protocol, and she wasn't even sure what that protocol was. Maybe she'd just put the whole mess someplace where it would be safe. She imagined stuffing it into a canning jar, labeling it, then sticking it in the back of the freezer. The label would say GOULD with a red diagonal slash across it.

She was tempted to tell him she'd stayed in a hotel, but she wanted to stop with the lies. But wasn't her entire existence a lie right now? Not an outright lie, but a lie of omission? Of many omissions? "The plantation," she said like someone who was tone-deaf.

"Oh, that's great. Out there by yourself. Middle of nowhere. Poor cell service." He took a swallow of coffee. "Ghost in the pool."

Now he was making fun of her. "It's almost on the edge of town," she pointed out, dropping her bag on her desk, which faced a window overlooking Colonial Park Cemetery while David's desk faced a brick wall. His choice.

"You know what I mean."

Mouth against hers, soft and warm. Bed and clothes and buttons and buckles. Laughter.

"Nothing happened." Nothing she could tell him about. *My birth father might not be dead. My aunt definitely isn't dead.*

She turned her back to him and squeezed her eyes shut. "How far did you run this morning?" It was a question she often asked him. Today it was her attempt at a return to routine.

"I didn't."

That was unusual. He ran almost every morning. Said it was his therapy. Had last night upset him that much? Maybe she'd been too hard on him, but root work was a hot button for her. And yet this morose distraction seemed more than a product of their fight. They'd fought before, and he usually shrugged it off.

A flurry of activity at the open door, a knock, then Avery stuck his head inside, hand on the doorjamb. "Got a live one downstairs," he announced in excitement. "Interrogation room. Picked him up this morning."

"Tremain?" Elise asked.

"No. You know the prints we got from the newest killing? This guy's a match."

Gould and Elise were on their feet before Avery was done talking. Gould grabbed his jacket from the back of his chair; Elise grabbed his coffee and took a long swallow before handing it to him. And then they were off, striding down the hallway, Avery in front of them, Elise moving slower than usual because of her ankle. Gould took in her antique cane, carved with flowers, the handle worn smooth by dead hands, but said nothing.

At the elevator, Avery hit the "Down" button while continuing to fill them in. "He's had his rights read to him. Refused a lawyer. Says he doesn't need one. Same old song."

"Are you ready for this?" Gould asked Elise once they exited the elevator on the first floor and were approaching the interrogation room. "I can do it."

"I'm okay." The department had long ago realized Elise was the best interrogator they had, and she got better results when she interviewed the subject one-on-one.

"We can do the old good cop, bad cop," David offered, still worried about her mental state.

"I'll be fine."

The suspect ended up being a typical crime model. White, early thirties. Seedy and dirty and skinny and nervous. A record a mile long with a start in petty theft before graduating to drugs, assault, and felony. A repeat offender, with a prison stint under his belt.

"So, Zachary Creed." Elise sat down at the table across from him and opened his file.

"Zach," he corrected.

"You're on probation right now, is that right?"

The space was as bright as a school lunchroom, and just as stark and depressing. High in one corner, a camera recorded everything while Gould and Avery watched from an adjoining room.

"Did anybody offer you anything to eat or drink?" she asked.

He nodded, staring at his tattooed hands folded in front of him on the table.

The secret to Elise's high success rate in the interrogation room wasn't really a secret at all. She didn't browbeat people. She didn't play games. She simply talked to them in a straightforward manner. She simply treated them like human beings.

"Your fingerprints were found at the scene of a very serious crime," she said. She opened the manila folder and sifted through pages of criminal history. "I'm looking at your file, and you've had some arrests. Assault and battery, armed robbery, drugs, but I don't see murder on your record. That's good, since I'm sure you know Georgia has the death penalty. But I want to let you know that cooperation now could help you avoid a death sentence down the road."

He was listening, head bowed.

"Do you want to tell me how your fingerprints ended up at the scene of a gruesome murder?"

Fifteen minutes later, he was sobbing. "I didn't know he was so young. I didn't know that until I read it in the paper."

"How much money were you offered?"

"Two thousand dollars."

"For a life?"

"I know! I know!"

"I'm sorry, Zach." And she was. There were evil people, and there were people like Zach. Just really, really messed up. Without hope. And sadly, a lost cause with no chance of redemption. People like Zach could rarely be saved. She would have said never, but that seemed too bleak.

Now that he'd as much as confessed, he seemed eager to share information. And as his story unfolded about some unknown person contacting him about organs, her mind sorted through what he was telling her, and a suspicion began to form. These were not murders for the sake of murders. They were murders for profit. And deep down she sensed that Tremain was somehow connected. They had no evidence to back that up, and she knew it would be hard to convince anybody else of her theory.

"I think you should have a lawyer," she told Zach. "Would you like the court to assign you one?"

"Yeah." He wiped his nose with the back of his hand. "Yeah, thanks." He looked up at her. "What did you say your name was?"

"Elise Sandburg." She stood and held out her hand. They shook. "Good luck. Wait here and someone will be in to escort you to a cell. And a lawyer will speak to you later."

"Thanks."

Outside the room, Gould and Avery were waiting.

"Good job," Avery said. "As usual."

Her successful interrogation rate was said to be because she used hoodoo. A joke, but irritating all the same. Her strategy was simple: she treated the criminals as if they'd done nothing wrong. And many, in their twisted minds, didn't think they had. You had to meet them where they lived. It wasn't her job to hand down blame. Her job was to simply come out of that room with the truth.

Back in the hallway, Gould pushed the elevator button while Avery broke away to take the stairs. "His story pretty much supports what we were beginning to suspect," Gould said. "Black-market organs." The trafficking of human organs was a multimillion-dollar business.

They stepped in the elevator and the doors closed. "I don't think this is your typical organ black market," Elise said, fingering the handle of the cane Anastasia had given her. "The victimology is all over the place. Old people, young people. If someone wanted transplant organs, they'd want them taken from healthy eighteen-to-thirty-year-olds."

"Maybe the victimology seems random because the kills are opportunistic. The vic simply in the wrong place, wrong time. I mean, that guy . . . Zach. He's definitely no pro."

"I think the targets are very specific."

"I don't get it. What's your theory?"

The elevator stopped on the third floor. "I think they're being sold for root work and mojos," Elise said.

David blinked, then gave an almost imperceptible shake of his head. "No. Come on, Elise."

"And I think Tremain is involved."

"I disagree."

"Tremain could have been supplying the same person. Or persons." To back up her statement, she continued: "If the bodies were being harvested for black-market organs they wouldn't be using some street punk like Zach."

"I'm not so sure about that."

The elevator door opened to a cluster of officers waiting to board. Elise and David shut up and walked down the hall to their shared office. As soon as they stepped inside, David closed the door and said in a voice hardly above a whisper, "What about you? How do you fit into this?" The whisper was his attempt to protect her reputation. He didn't want her theory getting out.

"Daughter of a conjurer?" she asked. "Do you know why my father was buried in an unmarked grave? So he couldn't be dug up." Whether or not Sweet was alive or dead was immaterial. The reasoning behind an unmarked grave was the same either way. "Because his body would be worth a lot of money. A *lot* of money."

"And a conjurer's daughter?"

"Just as much. Maybe more."

"I don't want to start an argument, but this whole thing is so damn far-fetched. Why not just put some ashes—any ashes—in a bag? Or use dirt? Or ground animal parts? Why human? Why kill a person? If we're talking about a business rather than someone on a killing spree, the crimes have to make more sense."

"Belief, remember? Maybe it makes no sense to you, but for people who believe? That's different. You wouldn't give somebody flour when he needed penicillin. If my theory is correct, the people soliciting body parts are either true believers or they don't want an analysis of their product to prove it to be anything less than what they say it is."

"You have no basis for this supposition, and we don't have time to chase false leads," Gould warned.

This was the first time he'd ever argued with her about a theory. "I know," she said with doubt in her voice. It made sense that she'd see what she wanted to see in order to get Tremain the death sentence.

They both sat down at their desks, and Gould wheeled his chair close to Elise, elbows on his knees, hands clasped in front of him. "Okay, think about this. If what you say is true, then why didn't Tremain kill you?"

"He would have killed me; he just wasn't ready yet."

"Because he was obsessed with you."

"Right."

Gould stared at her, and she could see the resistance in his eyes.

"I want to go back to Tremain's house," Elise told him. "I expected to find something we didn't find. I think it's still there. I think we missed it."

"We combed that place. We went through every book, every drawer, every cupboard."

"I want to go through it again. I also think we need to put a few officers on the house."

"Already done."

"He'll know he shouldn't go back there, but he's going to want some of his belongings."

"Like the book of skin?"

"Exactly. One thing we do know, Tremain is obsessive. Not sure he'll be able to stop himself from trying to return even with cops watching his house."

"Okay, I'm with you on this for now. But just for now."

"Thanks."

"I need to tell you something that has nothing to do with the case," he said, his demeanor changing as he shifted gears.

"Is it about last night? Let's forget about that. At least for now. At least until we catch Tremain."

"I got a call this morning from a contact in Virginia."

"Oh." Gould used to live in Virginia. A lot of bad things happened to him there.

"It's my ex," he said. "She's being put to death next week."

That explained the distracted air. It hadn't been about Elise at all. Hadn't been about last night at all. Poor David.

"I don't know how much press it'll get, but I wanted to tell you in case it gets picked up by some of the major outlets."

"Are you going?"

"I need to be there."

She understood. Well, not completely, but a little. "Any chance of a stay of execution?"

"She's had two. I don't think it'll happen a third time, but you never know. I won't be gone long. Overnight, probably."

"I'm sorry you have to go through this, but maybe it'll bring you some closure."

"I hope so." He was quiet a moment, then he surprised Elise with something personal. "I thought I loved her once. I did love her. It's a weird thing. I don't really know where to put it, because I also want to see the bitch dead."

This was the sad David that very few people saw. She understood that he had to keep that David suppressed, otherwise he couldn't function. And she'd seen his inability to function.

But maybe his ex's death *would* give him closure. Knowing the woman was there, knowing she was on death row for what she'd done to their child . . . how could that not eat at a person? Elise was sure David blamed himself. For not seeing what was going on. For not understanding the level of her evil or insanity or whatever it was. Who would think that a mother would kill her child? Most mothers would die for their children. And Elise also took what Gould had experienced as a warning. *This is what happens when you get too lost in your work. You don't see what's going on in your own life.*

"I need to Skype with Audrey today," Elise said, her thoughts shifting to her own child. "I want her to stay in Sweden until we catch Tremain."

David straightened away from her. "I think that's wise."

They were back.

Maybe she'd remember how he felt, and how he smelled, and how he'd made her feel for those few minutes, but this relationship was the one they both needed. At least that's what she told herself.

And she mentally removed the red slash from the canning jar. It would just say GOULD. No, David. It would say David.

"I'm going to say this once," David said. "You're my partner and my friend." His words echoed her own thoughts. "I value that above all else. I would never want to do anything to jeopardize what we have here."

"Okay," she said.

"Okay." With that, David got to his feet. "I'm gonna get some fresh coffee. Want anything?"

"Maybe an orange if there are any in the break room. Oh, and a yogurt." She forgot she hadn't eaten breakfast. In fact, she needed to go shopping again to replace the groceries Anastasia had polished off.

"You got it."

Once David left, Elise caught herself staring into space, gently tracing a finger across her bottom lip. Then she came around and sent her daughter a text message, giving her a heads-up about the Skype call. Even though it was late, almost midnight in Sweden, they visited face-to-face, or as face-to-face as using Skype allowed.

Audrey looked good. So beautiful. How had she ever had such a beautiful daughter? Elise caught herself thinking about the man who'd shown up at the plantation last night, a man who might be Audrey's grandfather.

They small-talked for a while. Elise asked Audrey about her host family and about the school she was visiting. The weather. The food. Audrey asked her mother how she was feeling, and if she was healing from her injuries. Then Elise broached the tougher subject. "I have some bad news," she said. Rather than prolong Audrey's agony, she followed up with that bad news. "Atticus Tremain, the man who abducted me, has escaped."

Audrey let out a gasp and put her hand to her mouth.

"I'm sorry, honey," Elise said.

"I don't care about me! I'm worried about you!"

"I'll be fine."

"Oh, my God. Mom."

"I want you to do something."

"What? Anything."

"I want you to stay in Sweden until Tremain is caught."

Audrey shook her head. "No. I like it here. I love my host family, but I should be with you. I shouldn't have come in the first place."

"It's good that you're there. I think Tremain might use you to get to me. I want you to stay where you're safe."

"What about Thanksgiving? Will I be home for Thanksgiving?"

Elise didn't want to say it might be longer, but she didn't want to lie. "I don't know. I hope so." Her job was disrupting Audrey's life again.

"Why can't we be normal?" Audrey said.

"I'm trying." Elise didn't want to say that normal might always elude them.

Audrey had grown up a lot in the past year, but now, with the thought of not being back in Savannah for the holidays, she reverted to the resentful child of a year ago, always angry with her mother for never being there. "So I might not be able to come home for Thanksgiving because of your job?"

"I'm sorry." Someone was knocking on her office door. "Honey, I have to go. I'll talk to you again in a few days. Love you."

Audrey disconnected without responding.

This was their normal.

CHAPTER 28

Every case was different, but most often when a house was a crime scene the keys were passed to a relative after the initial sweep and evidence collection. In the Tremain case, no relative had yet come forward, and the police department still had the keys.

"And what are we doing here again?" David asked, hands on hips as he perused the living room of Tremain's house once more. "What are we looking for?"

"I started thinking he has to have a hiding place somewhere," Elise said. "Because there are things we didn't find. Maybe some hidden compartment in a wall, in a closet, in a cupboard. Under the floor."

"I don't even know where to start." David put a hand to his head and scanned the filthy space. "I can't believe you were here three days."

"Could have been longer," Elise said. "Could have been weeks." This was her new way of looking at it. For some weird reason, Tremain's escape hadn't turned her into a quivering ex-victim. Instead, she'd come out fighting, and her head was clear. Her confidence was back.

They searched closets and cupboards, and all the while Elise could tell David's heart wasn't in it. He was humoring her once again.

"Let's move the rug," she said. "I know that seems obvious, but—"

"Obvious is why most people still hide their valuables in their underwear drawer." David slid a wooden chair out of the way. A chair Elise had been tied to more than once. She wouldn't mention that. Maybe in her report that was still due, but not now. Not here, and not to David.

He crouched and began rolling up the carpet. It was some cheap blue remnant with ragged edges. "Sweet kitty, this is nasty." He tossed it on the equally nasty mattress, then they both began searching for loose floorboards.

"Let me ask you one thing, then I'll shut up," David said as he tried to pry a board loose, gave up, and moved to another. "What made you think the mojo worked?"

"Can we just stick to the task?"

"Were you briefly and inexplicably drawn to me?"

"Gould," she warned.

"What you're saying is no way in hell would you ever find me attractive under normal circumstances."

Let him think that. "Didn't we agree to put this behind us? And Strata Luna. Really."

"She came to me," he said. "And she likes you. She wanted to do something for you."

"I would have preferred a potted plant."

"You're the daughter she wishes she'd had."

"She's a madam. I'm a cop."

"Maybe you two could open that coffee shop together."

Now he was teasing her, but that was okay. "I can't quite see her serving lattes and wearing an apron."

"I can't see you doing that either." He shrugged. "I find the woman fascinating, that's all."

"You're smitten like all the other men in this town."

"Maybe." He paused and straightened. The front of his coat was covered in dirt and cobwebs. "We're good, right? You and me? Because you keep calling me Gould instead of David."

Elise's focus shifted to the board beneath her hands. "Loose."

"Now that's just way too easy."

He helped her pull it free, revealing bent, weakened nails—a sign of repeat traffic. Two more boards removed, and they were staring at a square metal box with a handle in the center. David lifted it from the hole and set it down in the middle of the floor.

After slipping on a pair of evidence gloves, Elise snapped the case open and pulled up on the hinged lid to reveal a tattoo kit complete with ink and needles and tattoo guns.

David looked from the ink guns, to her, back to the ink guns, quickly figuring it all out. "My God, Elise." He started to drop down on the bed, thought better of it, and just stood there staring at her. "Holy crap."

"Yes."

"This is blowing my mind."

"Everybody keeps asking me what he did to me those three days. This is a big part of it. He worked almost nonstop. He must have been doing speed or something, because I don't think he slept. I would doze off in the middle of it. No food, no water, but he just kept going. That might also explain how I was able to eventually take him by surprise."

"Why didn't you tell me?"

"I don't know. I felt dirty. Ashamed. I can't explain it. He violated me in this permanent way, and now I'll never get away from him." She'd even lied about the tattoo to the doctor who'd treated her, telling him she'd gotten it right before her capture, and she asked that he keep it to himself.

"He did more to you than the tattoo."

"I don't want to talk about that now." She snapped off her evidence gloves. "We're having a debriefing first thing in the morning." She tossed her cane and jacket aside, and began unbuttoning her shirt. "I want to include photos. No more secrets."

He took a stumbling step away. "Let's wait till we're back at the department. One of the women can handle it. With an evidence camera and better lighting."

"Let's do it here. Use your phone." She couldn't explain why it seemed fitting to take the photos in Tremain's lair rather than in some bright, sterile room at the police station, but it did. "I think your phone takes better images than our digital camera anyway, or at least just as good."

While David opened the blinds to let in light, Elise removed her blouse and dropped it on the wooden chair. She unbuttoned and unzipped her black slacks, pulling the low waistband down to her hips. And then she turned her back to him and unhooked her bra.

"Can you see the whole thing?" she asked.

She heard his feet against the floor, then felt his fingers moving her bra straps down her arms, adjusting the waistband of her slacks to reveal more skin. He took several photos, then said, "I think I got it."

She turned. "Let me see."

He handed her the phone, and she scrolled through the images. "I've never gotten a good look at it. At first I was afraid to see what he'd done, and later I just wanted to forget it was there."

"It's actually quite beautiful."

"So strange," she said. "So much talent gone to waste."

"Will you get it removed?"

"That's a lot of ink. And black is harder to get rid of."

Still staring at his phone, she zoomed in on the clearest image, hardly aware that David was behind her, fastening and adjusting her bra.

"I don't think this is a bunch of random images. I think this is about me," she said. "My life."

He looked over her shoulder as she moved her finger across the touch screen, zooming in on one area at a time. A cemetery, a tombstone, a grave, with what appeared to be a baby on it.

The site where Elise was left as an infant had been a secret known only to a few, but somehow word was getting out. She hoped news of the location wouldn't hit the mainstream, because she damn well didn't want coworkers going there, and she damn well didn't want her past ending up as part of some Savannah cemetery tour.

"There's the police station," David said. "And isn't that your house?" He pointed to a Victorian structure with ornate trim and a wrought-iron fence, then he pulled her toward the window and turned her so her back was to the broken light. He traced his finger across the images, going over them one at time. "Here's a pair of glasses."

"Conjurer's glasses."

"I think this might be Strata Luna. And here's a guy. Is that me? Who is that?"

"Maybe Thomas? My ex?"

"Yeah, maybe. I need to get a better look at this." He pushed the waistband of her pants halfway down her buttocks to expose the entire piece. "There's some lettering here. I think it's his signature."

"Oh, great. He signed me."

"Yeah." David was silent a moment, trying to take it all in. Then he said, "I don't think in my years of profiling I've ever seen such an extreme example of obsession. You have to understand that by submitting these images as evidence you'll never be able to put this completely behind you. This case and your body are going to be used in classes at Quantico."

The kitchen door slammed and booted footsteps shuddered across the floor. Mason and Avery appeared in the doorway, weapons drawn, hands bracing straight arms, guns steady.

"Whoa. Okay, wasn't expecting to see this." Mason lowered his weapon.

"We'll leave you two alone," Avery said, backing away. Mason remained where he was, staring at the two of them. But mostly staring at Elise in her bra and unzipped pants.

Elise shoved the phone into David's hand, pulling up her pants. "This isn't what it looks like."

"What it looks like is something severely kinky," Mason said. "Sex? In the perp's house? That's really messed up."

"What are you doing here?" David asked, pocketing his phone.

"We were staked out in the alley, thinking if Tremain showed up he'd sneak in the back. We saw the blinds open and figured it was our guy."

From outside came the sound of a million sirens and police cars descending on the house.

Avery made a face. "We called for backup."

Elise reached for her blouse. "Always a good idea. And Mason? Could you look the other way?"

He closed his mouth, made a choking sound, and backed out of the room. "Sorry," he mumbled once he was out of sight.

"Did you see her red bra?" came Avery's voice from beyond the room.

"I saw a lot more than that," Mason said.

Elise fastened the final button of her blouse. "I can hear you."

CHAPTER 29

S hould they send him? Could he handle it? Always the question, never verbalized, but there. Just under the surface. Nobody understood that these were the cases David had to take. They didn't understand that this was his penance and hopefully his salvation.

The Amber Alert went out thirty minutes after the abduction. Gender: Male. Name: Kenny Gage. Age: Eight. Skin color: White. Hair: Blond. That information was followed by blue eyes and a weight of forty-five pounds.

Twenty-four hours after Kenny was abducted on his way home from school and two hours after Elise and David's visit to Tremain's house, a child's body was reported by campers at Skidaway State Park.

Avery and Mason were still on surveillance, so that narrowed down the available homicide detectives to two. David drove while Elise rode in the passenger seat fielding information from incoming calls.

The white coroner's van was already on site when they arrived at the scene. Also on site were the expected police cars, along with someone from the Georgia Bureau of Investigation. First responders had been there awhile, the initial 911 call having come in over an hour ago.

A perimeter had been established with yellow crime-scene tape. John Casper met them at the end of the dock. "They're pulling the body out right now," he said.

There wasn't a lot that could be processed when a body was found floating in the water, but detectives, lab techs, and the medical examiner would do what they could. Reporters with TV cameras swarmed, and an open area under a grove of trees was packed with people hoping to see something.

The dead child was dragged from the water into a small motorboat and placed directly into a lined body bag. From there he was taken to shore, the bag unzipped for evidence collection and photos.

"Initial take on the situation?" David asked, barely glancing at the child.

"Body is pretty fresh, so I'm guessing it's the missing boy," John Casper said, his voice low.

Needing to step away, David nodded and strode to the end of the dock to stare at the sunlight reflecting off the water, marveling at the shifting pattern.

Of course he thought about that other time. How could he not? Same age, same size, same hair color. Water.

He could have let Elise come alone, but maybe he was a masochist. And he didn't deserve to look the other way or trade Avery for the stakeout gig. This was his punishment. For not being there for his son. This was the guilt parents lived with after losing a child, no matter how it happened. Even if they weren't to blame, which was most often the case. But parents were supposed to protect their children, keep them from harm. That's what mothers and fathers did.

Dr. Kicklighter thought he should quit homicide. She didn't come right out and say it, but it was the reason he still had to see her once a week. She didn't feel he was healed. And no, he wasn't.

And no, he couldn't quit. Because working homicide was one of the things that kept him going. People were always trying to fix the past. They deliberately, often unconsciously, relived events similar to something that had gone wrong. A bad decision, or a situation completely out of their control. That's what he was doing. Trying to fix what had happened. A sort of atonement. A sort of righting of his wrong life. He wanted to be the hero for a change. He wanted to save the life of a child.

And this recent thing with Elise. God, he'd been out of his mind. He'd failed her, just like he'd failed his son. She was right the other day when she'd said he hadn't saved her. That she'd saved herself. For once in his life, he wanted to be there for the person he loved.

Instead, she'd been her own hero. That was Elise. For a while there, he'd suffered from the delusion that she might actually need him. But she was back to her old self, and she didn't need anybody.

David returned to the group of people clustered around the body just in time to hear Casper pronounce the boy dead at the scene.

"Not really much to process," the crime-scene investigator told them. "Body was most likely dumped in another location, carried here by the tide. Once the ME gets a lock on the approximate number of hours the body was in the water, we'll contact a tide expert to see if we can come up with a rough guess as to drop location."

If the body hadn't been found in water, they would have documented everything on the spot, rolling him over to get both sides. Now the main objective was to keep any possible evidence inside the bag with the body, but everyone knew water usually erased all traces.

Some of the officials moved away while David and Elise stood over the dead boy. He was almost beautiful, with skin the color of marble. One eye was half open, the pupil a creamy white, like a cataract.

Elise pulled out her phone and scrolled to a photo of the missing Gage child. "It's him." She turned the phone so David could see the image. He nodded.

"The parents will have to give us a positive ID," she said. "I'll call them once the body is at the morgue. After that we'll set up a press conference."

They moved back so the crime-scene investigators and medical examiner could finish up. The body was tagged and the bag was zipped and lifted to a gurney. As David and Elise approached the crime-scene tape, microphones appeared from the crowd of people.

"Press conference once we have the details," Elise said.

David scanned the mob, looking for anyone suspicious. Sometimes killers watched the crime-scene drama. The perp could be taking it all in right now.

"Who found the body?" David asked one of the first responding officers. She pointed, and David and Elise briefly interviewed a gray-haired, semi-toothless woman with a baby in her arms, leaving her with a business card and contact information.

"If you think of anything you might have forgotten," Elise said, "give us a call. Anything you might have seen around the campgrounds that just didn't seem right. Trust your gut."

The woman nodded.

One reporter, a persistent woman David had seen on the local news, broke away from the throng. "Someone said it was a young boy. Can you confirm that?"

"No comment at this time," Elise said.

Another microphone, another question. "In your professional opinion, would you care to speculate? Was the MO consistent with previous murders? In particular, the Organ Thief?"

"I can't say." Elise kept walking. "I know you want your evening sound bite, but you're going to have to wait until the body is identified and we've notified next of kin."

At that moment, a man burst through the crime-scene tape and charged at the gurney being wheeled toward the coroner's van. People shouted. Cops jumped forward and tackled the man, bringing him to his knees.

"I'm the missing boy's father!" he sobbed. "I have to see!"

The cops dropped back, and the man staggered to his feet.

The agony in the father's voice triggered something in David. Suddenly the world wasn't moving at the right speed, and every second lasted too long. He was aware of matching Elise's stride, and aware of the way his coattails hit his legs. He could hear his heart beating in his head, and he kept hoping the kid on the gurney would be a John Doe. But of course he wouldn't be. And of course he wasn't.

Through a haze, David watched as the body bag was unzipped. And this time he looked longer than he'd looked before. Maybe to keep his eyes off the father's face.

Blond hair, plastered to a white forehead. Blue lips. Blue chest. A hole where the child's heart should be.

Mr. Gage let out a sob and fell across the dead body of his son. The air smelled of salt water and anguish. Brilliant sky, calling birds, a dead son with blue lips.

Elise was suddenly there, pulling the man away. "Mr. Gage, please. We haven't collected all of the evidence."

The man straightened, his awareness expanding beyond the small body on the stretcher, taking in Elise and David and the medical examiner, the cops. He swallowed and nodded.

"Is this your son?" Elise asked, looking directly at him, speaking very clearly. "Is this Kenny Gage?"

"Yes," the father whispered. "Yes." And then the guilt started, because it came that fast. "I should have been there. He shouldn't have walked home by himself. I should have been there."

David would like to have told him the guilt would go away, but that would be a lie.

"Where are they taking him?" the man asked. "Where's he going?" Then another thought, a painful thought: "I have to call my wife."

David was aware of Elise moving away, cane in hand, back to the edge of the crime-scene tape where the crowd had grown and more reporters were shouting questions.

David opened his jacket and flashed his badge. "I'm Detective Gould. Would you like me to call your wife? Do you have anyone else you'd like to contact? A family member? Minister?"

The words barely penetrated the man's brain. "No," he finally said. He pulled out his cell phone. He stared at it, then up at David. "I don't know what to say to her."

"If you dial the number, I'll tell her." David spoke softly, clearly, and compassionately. "You dial, then hand me the phone."

With a trembling finger, the man's hand hovered over the screen. "I can't."

"Would you rather we went there? To your wife? I can take you."

The man looked up. "Could you do that?"

"Of course."

David told Elise he was driving Mr. Gage to his house. She looked startled. "It'll be okay," he told her. "You can pick me up, or I'll catch a cab to the morgue."

"I'll follow you."

The boy's father stood there, numb. "I don't even know where my car is. I don't remember where I parked."

"Let me have your keys," David prompted.

Gage handed them to David, and David hit the "Lock" button a couple of times. A car responded, and the two men walked toward it.

It took fifteen minutes to get to the Gage home. Blocks away, signs appeared in every yard. Pictures of a smiling blond boy. In the car beside David, Mr. Gage buried his face in his hands, shoulders shaking.

The Gage driveway was full of cars, probably relatives and friends, watching, waiting, searching, the house having been turned into a command center. The yard was full of the same signs they'd seen on the route there, the house located in an average, well-kept neighborhood of matching brick ranch-style homes. Palm tree in the front yard.

The front door opened before they reached it. A woman, a young mother, long hair. Young. So young. "Kenny?" she asked, her eyes going from Gage to David. And he could see she already knew. Maybe she'd known hours ago.

David introduced himself. He started to speak, but Mr. Gage interrupted in a sudden need to be the one to tell his wife. In a sudden need to share his pain with the only person who could truly understand.

"Honey, he's gone."

"Gone?"

In situations like this, people needed more than vague words. Otherwise they couldn't process the information. Otherwise they turned it into hope when there was none.

"Your son is dead," David said. "I'm sorry."

Your son is dead.

Words someone had told him a day not so long ago. Because the passage of time becomes molasses when dealing with the death of a loved one. A month. A year. Two years. All the same. "I'm very sorry," he said.

The man and woman clung to each other, sobbing. People from within the house gathered at the door.

David produced a business card and approached a middle-aged man who hadn't yet fallen apart. David pulled out a small tablet and wrote down the address of the morgue where the young couple would need to go to sign papers. He ripped off the lined sheet and handed the address to the man. Then David left them to their grief, walking to the curb where Elise waited in the unmarked car.

He slid into the passenger seat, looked at her, saw the sympathy in her eyes, and looked away. "To the morgue."

CHAPTER 30

Elise pulled the car into the parking lot assigned to the morgue, a deliberately nondescript building on the outskirts of Savannah. The routine for entry was always the same, and required the buzzing of a black button at a gray steel door. But this time it was answered, not by coroner and medical examiner John Casper, but by a young girl with long dark hair and a red skirt just visible beneath her white lab coat. Bare legs. Un-sensible shoes.

"I'm the new assistant," she said as Elise and David introduced themselves and displayed their badges. "The medical examiner is expecting you."

So formal. Elise wasn't used to that.

The girl led them to a brightly lit, windowless room David and Elise were both way too familiar with. John Casper appeared and greeted them, then turned his attention to Elise. "I heard you had quite an adventure." Casper was dressed in his signature outfit: white lab coat, jeans, and red Converse sneakers. His dark hair looked even curlier than usual, most likely due to the high humidity.

"You could say that," Elise said. Not that she'd consider being abducted an adventure, but leave it to Casper to make an awkward and naïve comment.

"It's good to see you." His eyes got glassy with a rush of emotion. Embarrassed, he cleared his throat, looked down at his feet, then slapped David on the arm in a male greeting.

The two had bonded at their first meeting, laughing over a line from *The Wizard of Oz*, something about being most sincerely dead. After that, they'd spent a few evenings drinking beer and talking bodies. Casper was young and enthusiastic, and he tended to say things he shouldn't, which probably explained the rapport.

"Family will be here soon," David said. "Right now we'd just like to get your brief, pre-autopsy assessment of the body."

"As in, was this murder committed by the Organ Thief or a copycat?" Casper asked.

"Yes." The answer came in stereo.

"Come on." The young medical examiner motioned for them to follow him down the hall. "I'm engaged," he announced over his shoulder with no preamble—typical behavior for Casper.

"Wow." David sounded surprised. "Congratulations."

"You met her. My assistant, Mara."

"She seems nice," Elise said. "And she smelled good."

Casper laughed. "The weird thing is that I gave up on dating a long time ago. Decided I was going to be a bachelor because the women I met just didn't get my hours or my obsession with bodies and forensics. They were either freaked out by what I did, or they were a little too interested in it."

In the autopsy suite, they gathered around the metal table where the child's body had already been placed. Casper stood on one side, David and Elise on the other.

"I quit looking, really. And then I met Mara at a coroner's conference. We just clicked. The job opening came up here, and she transferred from the coroner's office in Dallas."

"I'm happy for you," Elise said. "But working together. In the same field. In the same office . . . Is that a good idea?"

"I think it's a great idea. What could be better?"

David looked at Elise, raised his eyebrows, and smiled.

She changed the subject, settling on her own form of small talk, which tended to involve holidays and the weather. "So, what are you and Mara doing for Thanksgiving?"

"Not sure. Mara's family lives in Texas. And honestly, I have some relatives around here, but I try to avoid them."

And then they got down to business. "Okay," Casper said. "I already have a preliminary, but let me start out by saying I'm ninety-five percent sure we're dealing with the Organ Thief. The incision is precise, like the early murders, and in no way sloppy like the Kingfield murder."

"That pretty much answers our question," David said. He suddenly seemed eager to get moving.

"Once the family leaves I'll start the autopsy," Casper said. "I know you want a report as quickly as possible. If you're staying, you'll have to gown up. You know where everything is."

Elise was about to tell him they planned to observe when she glanced over at David to see that he'd gone chalk-white, his forehead and upper lip beaded with sweat as he stared at the dead child on the table.

"I think we have the information we need," Elise said. "If anything changes, or if something pertinent comes up, give us a call no matter the time."

"Will do."

She grabbed David's arm and steered him out of the room and down the hall toward the back door.

"Bye!" Mara said with a wave.

"Cute girl," David said as they stumbled outside into the sunshine and fresh air. He lunged for a wall and pressed his back against it.

"Maybe you should sit down," Elise said.

"I'm okay."

"You don't look okay."

"Didn't you almost faint here once?" he asked.

"That was you."

"No, I'm pretty sure it was you."

"And you threw up. Right over there." She pointed to a curb and a grassy area.

"Oh, right." He collapsed in that very spot and rested his head between his knees while she leaned against the car and waited for him to recover.

"I'm okay." He took a deep breath and palmed his hair back from his forehead with both hands while tilting his face skyward. "You don't have to babysit me. Go back in and watch the autopsy."

"I'm sorry. I wasn't thinking." She would have added that he shouldn't have come, but she didn't want to imply that he couldn't handle a basic part of his job. And she would have sat down beside him, but her ankle injury would make for some graceless maneuvering.

Now that David's complexion had improved, going from chalk white to eggshell, she asked, "What do you think? Was it Tremain?"

David squinted his eyes against the sun. "How in the hell can a guy who was in a coma murder someone forty-eight hours later?"

"We need to talk to a coma specialist, but I think it's probably possible. If not, it means Tremain isn't working alone, although I really had him pegged for a loner. But a partner would explain how he got out of the hospital and went into hiding so fast. If that's the case, I don't get why there was no one else on the surveillance tape."

"Did you ever have reason to think Tremain was working with someone when you were at his house?" David asked.

She shook her head. "I never saw anyone else, and never heard him talking to anybody. But three days isn't that long." Not the eternity it seemed at the time. She extended her hand. David considered it a moment, grabbed it, and let her help him up.

In the car, David drove while Elise called in the preliminary details to Major Hoffman.

"I'll hold off on the press conference until we have the autopsy report," Hoffman said. "And we'll need to fill in all officers with this new information. I'd really like to get a task force together, but unless I request help from the outside I'm not sure that's going to happen. Quantico might send a couple of FBI agents, but quite frankly I think we can do just as well ourselves. Outsiders can some-times drop in and slow down an investigation. Gould is ex-FBI, and you know the killer as well as anybody, but I'll keep you in the loop if anybody decides to drop in and surprise us. In the meantime, I'm scheduling a debriefing. I'll get back to you with a time."

Elise spotted a parking spot in front of a deli on Oglethorpe and motioned for David to pull over. It was easy to forget about food when immersed in a case, but the awning and neon "Open" sign reminded her they'd hardly eaten anything that day. Not miss-ing a beat, David whipped the car into the empty space and cut the engine.

"We're stopping for lunch, then doing some fieldwork," Elise told Major Hoffman. "I'll let you know if anything new comes up." They ended the call.

Elise and David ate sandwiches in the privacy of the car while putting together a game plan for the rest of the day. By the time David gathered up the wrappers and tossed them into a nearby trash container, his color looked almost normal.

Their first stop was a head shop on Drayton that sold tattoo guns, needles, and ink.

"Oh, yeah," said the guy behind the glass counter. He passed the color photo of Tremain back to Elise. "I know him. Well, I don't know him, but he used to come in here sometimes. Bought an ink gun that was pretty damn nice. Not one I could afford to carry in the shop, so I special-ordered it for him. He had some major skills, that guy. And what was weird is that he was kind of a geek, and he didn't have any visible tattoos. I've never seen a tattoo artist without tattoos, know what I mean?"

"Did he ever talk about himself? As in places where he might hang out, things he might do?" David asked.

The guy thought a few moments. "No, not that I remember. And it's been maybe a year since he was here. Used to come all the time, then he stopped. I kinda wondered what happened to him. Never would have guessed he was doing such crazy shit." He looked at Elise. "Hey, you're the chick he abducted, right?"

She wasn't going to get out of this one. "Yeah."

"I'm glad you got away. Saw it on the news. Recognized Tremain right off. Had to call my buddies. We couldn't believe it. He seemed like an all-right guy."

"Don't they all," David said. "Thanks." He pulled out his card and gave the shop owner his usual spiel. *Call if you think of anything.*

And then they were off to the next place on their list.

An hour later, they'd hit two shops that sold herbs for root work and spells. Nobody had ever seen or heard of Tremain.

"Either they're lying or he's too big for the small shops here," Elise said, once they were back in the car. "And honestly, a real root doctor wouldn't go to a shop in Savannah to buy supplies. These places are geared to tourists, not professionals."

"What about Strata Luna?" David said. "I know how you feel about her right now, but she has connections. Underground connections, I'd guess. And she likes you."

Elise's phone buzzed, indicating a text message. She checked the screen: Audrey.

I'm coming home.

Elise replied: *No you aren't. Don't argue, Audrey.*

"Something wrong?" David asked.

"Audrey. She says she's coming home."

Another text: *I want to be there with you. I shouldn't have come here. I'm too distracted.*

Elise replied: *You're safe there. You wouldn't be safe here.*

I don't care. I'm coming home.

No you aren't. I plan to call your host mother later today. I'm sure she'll agree that you should stay.

No response. Disconnect.

Elise shook her head. "She's so stubborn."

"Wonder where she gets that."

She shot him an annoyed look, and since it appeared that Audrey had once again gone off in a huff, Elise put in a call to Strata Luna.

"Come right over," the Gullah woman said. "I'll have tea ready." She sounded quite pleased, and Elise suspected she wanted to follow up on her little matchmaking endeavor.

CHAPTER 31

Sitting in the courtyard of Strata Luna's house on the edge of the Victorian District, one could almost forget the rest of the world existed, and almost forget that bad things were happening not that far beyond the iron gates that had closed behind Elise and David's car when they'd pulled in fifteen minutes earlier. The sky was blue, Strata Luna's house was pink, and the camellias and Christmas roses were blooming. Not far off, the sounds of a fountain added to the overall sensory experience.

But like everything in Savannah, if you dug deep enough... The fountain that sounded so wonderful was the very fountain Strata Luna's daughter had drowned in years ago. And the beautiful pink mansion with black shutters had once been a morgue and still held many secrets, secrets that had almost killed David.

As Elise sipped her tea, she was aware of a softening in the woman sitting at the small bistro table with them. And maybe a complacent sorrow. Strata Luna still gave off a sense of power and a sense of mystery, but there seemed to be an acceptance of her life and all that had happened to her that hadn't been there before.

Did the older woman have any friends? Real friends? Because Elise was pretty sure she didn't have any family left. There was the new "houseboy" who'd answered their knock. The young men were almost interchangeable. The last one had been beautiful and sweet, with luminous brown skin and a charming smile. Enrique. Gone now.

Strata Luna had mourned him, but he hadn't been her equal. She claimed no man was her equal, but Elise often wondered what would have happened if she and Jackson Sweet had stayed together. They would have made a powerful pair.

Right now Strata Luna was looking at the detectives over the rim of her dainty floral teacup, a smile on her lips and a smile in her eyes. *Here we go*, Elise thought. Beside her, David shifted uncomfortably, and raised his own dainty cup to his mouth.

"So," Strata Luna began. "How are you two doing?"

Elise had never seen her in anything but a voluminous dress that swathed her in black from chin to toe. But she had to wear something else at night, didn't she? Yet it was hard to imagine her in anything but the outfit before them.

Her voice was almost as deep as a man's, and intoxicatingly smooth and soothing. Elise could swear that the tone of it did something to her brain, made her limbs go weak, made her body relax.

David must have been experiencing the same sensation, because he shifted in his chair until he was practically lying down, his dark sunglasses resting on top of his head, jacket tossed aside as he soaked up the afternoon sun. "These cookies are great," he said.

"Javier makes them. Out of freshly squeezed limes. He's a treasure."

"A man who can bake," Elise said.

"He can do anything. I mean *anything*." Strata Luna smiled in innuendo.

David made a choking sound and attacked his tea again.

"But really," Strata Luna said. "What's going on with you two? I mean, are you . . . together?"

Elise had hoped to avoid the whole love-spell thing. "Detective Gould and I aren't a couple," Elise said. "We've never been a couple, and we will never be a couple. And I have to tell you since you brought it up, I don't appreciate your giving him a mojo." She glanced at David, who was staring into his cup with the intensity of a tea-leaf reader, his face flushed. "He doesn't understand"—Elise corrected herself—"he doesn't believe in such things."

"He doesn't need to believe."

"That's the problem. He doesn't realize what he's dealing with."

"I'm sitting right here," David said, pulling his sunglasses off his head and covering his eyes.

"So you tried it." Strata Luna smiled. "And?"

"He put it under his pillow."

"I'll just leave," David said. "You two can talk girl talk."

"Stay. It doesn't matter." Elise glanced at him before turning her attention back to the older woman. "It did what it was supposed to do, but I discovered it in time."

"That's too bad," Strata Luna said.

Elise put down her cup, crashing it against the saucer. "No, it's not." They weren't here to talk about David and his silly mojo. "Let's forget about that."

David returned his sunglasses to his head. "Let's."

"We're here because of the Tremain case," Elise explained. "I'm sure you heard he escaped. Well, two hours ago a child's body was found mutilated."

"And we have reason to believe it was done by Tremain," David added.

"What we're about to tell you hasn't been made public." Elise leaned forward. "And we want you to keep it confidential."

Strata Luna nodded. "Poor child. Poor, poor child." Her eyes got a faraway look, and Elise knew she was thinking of her own baby, the girl who'd died just yards from where they sat. And David. The two of them had forged an unspoken bond, both having lost children in a water death. And now this boy, also found in the water. Elise hated that she was constantly reminding them of a past they tried to put behind them on a daily basis. But a parent never forgot that kind of thing. It wasn't possible.

As Elise focused on the reminders of their loss, David picked up the thread of the conversation she'd started. That's how it was with them. She would start; he would finish. Or the other way around. They were like a couple. As hard as she tried, she couldn't deny it. But it was common for detectives to form twin-like relationships. Sometimes detectives knew each other better than they knew their own spouses. And it felt as if she'd known David forever, but two was ten in cop years.

"We have reason to think that the murders aren't just random serial killings," David said.

"It's the body parts, isn't it?" Strata Luna asked.

David did a little double take of surprise. "Yeah."

"That's what I thought."

"I think someone might be selling them for root work or spells," Elise said.

"We've been to the shops in town, but that was a dead end. Do you know anything that might help us track down the person or persons Tremain might be supplying?"

"I want to help in any way I can. Children shouldn't die. Children shouldn't be murdered. If you hadn't come to me, I would have come to you. This has to stop. The problem is that the shops you visited don't sell real ingredients. Some of the potions might have some results, but most are just play powders wrapped in interesting packages. Those people aren't going to deal in the darker herbs. What you're talking about is black market. Those people don't leave trails. The person in charge might not even live in the United States, but I have some people I'll contact. See if they've heard anything."

"Thanks," Elise said.

Strata Luna took a bite of lime cookie, then wiped the powdered sugar from her lips with one long-nailed finger. "You should stay with me."

Elise and David looked at each other, trying unsuccessfully to hide their surprise.

"I mean it." She put the unfinished cookie aside, and brushed her hands together. "My house has a ten-thousand-dollar security system. Nobody can get in or out without triggering alarms."

"I appreciate the offer," Elise said. "I really do—"

"It's not safe for you out there, Elise. Not with this Tremain man on the loose. You should have killed him while he was in the hospital. I thought of doing it myself, but I knew I couldn't get in and out undetected. You two, on the other hand, could have easily ended his life without suspicion."

"We can't really do that kind of thing," David said. "We're cops."

She made a familiar sweeping-hand gesture, combined with a scornful sound of disagreement. "Foolish laws. You can't always pay attention to these things. Not when lives are at stake. And now a child is dead."

Neither Elise nor David had an answer to that, especially since they'd both considered the very thing she was talking about. Elise regretted not ending Tremain's life when she had the chance, and she suspected David felt the same way. A child was lying in the morgue right now because of that decision.

"Think about my invitation," Strata Luna said. "Try to talk her into it, David. You know I'll take care of her. I can even put a no-harm spell around the house, and at night she can sleep with a mojo under her pillow and Javier outside the door."

David got to his feet, shrugged into his jacket, and pulled his sunglasses back down. "Thanks, but I think we've had enough spells."

"Staying at Strata Luna's might not be a bad idea," David said as they drove back to headquarters. "I think you'd be safe there."

"That would be a nice addition to my already freakish résumé. A homicide detective staying with a madam."

"I don't think of her that way."

"How do you think of her?"

"As a businesswoman." David stopped the car at a red light. "And you have the Black Tupelo art on your back, so you must feel something for her, and must trust her to some extent."

"I trust her, but I don't want to stay at her place. And I don't want to stay at your place."

Elise was thinking of Anastasia, alone at the plantation. If Tremain somehow tracked Elise there, then Anastasia could be in danger. She needed to go back to the plantation and talk to her aunt. The situation was more than Elise could deal with right now and definitely something for the back burner, but she had to figure out what to do with Anastasia in the meantime.

"Tremain isn't some kind of mastermind," Elise said, organizing her thoughts and putting a plan into motion. "He's just a psycho-path with an obsession. In some ways, I think the plantation might be the best place for me to stay, but I'm not a fool. I don't want to leave Audrey without a mother, so I'm going to drive out and pick up my things."

The light turned green. David drove through the intersection, then made a left turn. "What if I stay there with you?"

"No." Her reply was a little too fast and emphatic. She wished she could tell him about Anastasia. Maybe she should, except that she'd promised to give her aunt some time. And she wanted Anastasia to come forward on her own. If she didn't, Elise would have to do what she had to do. "I'll be fine. I'll just be gone an hour, tops."

"I want you to come back to my place."

"There's no guarantee I'll be any safer there."

"Oh, man. That hurts."

"Nothing personal. Your building is old. Filled with transients. Windows that aren't secure. Doors that could easily be kicked in. That's all I meant."

"No place will be one hundred percent. But two detectives in the same space? That gives you better odds. That's all I'm sayin'. Let me know what you decide. My place. Strata Luna's. Headquarters— for real, this time. But not the plantation."

And speaking of headquarters . . .

David parked the car in the lot off Liberty, and they walked through Colonial Park Cemetery to the police station.

"Is your report ready?" Major Hoffman asked, when Elise stopped by her office.

"Almost."

"Get it done, because your debriefing is scheduled for two o'clock tomorrow afternoon."

"It'll be ready." But would *she*? Elise dismissed herself and headed for her car while David and Major Hoffman prepped for the press conference. Thankfully they'd decided she should avoid it.

"We want to keep your face off the five o'clock news," Hoffman said.

CHAPTER 32

E lise hoped to make it to the plantation before dark, but that didn't happen. Now she turned into the lane and pulled to an abrupt halt, headlight beams illuminating cars parked on both sides of the narrow dirt road. The plantation house wasn't in view, but she could see a glow of lights where the building hid like some alien spaceship over the horizon. She backed up, then squeezed her Saab into the only parking spot left. She cut the engine, grabbed her cane, and quickly exited the vehicle, approaching the house with stealth.

As the distance fell away, she heard a shout followed by a scream. Instinctively she reached into her messenger bag for her gun, then paused. No, a woman *laughed*.

Music was playing. Blaring, actually, windows open, rectangles of light falling across the ground.

Moving faster now, Elise pounded up the wooden steps and across the porch. Through the front window, she saw people holding wineglasses. Men and women, talking and laughing. She opened the front door and slipped inside, the heat from the packed bodies hitting her like a wall. The noise of conversation was deafening, and nobody noticed her. Melinda? Having a party at her mother's house?

Elise squeezed between conversations. "Excuse me. Coming through."

It was like the apartment scene in *Breakfast at Tiffany's* where the room was filled body-to-body, although the plantation house wasn't nearly as bright. The living room was lit mainly by candles and a few low-watt bulbs beneath red lampshades. People bobbing up and down in an attempt to crowd dance.

"Oh, Elise!"

She turned to see Anastasia weaving her way through the throng to finally reach her niece, her body pressing against Elise as someone jostled her from behind. "You have to try the stuffed mushrooms. They're wonderful."

"What's going on?"

"I'm having a party, dear. Obvious, isn't it?"

"But you're supposed to be dead."

"This is my I'm-not-really-dead party. I decided if I'm going to prison for my little fib, then I'm having a party before I leave. So I called people, and it was all impromptu, but isn't it great? Just like the old days."

She was right about that. With a lot more people.

The scent of marijuana wafted in their direction.

Anastasia caught her alarmed expression, and said, "Please, Elise. Just tonight. Pretend you aren't a cop. Just have fun. Here—" She handed Elise her full glass of wine. "Let me get you a plate. So much good food. Everybody brought something. Oh, I missed this. I *will* miss this. But the place wasn't the same when I was dead. I couldn't have my parties. I couldn't have the music and company. I was so lonely even though Melinda came when she could. I need people around me."

Elise didn't want to vocalize what she was thinking: that Anastasia would have plenty of people around when she went to prison. And that immediately made her incredibly sad. This woman in prison. Really, what had she done? She hadn't killed anybody. Oh, wait. Elise took a big gulp of wine. Maybe not killed, but Anastasia had been somewhat of an accomplice.

Anastasia smiled and squeezed her arm, then leaned close and shouted in her ear. "I'm so glad you're here! I have to mingle, but try to have some fun. You deserve it, my dear." In a swirl of India-print fabric, she vanished into the mob.

A nudge on Elise's arm had her looking to see a sixty-something-year-old man offering her a joint. She shook her head and dove toward the kitchen area. She *was* hungry.

And Anastasia was right. What a spread.

She put her cane aside while she filled a plate with lasagna, pulled chicken, and various salads. Her wineglass was empty, so she refilled it from one of the numerous open bottles on the countertop.

She drank the wine so fast that her face felt hot, and her limbs had that warm glow that only wine or a fever could generate. The kitchen wasn't as crowded as the living area, and she found a corner where she put down her glass and attacked the food with a fork.

Delicious.

Beyond the sea of humans, she saw lights moving outside. Anastasia's famous lanterns. People were carrying them, moving toward the river and the dock. Several lanterns hung from trees.

A bittersweet feeling of nostalgia washed over Elise as she found herself embracing the moment, just letting it flow over her. Anastasia's time machine . . . And really, it hadn't been all that long ago that nights like this were the norm, and Anastasia's parties were the place to be.

Someone called her name, and Elise turned to see Melinda standing there, a beer bottle in her hand, a guilty expression on her face.

"I'm sorry about everything," Melinda said. "I feel so bad." She was talking fast, as if expecting Elise to turn and walk away. Or, at the very least, slap her silly. "I tried to talk Mom out of the whole insurance thing, but you know how she is. She's such a force. How can anybody tell her no? And I have to admit that I didn't try all that hard because I didn't want to lose the plantation either."

She took a long swallow of beer, fortifying herself. "I know there's no excuse, but I just wanted to tell you I'm sorry you got caught in the middle of it. And I'm sorry about the pool. I was bringing food over at night, and you know how Mom likes to swim."

What did a person say in a situation like this? The girl was looking for some sort of absolution, and Elise knew how persuasive Anastasia could be. She actually felt sympathy for Melinda. How could any child stand up to a mother like hers? "It's okay."

"Really?"

"Yes."

Melinda beamed, gave Elise's arm a squeeze, then turned and practically skipped away to reunite with an equally beautiful young man who seemed to be waiting for her.

With a sigh, Elise put her unfinished plate aside, filled her glass again, and moved through the crowd and out the back door. She picked up a lantern, left there for just that purpose, and, with the aid of her cane, followed the stone steps down the hillside, to the dock and river.

She thought about what Strata Luna had said earlier that day. About right and wrong, about the need to do things even if they didn't fall within the law. Both she and David had wanted to end Tremain's life. But they didn't. If they had, a child would still be alive. And years ago, a man had attacked Elise on a night very much like this night. And someone had killed him. And saved Elise.

She passed a hand over her forehead in an attempt to erase her confusion. She'd always clung to the law. Always. But was Strata Luna right? Was Anastasia right?

Her own father had been known for working outside the law, exercising his own brand of justice. Maybe he'd been right too. Maybe *she* was wrong.

"More wine?"

A man about her age stood with a bottle in his hand.

She smiled and held out her glass. He filled it, and they began to talk. And it was nice. He had no idea who she was. She could be anybody. Not a cop. And the boy who was now lying in the morgue? She would try to forget about him, just for the night. Just until tomorrow.

Someone shouted. That was followed by a loud splash and a shriek. People were swimming in the river. In November. Pulling off their clothes and jumping in, even though the temperature was what? Sixty?

"How about a swim?" the man who didn't really know her asked.

Her initial impulse was to say no. Then she thought, *What the hell?* "Why not?"

She tossed her cane and messenger bag aside, and shrugged out of her jacket and blouse.

"Awesome ink."

She glanced over her shoulder, as if able to see her back. "Thanks." Then she reached for the button of her slacks, unfastening, unzipping. She was ready to shuck them down her thighs when a male voice came out of the blackness beyond the lantern.

"Elise?"

An all-too-familiar voice. "David?"

He stepped out of the dark and stared at her as if seeing a stranger who looked like his partner. "No wonder you didn't want to come to my place."

She pulled up her pants, buttoning, zipping. "You go ahead," she told the man who'd asked her if she wanted to swim.

"Everything cool here?" He looked from Elise to David.

"Fine."

"Just checking." He walked away, tugging his T-shirt over his head as he went.

"What the hell is going on?" David's words came more as a statement than a question. He pointed over his shoulder. "There are naked people in the pool. Then I come out here, and—" He stopped, still trying to process. "You could have told me about the party," he said, sounding hurt. "And that guy . . . Who was that guy? I didn't know you were seeing anybody. Where the hell did he come from?"

She picked up her shirt and slipped it back on. "I don't know who he is. I just met him."

"There must be a couple hundred people here. I didn't even know you *knew* that many people. I didn't even know you knew people at all." He turned back in the direction of the house to stare at the lights. Music was blaring. Something retro and bluesy and druggy. "It's like the sixties here. It's like Woodstock."

"It's kind of a going-away party," Elise said, buttoning her shirt.

He swung back around. "For who?"

At that very moment, her aunt spotted them and came gliding across the grass, zeroing in on David. "Hello." The tone of her voice said she found him extremely attractive.

"The party is for . . . Gloria, here," Elise ad-libbed, grabbing her jacket, messenger bag, and cane.

"You're adorable," Anastasia told David. "How do you feel about older women?"

"I think they're groovy."

Elise laughed.

"I don't think I'm cool enough to be here," David said, glancing around. "Where are you going?" he asked Anastasia. "Elise said this was a going-away party."

"On a kind of spiritual journey," Anastasia said.

David nodded as if he understood.

Elise's aunt floated off, and David said, "Want to introduce me to some of your friends?"

"Maybe later," Elise said. "What are *you* doing here, David?"

"I was worried about you. Remember telling me you would let me know as soon as you were back in town? That was hours ago."

She gave herself a mental smack on the forehead. "Sorry."

"Why didn't you just say you were having a party?"

"I don't know."

"So you aren't coming back to town tonight?"

"I'll be fine here. All these people. No way would Tremain get away with anything in a crowd this size."

"Or he could blend pretty easily," David said. "In the dark. Everybody wasted."

"You're a fine one to talk about that. And you're always telling me I need to have some fun."

He let out a breath—a sound of resignation. "I'm heading home. I'll see you in the morning."

"Would you like to go swimming first?"

"No, I don't want to go swimming. I don't swim."

"Why are you mad?"

"I'm not mad. I'm just . . . confused. None of this makes sense."

"I was just thinking . . . I don't know. Maybe we should all live our lives as if we were going to prison. What would you do if you were going to prison tomorrow?"

"I'd probably hire a damn good lawyer and file an appeal."

She laughed.

"Do you remember that article I showed you a few months ago?" David asked. "About the scientist who claimed that toxoplasmosis in cat poop could actually change the behavior of people?"

"You're the one with the cat."

"I thought maybe you got a little too close to the litter box," he said.

"There's nothing wrong with having some fun. I almost died not long ago. That changes a person's perspective."

"There's fun, and then there's out of character. I have to go, Elise. I couldn't find a place to park, so I'm blocking the lane. I'll see you in the morning." He looked at her with such intensity and annoyance that she wanted to kiss him and laugh at him at the same time.

He made an irritated sound, and turned to leave.

He *was* adorable, Elise decided.

"Wait," Elise said. "Don't go away mad."

"You're drunk. Not that there's anything wrong with that. It's just a little unsettling since I've never seen you like this."

"I've been thinking." She wanted to touch him, but she stopped herself. "Strata Luna was right. That day in the hospital. We should have killed Tremain. It was just the two of us there. Just us. We should have done it. You and me."

"I know." He nodded solemnly. "I have to go. Be careful. I'll see you tomorrow." He smiled a kind of sad smile. "Helluva party."

He left.

She wished he'd stayed. She thought about the mojo, torn, scattered, her name paper shredded into pieces and stuffed into a corner of her suitcase. For a few moments she thought about putting it back together. For longer moments she wished she hadn't found it the other day.

Sometimes it was better to not know what was under the pillow. Or who was hiding upstairs. Or what was in the trunk. All knowledge that didn't help her, that didn't really move her life forward. Instead, it tripped her up.

Strata Luna had been right about Tremain. Maybe she was right about David too.

Long after David left and the party was winding down, when the day to come was closer than the day left behind, Elise and Anastasia sat in chairs on the front porch, telling people good-bye as they left.

"I'm sorry I blew your cover," Elise said.

Anastasia waved a ringed hand. "I was tired of being dead anyway. You were right. It was a bad idea."

"At least you got to come back from the dead."

They both looked into the distance, listening to the birds singing in the dark, watching the sky turn a lighter shade of black.

"Yeah," Anastasia said. "That was fun."

Back at Mary of the Angels, David couldn't sleep. The party. Elise. Not that it hadn't been cool, and not that it hadn't been fun, but, as he'd told Elise, it was out of character. And while they were in the middle of this case.

He grabbed his laptop and got back into bed, pillows propped behind him. With the glow of the screen almost blinding in contrast to the blackness of the room, he did an Internet search for funerals that had taken place in Chatham County over the past few months and came up with an Anastasia Green. An image search brought up several photos of the woman from the party. Elise's dead aunt.

"What the hell are you up to, Elise?" he said.

Instead of trying to sleep, because who the hell could sleep now, he put on his running clothes and running shoes, and hit the streets as birds announced the predawn.

He solved a lot of things when he was running. But today, no matter how far he ran, he couldn't come up with an answer. Elise's aunt was alive, which must have meant she'd faked her own death. Insurance? Maybe. But then some people wanted to vanish for other reasons. After seeing the party last night, David would guess vanishing was no longer a part of her agenda. And Elise. Was Elise in on it? Had she been in on it from the beginning?

He was confused as hell. The worst part of the whole deal? His partner, someone he should be able to trust, was lying to him.

CHAPTER 33

When Elise arrived at the office the next day, David was waiting with a glass of water and Advil.

Wordlessly she plucked the pills from his palm, tossed them into her mouth, and washed them down. Then she eased herself into her chair to finish putting together her report for the debriefing.

Not only was she hungover, she'd gotten no sleep after the party. She and Anastasia had stayed up talking, but Elise could at least relax knowing her aunt would be staying with Melinda for a few days while they found a good lawyer to advise them on how best to proceed.

"How to handle returning from the dead isn't something that's easily answered with an Internet search," Anastasia had said.

By noon Elise was feeling almost human, and by two o'clock, as she handed out her prepared material in the downstairs meeting room, all remnants of her hangover were gone.

"Here you'll find a more thorough report of my time spent with Atticus Tremain," she said. "I didn't cover everything, but some of what happened to me is nobody's business." She spoke those words without looking at Major Hoffman, who stood imposingly near the door. "Someday I might choose to talk about it, or I might not. But let me say here and now, the information I left out has no bearing on this case. I didn't supply you with an hour-by-hour, minute-by-minute timeline. What I have supplied you with is information that might help us find Tremain. I know some of you have been concerned about me, and I thank you for that. But I'm back. I'm one hundred percent, and I want to catch this man."

People settled into their seats, paper was shuffled, and heads were bent as they studied the material. If this were a high-school classroom, Avery, Mason, and Gould would be the vagrants lounging in the back row, while outside, from the vicinity of the cemetery, came the sounds of children playing.

"The material in the handout is pretty self-explanatory," Elise said. "But I'll go over it for the sake of clarity. If anybody else has anything to add, please feel free to jump in at any time. I'm not in charge of the case; I'm just facilitating. I think it's fair to say we're all equals in our endeavor to catch Tremain and whoever else is behind these disturbing murders."

Major Hoffman broke in: "Before you start, I want to welcome you back, Detective." She stepped front and center. "I also want to address the issue of Tremain's escape from the hospital. The department is getting a lot of negative press about this, and one officer was accosted in his patrol car yesterday. He's fine, but the assailant took a ball bat to the vehicle, causing a lot of damage. I want you to know that our officers are in no way to blame for what happened. This shameful turn of events falls on a budget that's collapsing under us. We can't afford to put enough officers on the street, and we certainly can't afford to pay them to stand guard over a comatose patient. I could point fingers at the doctors who said Tremain would most likely never regain consciousness, but I think that would be unfair. Let's move forward. Let's catch this guy or these guys, and in the interim I plan to make the press fully aware of our fiscal situation. I hate to use this latest tragedy as a way to drive home the funding issue, but there it is. I can't deny it. If it's anybody's fault, it's our mayor's, who continues to cut department funding."

People clapped and Major Hoffman took a seat, giving her suit jacket a sharp tug.

Elise picked up where she'd left off. "In the first pages of the material, you'll find a profile of Tremain. White male, forty-five years old. His given name was Joel Francis, but he changed it to Atticus Tremain when he was twenty-two. Lived in Savannah a large part of his life, moving back and forth between Florida and Georgia. Attended Mercer University where he aspired to become a doctor. Lasted two years before he was kicked out. School records give no indication of why, but we're looking into that. He took gross anatomy, where he probably became a bit experienced with the scalpel. Raised by a single mom, Ella Francis, who lives outside Atlanta. We know she visited him in the hospital, and we've requested help with the local department up there, asking that they question her. But anyway, somewhere along the way, Tremain became interested in root work and spells. And somewhere along the way, he became interested in tattooing."

"That's pretty ambitious for a scumbag," someone said.

"That's why his profile steps outside the norm. He's an artist. A very good one. If you look deeper into your packet, you'll find an example of his work."

Officers dug. Paper rustled. The room was in agreement about the good part.

"Nice work," an officer said.

"Nice back," someone else said.

David coughed into his hand.

"One more thing you should probably know." Elise straightened to deliver the punch line: "The back? It's mine."

Gasps.

"Oh, sorry," said the cop who'd mentioned the nice back.

Avery and Mason were whispering to each other, probably figuring out what had really been going on in Tremain's house when they'd caught Elise half dressed.

"Still a nice back," someone said.

People laughed, lightening the mood.

One of the officers, a young female in the front row, spoke up: "I'm confused. Are you saying you two knew each other before you were abducted? You went to him for tattoo work?"

"I'm saying he gave me the tattoo when I was being held against my will."

An officer whistled. "That's a lot of ink for three days."

Elise wrapped up with the autopsy report on the Gage boy, and threw the most recent theories out there. "I might be proven wrong, but my feeling is that Tremain is the key to all of this." She looked around the room. "Anybody have any thoughts or additions?"

Hands shot up. Elise pointed to a young male officer seated in the front row.

"You've given us a fairly thorough bio on Tremain," he said, "but I'm wondering about his emotional makeup. What makes him tick."

It was a question Elise had hoped to avoid because she'd worked so hard to create a work persona far removed from her background, but if she faced this thing head-on, which she'd decided to do, there would be no sidestepping. "Tremain is obsessed with root work. With spells and conjuring. I think that obsession became more fully realized once he abducted me." It was hard for her to admit to the connection between her own history and Tremain's obsession, but there it was.

The officer didn't back down. Young. Smart. Foolish. Enthused. All of those things. Elise checked his name tag. Felix Taylor.

"In your opinion, is he insane?" Felix asked. "Evil? Or is he on a journey? A quest? Does he think he's doing something that needs to be done?"

How many nights had she spent drinking and talking to fellow detectives and officers about the line between sanity and insanity? How did you differentiate between evil and a person who gave in to sick compulsions?

Strata Luna said evil was everywhere, and it didn't need a reason to exist. Maybe that was true, but Elise had yet to meet a criminal who seemed one-hundred-percent evil. They all had a soft spot somewhere. And as twisted as it seemed, she believed Tremain had demonstrated a soft spot for her. Otherwise he would have killed her. And by branding her with ink, he'd made her truly his. In his mind, anyway.

She'd sworn to be straightforward, but all of these thoughts bordered more on confession than on the sharing of pertinent information. Or at least that's what she tried to tell herself.

David picked up on her discomfort and joined in. "At the core of it all, it appears that the murders are for profit. And like all happy freelancers, he was able to combine his obsession with work. We think he believes he's providing something necessary and important."

The officer nodded. "Justification."

"Exactly. We all do it."

"But wouldn't you expect him to leave town?" someone else asked. "I don't get this new murder, right here in Savannah."

"He's probably feeling cocky and untouchable right now," Elise said. "After his escape. Our records show that he lived in Savannah off and on his entire life. He always came back here. This is his town, and he knows the streets and alleys, and probably the tunnels.

I don't think it seems that odd. If he's going to commit crimes he'll want to be on familiar territory."

"One more thing," David added. "I'm not convinced this last murder was for profit, because I'm guessing his contacts are lying low and avoiding him. He's definitely escalating, and I think he did it for attention. He's thumbing his nose at us." He looked at Elise. "And he's showing off to Detective Sandburg."

"If that's the case, what about you?" Felix asked, addressing Elise. "Do you expect him to come after you?"

Elise was quiet a moment. She glanced at David, then at the young officer. Now was the time for honesty. "Yes," she said. "I do."

CHAPTER 34

The bad thing about putting out an all-points bulletin and scrolling the tip line number across local and national television? So many false sightings. It always happened, and the officers sitting at desks fielding calls were burning out. Four days had passed since Tremain vanished from the hospital, and in those four days his face had been plastered on the front of *Savannah Morning News* and all over the Internet, plus local and national television. The phones hadn't stopped ringing, and two extra officers had been assigned to the tip lines to try to keep up.

Most calls were from people who desperately wanted to help, so much that they'd convinced themselves they'd spotted Tremain at the gas station, or the discount store, or walking down the street. But there were also the nut jobs, the people who wanted to connect themselves to someone famous, even if that famous person was a cold-blooded killer.

All leads couldn't be followed. Officers manning the phones needed to be astute. They needed to be able to read people without the aid of visual contact. Elise and David had gone on four false leads so far. And now they were probably heading for the fifth: a report of a theft from a small used-car dealer who'd caught the perpetrator on camera.

"Wanna make a bet?" David said as they headed down Abercorn in the direction of the car lot. He was at the wheel, a chocolate chip cookie in one hand. Elise was eating from a bag of potato chips, both snacks grabbed on the way out the door.

Elise had spent the past few days sleeping in her office on an air mattress, and she had to admit that Strata Luna's invitation was sounding better all the time. A comfortable bed. High thread-count sheets, a shower that hadn't been used by off-duty officers. Maybe some privacy, not to mention clean clothes. She'd been wearing the same black pants and top for the past three days, and as soon as she got a second of free time she planned to stop by her house to pick up a fresh outfit.

"I'll bet the person on the security footage looks nothing like our guy," Elise said.

David agreed, but a visual was a lead they had to follow.

They located the dealership and talked to the owner, who took them into his cramped office to view the video.

"Look at the time stamp." Elise pointed.

David leaned closer to the screen. "Yesterday, five a.m."

The footage was of such poor quality that there was no way to know if the thief was Tremain, but David and Elise collected the information about the stolen car, a silver Chevy Malibu.

"Dealer plates?" David asked.

"No."

Didn't matter. The thief would most likely have changed dealer plates for stolen ones anyway. They thanked the shop owner, then headed back to headquarters, grabbing carryout on the way.

Avery poked his head around the corner just as Elise and David sat down in their office with sandwiches and sweet tea.

"We got somebody on the phone you're gonna want to talk to," he said. "We'd put the call through to your desk, but we're afraid we might lose her."

David and Elise shot him a question-mark expression, then both glanced at the sandwiches in their hands.

"Says she's Tremain's mother. And we have confirmation that the call is coming from north of Atlanta."

Sandwiches dropped. Elise and David scrambled to their feet and hurried down the hall, talking as they went. "If Tremain stole the car yesterday—" David began.

"Then the timeline fits," Elise finished.

In the command center, a blond uniformed officer was talking into a black desk phone. Her name tag read "Meg Cook." She spotted Elise and David and her eyes widened. "Just a minute, Mrs. Francis. I have Detective Sandburg here with me right now." She passed the phone to Elise, and whispered, "She specifically asked for you."

Elise spoke into the receiver, introducing herself. Her voice sounded normal to her ears, but inside she was shaking.

The woman was nervous, whispering into the phone. Elise imagined her sitting in her bedroom, or some corner of an eighties kitchen clutching the receiver while casting terrified glances over her shoulder.

"He's here," she said, her words broadcasting to the room through a speaker on the desk while a tech made certain it was all being recorded. "He got here late last night."

"Have you been injured in any way?" Elise asked.

"No."

"Has he threatened you?"

"No."

"Where is he right now?"

"He's asleep. When he got here, I cooked for him. I made him pancakes and sausage. He used to love that. He ate, and then he went to his old room. His bedroom, and shut the door. I haven't heard anything since. Well, I heard him snoring, and I heard him turn over in bed." She let out a trembling sob. "What should I do?"

Elise wanted to tell her to leave. To get the hell out of there as fast as she could, but if he woke up and found her gone, he'd run. Better to keep things as normal as possible. But that put Tremain's mother in danger.

Everybody in the task-force room was focused on the phone call. Elise's heart had been pounding before, but now it began to slam in her chest. "Mrs. Francis," she said. "You can leave right now. You can put down the phone and walk out the door. Nobody would fault you for that. Do you understand?"

"Yes. Yes, I do."

"Or you can stay, and when your son wakes up you can act as if nothing unusual is happening. Make him lunch. Talk to him about little things. Try to avoid topics that might upset him. But it's your choice. Leave now, or stay."

After a brief silence, the woman said, "I'll stay."

Elise's shoulders relaxed. "Good. We just want you to try to keep him there. Just keep him from leaving until the police arrive."

"When will that be? When will they come?"

"As soon as possible."

"How long?"

From research, Elise knew the Francis house was in a remote area of Lumpkin County, north of Atlanta. It was a different world up there. Even under the best of conditions, it would take time to put together a group of professionals, which would be composed of a SWAT team.

Most police work was stymied by bureaucracy, but thank God SWAT team units were set up to respond quickly. But getting to the remote location . . . Elise would guess it would take several hours at best. Plus it wasn't their jurisdiction. They would have no control over how Tremain was captured. Regardless, Elise wanted to be there when it went down.

David handed Elise a note. *Ask about the car.*

"Mrs. Francis, how did he get to your home?"

"He drove."

"Do you happen to know the make and model of the vehicle?"

"Just a minute." Elise imagined her pulling aside a curtain. "A silver Chevy Malibu," the woman said.

Elise looked up at David and nodded.

"I have to go," Mrs. Francis said in a frightened whisper.

Before Elise could reply, the woman hung up.

David squared his shoulders and checked his watch. "We can catch a flight to Atlanta, rent a car, and be at the house four or five hours from now."

Elise and David were heading out the front door of the police station when Elise's phone rang. She checked the screen, recognized the country code, and answered.

"Elise?" A woman's Swedish accent. "This is Sonya." She sounded on the verge of hysteria, and Elise froze in the middle of the sidewalk.

"It's about Audrey."

Elise's world shrank. She forgot about Tremain. She forgot about the woman she'd just spoken to on the phone in the command center, and she forgot about her need to catch a man who was still murdering innocent people. She forgot about the police station and Savannah and the sidewalk and the street and the airplane that was supposed to carry her and David away. She almost forgot about David, whom she sensed beside her.

"Audrey?" Elise said. "What's happened to Audrey?"

Here she'd sent her daughter to Sweden to keep her safe. "Is she hurt?" Please let her be hurt. Hurt was better than dead. "Is she okay?"

"Oh, Elise, I'm so sorry. It's all my fault."

Elise didn't want to know. She couldn't bear to hear Sonya's next words.

She let out a sound of anguish, and her legs went weak. She didn't recall walking, but she found herself behind the police station, in the cemetery. She groped blindly and sat down on one of the aboveground burial vaults.

David was still there. Hovering. She couldn't look at him. There were his black shoes. Plain black shoes with skinny laces. And the green grass. The green grass was there too. And white blossoms that had blown from a nearby tree.

"What happened?" Elise said, her voice flat and emotionless. She hadn't thought about turning herself off. The psyche just did that. How fast it could build a protective shell around a person, shutting you off from the crushed blossoms and the black shoes.

"It's all my fault," Sonya repeated in her heavy accent that up until this moment Elise had loved. Now it was threatening. Now it represented something bad.

"She told me she was staying the night with friends. I gave her permission to do that, but then she didn't come home the next day."

"And . . .?"

"I went to her room, and on her desk was a letter for me. Right now she's on a plane heading home."

Elise struggled to comprehend. "What did you say?"

"She caught a train to Stockholm yesterday, and she's flying back to the States. I'm so sorry. I should have watched her closer. I should have asked more questions."

"She's alive? She's okay?"

"She's perfectly healthy. I fed her well. I took care of her." Now Sonya was beginning to sound irritated. "You know how she is. So headstrong. So emotional. She was a lot of work."

"I know. She is. She can be."

Alive. Okay. Elise couldn't be mad. Maybe later, but now she was basking in the good news. The wonderful news.

"She was worried about you," Sonya said, her voice taking on a placating tone. "She kept wanting to come home."

"That's okay, Sonya. I understand."

Elise wasn't exactly sure what was said from that point on. Some more sentences, followed by a good-bye and a promise to let Sonya know when Audrey was back safe and sound. And then they disconnected.

For a moment Elise stared at David. And then the past weeks, days, and minutes swamped her. Her capture by Tremain, her escape, Tremain's escape, the phone call with Tremain's mother, and then this. Audrey.

Elise had never broken down on the job, but she broke down now. She burst into tears. Horrified, she pulled herself together in less than a minute, sniffling, wiping her nose with the back of her hand while David sat beside her, waiting. Once she calmed down, she told him what had happened, and how Audrey was on her way home. David laughed. He laughed!

He shook his head, but he was smiling. "She's got a mind of her own."

"She's fifteen."

"I'll bet you were just as stubborn at her age."

Yeah, she was. "I was younger than that when I put a love spell on a boy."

"Did it work?" he asked, humoring her, because Elise knew very well what he thought about such things.

"Oh, it worked. That's why I believe in them. That's how I know you can make someone love you, and how I know mojos can create false emotions."

She saw that her words gave him a small blow, and she instantly wished she could take them back. For a split second, she saw that she'd hurt him.

But in true David fashion, he shrugged it off. He got to his feet and turned to stand in front of her, hands in his pockets. And it was like the depth of field opened up and her world that had shrunk during the phone call now expanded. The sky was a brilliant blue, and the sun was warm on her face. David stood there, smelling of wool and leather, with his hair and his eyes, his calm demeanor, his presence a comfort. This is what she never wanted to lose. This feeling of absolute comfort and trust. She wished she hadn't brought up the love spell.

David crouched down. "Tell you what we're going to do. I'll go to Atlanta alone. From there, I'll fly to Virginia."

"Virginia?"

"The execution," he reminded her.

She'd forgotten about David's ex-wife. How awful that she'd forgotten.

She started to protest, but he held up a hand, stopping her. "Hear me out. Audrey is coming, and you need to be here when she arrives. You need to meet her at the airport."

He was right.

"Stay here. Meet Audrey. Take care of her. Yell at her. Fight with her. Hug her. Love her. Whatever you need to do, do it. I'll go to Atlanta. I'll take care of Tremain."

His words held an ominous tone.

"You aren't going to kill him, are you? I want him dead as much as you do, but, David, please, please, please promise me you won't do anything stupid. I need to know you aren't going to kill him."

She could see it, read it in his eyes. That's exactly what he was planning. And if she stayed in Savannah, she wouldn't be there to stop him.

"Don't," she said.

"He needs to die," David whispered. "We both know that."

"If you kill him, you'll go to prison."

"That's okay. I'm okay with that."

"I'm *not* okay with it. Don't do that to me. Don't you dare do that to me."

He was taken aback for a second time. His brow furrowed as he tried to figure out what she was saying. "I don't understand." And then his face cleared as he put it together. "Don't feel guilty. I want to do this. I have to do it."

"It's not just the guilt," Elise said. "What will we do if you go to prison?"

"What do you mean?"

"Me. Audrey." Didn't he know? Didn't he understand? "We *need* you."

He looked surprised all over again.

"Promise me," she said. "Promise you won't kill him."

He took her hands in both of his, and he rubbed them, as if trying to warm her up. She hadn't realized her hands were cold, but they were. He'd known before she'd known. "Okay," he said quietly. "I won't kill him. I won't kill Tremain."

She let out her breath in relief. But the relief was short-lived. Her phone rang. She pulled her hands from David's and reached into her pocket.

The call was from Medical Examiner John Casper. "Hey, Elise. Don't know if you heard about this, but we got a body in here you and David might want to take a look at."

She glanced at David, who'd gotten to his feet.

"White male, early twenties, I'd say."

"And?"

"I'm not even sure," Casper said. "You just need to come and take a look."

She disconnected, shared the call information with David, then stood up. "I'll head to the morgue, and you head to Atlanta."

He nodded. "Call me if you discover anything new."

"You too."

"And, Elise?"

She paused and turned back to him.

"Don't be too hard on Audrey. She loves you."

He was right. And the fact that her daughter was coming home because she was worried about her mother . . . how could Elise get mad at her for that? "She was safe over there," Elise said. "At least safer than here."

"We'll get Tremain. She'll be safe again. You'll both be safe again."

Elise's phone signaled another call. It was Strata Luna.

"Come by my place," she said. "I have something for you." With that cryptic message, she disconnected.

CHAPTER 35

Elise leaned out the car window and pushed the "Call" button. A quick "It's me," and the black iron gate that marked the boundary of Strata Luna's mansion swung open, then closed behind her. Elise parked, and, like before, Javier met her at the front door.

"She's in the garden," he said. "I'll show you the way."

Ceiling fans silently stirred the air and their footsteps echoed across Spanish tile as they passed a massive oil painting of Strata Luna hanging on a red wall. Elise had never been in this part of the mansion, and as she followed Javier in his crisp black pants and even crisper white cotton shirt, she tried not to gawk. Then they were back outside moving down a curved passageway that opened up to fountains and massive live oaks.

"Take the path," Javier said, pointing. "You'll find her."

Elise thanked him. Then, with the help of her cane, she ducked under branches and curtains of moss that blocked the sun. The path finally opened up, and there was Strata Luna in her signature black garb waiting on a cement bench.

She smiled at Elise, but there was strain in her eyes. "I'm sorry to be so mysterious, but a person just doesn't know today. We live in a time where it seems a record is left of everything, and even the walls have eyes and ears."

"You said—"

Strata Luna put a finger to her lips. *Shhh.* "Come with me, darlin' girl." She took Elise's arm and linked it in hers. Side by side, they walked down the path. After stones gave way to dirt, they continued until they reached a narrow river where a small boat was tied to the trunk of a tree.

"Do you know how to row?" Strata Luna asked.

"You don't grow up in the Lowcountry without holding an oar or two," Elise said.

Strata Luna laughed, untied the boat, and tossed the rope aside. Then she stepped in and took the far seat, her weight lifting the bow from land. "Hurry," she told Elise, as the skiff began to drift while Strata Luna picked up one of two sets of oars.

Leaving her cane on the bank, Elise stepped into the boat, sat down facing the Gullah woman, grabbed an oar, and pushed off.

"It's so quiet out here," Strata Luna said minutes later.

The rowing movement stirred up pain, especially to her ribs, and Elise was forced to take it easy. Not that it really mattered, since Strata Luna seemed to know what she was doing. With each sweep of the woman's oars, the boat shot forward until the water opened into a large lagoon, swamp trees with thick, tangled roots reaching deep into black water.

Strata Luna stopped rowing and rested her oars inside the small craft. "You look tired, sweetie," she said.

"I am. And as lovely as this is, I'm really not feeling up to a boat ride. I was on my way to the morgue when you called."

"This won't take long."

Strata Luna's hand vanished into a fold in her skirt, then reappeared holding three small drawstring bags made of blue velvet. She gave the bags a light toss so they landed at Elise's feet.

"If you wonder why I brought you out here . . . I don't trust Javier. If offered enough money, the boy would turn on me. And no one must ever know where you got these. If my name is associated with this I could be killed. Do you understand? No one must know."

Sometimes deals had to be made in order to catch a criminal. This was one of those times. Elise scooped up the bags. "I won't tell anyone."

"They contain ingredients for powerful mojos," Strata Luna explained. "Mojos that will make a person wealthy, extend a person's life, and make a person a sexual animal. I can see you don't think that's unusual. The difference is that these are said to contain the ground-up brain of a business tycoon, the heart of a one-hundred-year-old man, and the penis of a twenty-year-old."

The very body parts taken from the first three victims murdered before Tremain captured her. Elise eased open the drawstring on one of the bags and peered inside. It looked like dirt and ashes and coffee grounds. "And you believe it?"

"You asked for help." Strata Luna shrugged. "I did what I could."

"I'll send these to the DNA lab in Atlanta. They'll at least be able to tell us if there's anything human in here. And if your suspicions are right, they should be able to match the victims." She closed the bag, then tucked all three in the pocket of her jacket. "I won't disclose my source."

At the same time, Elise doubted the contents of the bags held anything human. How handy for an unscrupulous conjurer to hear the news of the murders, toss some dirt and ashes into a bag, and sell it as something real.

"Just rest, my dear," Strata Luna said, picking up her oars once again. "Lean back and let the sun heal you while Strata Luna takes us home."

Elise reached for her set of oars then stopped, leaned back on her elbows, turned her face to the sky, and closed her eyes while Strata Luna rowed.

Too soon the bow slid up the grass bank and Elise stepped out while the boat was still moving. Strata Luna followed, tying the small craft to the tree. Together the women walked up the slope through a canopy of trees, Elise with her cane, Strata Luna with her rustling gown.

"Would you like to come inside?" Strata Luna asked. "I could have Javier make us something. He could even give you a massage. He gives the best massages. And he could do more for you, if you have the mind. Take the bedroom upstairs at the end of the hall. I can send him to you."

"That's okay," Elise said.

Strata Luna smiled. "I was teasing. I know you wouldn't do that. I know you think sex is evil."

"I do not."

"Then why were you so upset about the mojo I made for David? He told me you found it and tore it up."

"I just don't want a relationship that isn't real."

"Oh, my dear. You should know a mojo can't make a person do what she doesn't want to do. Deep in your heart, you wanted him to lie down with you. I can see from your face it's true."

"I can't talk about this now."

"Okay, but that man is crazy about you."

"He's not."

Strata Luna laughed and shook her head. "You don't know nothin' about men."

"Do you believe in love?" Elise asked. She was curious, because Strata Luna always surrounded herself with men who weren't her equal, and men she could easily walk away from. Toys. Beautiful toys.

The Gullah woman got a far-off look in her eyes. "I don't know about love. The closest I ever came to experiencing love was with Jackson Sweet. Did I love him? I don't know. But sometimes, when I remember him, when I think of him, I get a pain deep inside."

Her nostalgic words made Elise wonder anew about the man who'd shown up at the plantation. Strata Luna was talking as if Jackson Sweet were a part of her past, dead and gone. Or, if the mystery man *was* Jackson Sweet, then maybe Strata Luna had closed that door when he ran off years ago. Maybe he was as good as dead to her.

After leaving Strata Luna's, Elise swung by the police station with the mojo bags, leaving them in the care of Avery and Mason with instructions that they be hand-delivered to the DNA lab in Atlanta even though it would take over three hours to get there. "Ask them to rush it."

Then, finally, she was heading for the morgue on the outskirts of town. As she pulled into the parking lot, her phone went off again. Not David, not Strata Luna. A picture of Audrey filled the screen, and Elise hit the "Answer" button. They both started talking at the same time. Questions. Explanations. Excuses.

Finally the number-one reason behind Audrey's call: "I missed my flight, and I'm stuck in London," she said. "I'll text you the new flight information."

"Audrey, you're fifteen." Talk about stating the obvious.

"I'm sorry, Mom. I needed to come home. I knew you wouldn't let me, so I decided to do it myself."

Elise didn't want to argue with her over the phone. "Be careful."

"I'll be okay. I'm just going to sleep at the airport. My flight leaves early in the morning London time, then I have to switch planes in New York before heading to Savannah."

Fifteen. Alone in London. "Don't leave the airport, do you hear me?" Elise said.

"I won't. Mom?"

"What?"

"Are you mad?"

"Let's don't talk about this now. I'll see you tomorrow."

"Are you picking me up?"

"Of course."

"Is my room done?"

"No. I have no idea where we'll stay. Maybe at the plantation, but I'll be at the airport. I'll even get a pass to come through the TSA checkpoint so I can meet you at the gate."

Elise wanted to watch the plane land. She wanted to watch it pull up to the walkway. "I have to go," Elise said. "Text me when you wake up. Text me when you board. Text me when you land."

"Okay. I will."

"I love you," Elise said.

"Me too."

They disconnected, and Elise stared at the picture of Audrey on her cell-phone screen. Then she slipped the phone into her pocket and got out of the car.

John Casper was waiting for her in the morgue. He seemed a little more wired than usual. Nervous, excited, smiling, and jumpy. He sure did like his dead people.

"Mara's out of town," he said, explaining his lack of girlfriend and assistant. "She went to Texas to pick up the last of her stuff she had in storage." Then he asked about David.

The new development was confidential, so Elise simply told him David couldn't make it. They didn't want anyone knowing about Tremain since the element of surprise was crucial to catching him.

"Here's the deal," John said. "This body was pulled from the Ogeechee River last night. At first they thought it was a drowning. You know how it is with bodies and water and current and nibbling fish . . . It's just hard to tell what's going on. So anyway, it didn't seem that strange."

"Are any organs gone?" She'd normally let him talk and talk until he finally got to the point, but she had too much in her head to wait. And she was having trouble concentrating.

"You okay?" John asked, looking at her a little more closely.

"A tough day."

"You have pain lines. Between your eyes. Headache? Need something? Tylenol? A glass of water? Coffee? I just got this latte machine, and I can make you a latte. Some caffeine might be just what you need."

"That's okay." She'd forgotten her cane in the car, and her ankle and ribs were killing her. She would take a pain pill when they were done. "The body—does it have anything that leads you to think it might be connected to Atticus Tremain? The more murders we can pin on him the better, and the more likely he'll be to get a death sentence."

"Nothing similar." They continued down the hall, toward the autopsy suite. "I just thought you and Detective Gould would want to see this."

What he meant was that he needed to share his enthusiasm.

In the center of the autopsy suite was a metal gurney and a body covered in a sheet. She'd seen the scene a million times.

"So," John Casper said. "We get this body, and I come in here today expecting the usual kind of water death. I prepare to start the autopsy and quickly realize this guy didn't die recently." He pulled back the sheet to reveal what, at first glance, looked fairly typical of a body that had been submerged for a length of time. Male. Hard to tell the age. Skin that had turned white, tissue sliding from bone, fingers and toes nibbled off by fish.

"Do we have an ID?"

"No. I have to get some statistics to your office in hopes that they can pull something together. But like I was saying, the weird thing? This guy has been dead awhile."

"What's awhile? Are you talking weeks? Longer? It could be a Tremain murder. Maybe it happened before his coma."

"No, I'm talking a long time ago."

Casper liked to drag things out. "How long?"

"Years."

"Care to take a stab at how many?"

"I can't really tell from my preliminary and cursory exam."

"John, give me an educated guess. I won't hold you to it."

He nodded. "Okay. Keep in mind that we're talking pre-autopsy . . . but I'm going to say he's been dead twenty years or so."

"How can that be? How can a body last so long in water?"

"That's the weird thing. I don't think he was in the water that long. Maybe forty-eight hours, max."

"So are we talking grave robbery?"

"I don't think so. Again, I can't say, but this doesn't look like an embalmed body to me."

"White male. Dead twenty years. No embalming." She didn't like where this was going. "Were there any clothes on the body?" she asked.

"That's another thing," Casper said, his voice rising with renewed enthusiasm. "I mean, the clothes could have come from a vintage shop, but they were definitely old. Everything on him was old, and everything on him looked to be from the same time period. The jeans, the belt, the shirt . . ."

"Can I see the clothing?" Her heart was beating in fresh dread, and at complete odds with John Casper's innocent excitement.

"Over here."

She followed him to a corner of the room. Spread out on a table, as if the body had simply evaporated, leaving the fabric behind, was a shirt, a leather belt, and a pair of jeans. But it was the shirt that got Elise's full attention. Flannel. Plaid. And not your average plaid. This one was yellow and black.

She made a big deal out of checking her watch. "I have to go," she said.

True. She had to get out of there. Get back to the plantation. To the third floor and a certain trunk. And also, Casper was surprisingly astute. He read people. And she didn't want him reading her. "Let me know what you find during the autopsy." She already knew what he would find. Death caused by blunt-force trauma to the skull.

CHAPTER 36

Thirty minutes later Elise pulled up to the plantation house. Above her, clouds were moving fast, darkness coming on even though it wasn't night. That weird kind of darkness that made her feel both excited and nervous.

She got out of the car, closed the door, and just stood there a moment staring at the house in the pre-storm silence. John Casper had been right. She was in pain. A great deal, in fact. Pushing herself too hard with the Tremain case, but the attempt to row Strata Luna's boat had been the kicker. And now, on top of everything, her head was pounding, maybe due to the threatening storm and sudden drop in barometric pressure.

Unable to step out of cop mode, she did a mental appraisal of the situation. Tremain would soon be taken care of, Audrey was coming home, and Elise would pick her up in the morning. And Anastasia? What about Anastasia? And the body at the morgue . . . Not good, but not life threatening. Not evil-psycho-killer stuff, but now that the Tremain case was under control, and now that they might have a lead on the people trafficking body parts, she had to deal with her aunt. It wouldn't be pleasant.

Why, oh why had Anastasia dumped the body? A jury might sympathize with her when it came to insurance fraud, but failing to report a murder, then covering it up? Then disposing of the body? Anastasia had made the mistake so many criminals made. She didn't stop when an arrest was inevitable, and she'd instead embarked upon something that would only make things worse for her in the end.

Elise walked up the plantation house steps, opened the door, and stepped into the kitchen. The table had been set with one plate. Something porcelain and vintage, decorated in a pink-rose design. A cutting board, a knife, a loaf of French bread. An unopened bottle of red wine. A delicate wineglass. A bouquet of some type of wild-flower with yellow blooms. Next to the plate was a sheet of unlined paper, folded once in the center.

Elise picked it up and opened it: a handwritten note from Anastasia.

My dearest Elise,

I will cherish our recent time together, and it breaks my heart to think I will never see you again. I wish we could have visited more when you were younger, but I'm grateful for the time we did have. You know that I'm a free spirit. I cannot be contained or held down or confined. The idea of prison hurts my soul even as I write this. But rest assured that I will always carry a bit of you in my heart, and I never meant to deceive. I just wanted to keep my precious plantation. That was wrong. I understand that now.

I am off on a new adventure. Maybe I will leave the country and give myself a new name. I will paint under a blue sky, and I will wear a red scarf around my neck and ride a bicycle and drink wine. In other words, I will live. Please don't ask Melinda where I've gone. She's been compromised enough in this ordeal. Just believe me when I say I love you. Be happy, and dance in the moonlight.

Anastasia

PS: Look in the refrigerator. I've left you something, lovingly prepared by me.

Elise put down the note and stared into space. *What the hell?* Didn't anybody in her family do what they were supposed to do? Audrey, not staying in Sweden. Anastasia, bolting. Not only bolting, but apparently attempting to dispose of a dead body before hitting the road. Jackson Sweet, possibly pulling a return from the great beyond.

How long had Anastasia been gone? Elise wondered. She needed to give police a heads-up so airports could be notified.

If leaving the country, would Anastasia fly out of Savannah? Maybe Jacksonville. Jacksonville would give her a better chance of a direct flight abroad. But then Elise thought of her aunt in that red scarf, sitting outside a café in some country far, away. And then she thought of her sitting in a prison cell.

She didn't need to check, but she checked anyway. With the help of the antique cane, she went up the three flights of stairs, to the room at the end of the long hallway, past the walls that had been stripped down to the lath, wood that whispered and smelled of a hundred years gone by, and wallpaper that might have come from France. Peeling, but still beautiful in its decay.

Anastasia's room was closed. Elise reached for the glass knob and opened the door. Inside, she turned on the light near the bed, the light with the red shade and the claw feet. Everything was as it had been the day she'd found her aunt living there, down to the dirty dishes and the coffee cups with lipstick stains. Elise could smell Anastasia's perfume, that mixture of vanilla and lavender, along with a hint of something woodsy. Like moss. Like crushed live-oak leaves. Like the damp soil along the edge of the river. All of those things were Anastasia.

There was the record player. Elise turned the control dial and placed the needle on the waiting LP, feeling a need to hear the music her aunt had last listened to. A song filled the small space. The Everly Brothers.

Even though Elise didn't have to look, she walked across the hall to the steamer trunk and lifted the lid. Women's shoes. The black bathing suit. A rubber swimming cap, and a towel. But no body. Of course there was no body.

Downstairs, Elise went to her room, or rather to Anastasia's old room, and searched through the bedside dresser for the pain medication she'd avoided taking for several days.

She popped a pill and removed her holster and gun. Then, in the kitchen, she found a homemade apple pie in the refrigerator, along with a platter of cheese covered in plastic wrap. She cut a slice of pie, poured herself a glass of wine, and sat down at the table. An idiot knew not to mix pain medication with alcohol, but she planned to take just a few sips in honor of her aunt.

Her phone buzzed, indicating a text message.

David, with an update on the Tremain situation.

I tried calling, but it didn't go through. We have the house surrounded. SWAT team is here. Sharpshooter on a nearby hill. It's getting dark, so we're hoping to complete the capture before the sun goes down. If not, we'll stick it out as long as we have to.

Elise told him about Audrey. About how Audrey was stuck in London. *Her flight gets in late tomorrow morning. I don't know the exact time yet.*

Go easy on her.

I will.

What are you doing right now? David asked.

I'm at the plantation, eating homemade apple pie and drinking a glass of wine.

I'm glad you're relaxing. Get a good night's sleep. I gotta go. They're ready to storm the house. This will be wrapped up soon. I'll text you when it's over.

Elise let out a giant sigh of relief, put her phone aside, and took a bite of pie.

CHAPTER 37

Everybody lies.

Those little lies you tell when someone asks if you feel okay, or if you liked a song, or if you liked a movie, or if you liked the meal a friend just spent hours preparing. Then there were the other ones. The embellishments. Rounding up. Five days of torrential rain instead of four. Two thousand miles instead of 1,800. A temperature of 110 degrees instead of 107. Those things that you find yourself doing just to give your story a little extra punch.

Earlier that day, David told Elise a big lie. A huge lie. The one about not killing Tremain. Now, as David and the SWAT team waited for darkness to give them the cover they needed to approach the Francis house, David didn't feel bad about his lies. He'd kill Tremain and go to prison. That was okay. And Elise was wrong about not being able to get by without him. She'd gotten by without him before; she could do it again.

David wanted to do something right. This was right.

The SWAT team and the Lumpkin County Police Department had no problem allowing him to tag along. His old FBI credentials got him into a lot of places his detective badge couldn't, and he was not ashamed to play that card. He hadn't lied about being an FBI agent. They knew he was ex-FBI, but that was more impressive than never having been FBI. It actually might have given him more leverage, because there was none of the resentment that came when FBI agents were sent in to save the day with their brilliance. Been there, done that, had the footprint on his ass to prove it.

"Ten minutes until we move." That came from the commander of the SWAT team. David nodded and went back to his prison fantasy.

Hopefully inmates wouldn't know he'd been a detective. Yeah, they'd know. He'd most likely be put in some special area where he wouldn't be killed the first day.

He and Elise would write letters and she'd come to visit. Maybe at some point she'd meet someone, remarry. Erase that. He didn't like thinking about that.

Focus.

He rechecked his weapon and slipped it into his shoulder holster under his jacket. He wished he'd had time to write Elise a letter. But what would he have said? Given her his recipe for pumpkin bread? Because anything more would just make her feel bad, feel worse, and that was the last thing he wanted to do. Maybe he would have explained that he was doing this as much for him as for her. Yeah, that was good. So she wouldn't feel guilty.

"Ready to move."

The house was under heavy surveillance, with the SWAT team a quarter of a mile away. Now they moved through the woods, their feet silent on the needle-strewn forest floor. No one spoke, and the only illumination came from one flashlight pointed at the ground.

Everybody in black. Helmets. Boots. They'd made David put on a bulletproof vest, but he'd told them he'd stay out of their way. Another lie.

He wondered if Audrey was flying into the Savannah airport. And what would Elise do? Hug her daughter and tell her she was glad to see her? Because that's all that really mattered in the end.

There was the house.

A one-story shack with lights burning behind thin curtains. No sign of life. No sign of movement. In the driveway was the silver Chevy Malibu that had been stolen from the used-car dealership in Savannah.

They moved forward.

How could such big men move so quickly and so silently? But they did. Running in a crouched position, flanking the front door while more men in their black gear moved to the back of the house to guard the only other way in or out.

It was all about speed and surprise. The idea was to take the perpetrator down in a minute or less. It could be done, and when the carefully choreographed dance went according to plan, it was beautiful to behold.

There was the signal.

The door was kicked open, and now the boots were no longer silent. Now the men shouted and ran, weapons drawn but pointed toward the ceiling. David drew his own and followed, bracing it in two hands, muzzle pointed at the floor in the way he'd been trained.

A woman. The mother. Sitting at the kitchen table. Getting to her feet, hands raised, mouth open wide.

Boots thundering through the house. Boots returning. The leader reporting. "Nobody."

David did a mental shake of his head, a clearing of his ears. "Check again."

"There's nobody else here."

"A crawl space. A cellar."

"No."

David pivoted to the woman. "Where is he?"

Tremain's mother was in her late sixties and dressed in a pale blue T-shirt, jeans, and white sneakers. Overweight, with teeth that needed work, and two inches of gray roots, the rest of her hair a faded orange. "I don't know," she said.

"When did he leave?"

"A few hours ago."

"I've been here five hours," said one of the men who'd watched the place from a nearby hill. "In that time nobody has come or gone. I never blinked. I never took my eyes off the house."

Everybody lies.

David introduced himself, then asked, "How long ago did your son leave?"

"Maybe it was more than a few hours," she stammered, lowering her hands. "I don't know. I tried to keep him here like the detective said, but he wouldn't stay."

"She's lying," David said to the others in the room.

And worse, he was beginning to suspect they'd all been tricked. "Your son was never here, was he?"

"He *was* here."

"We'll find out eventually," David told her. "Dust for prints."

He could see her brain falter. See her doubting her lies, wishing she'd told better ones.

"I understand," David said. "You were trying to protect him."

She relaxed a little.

"Where did the car come from?" he asked. "How did it get here?"

She didn't answer.

"You know you're going to be arrested for aiding and abetting a fugitive and suspected murderer, don't you?" He just threw the suspected in there, because they all knew damn well Tremain was guilty.

Someone slapped handcuffs on her, and another officer read the woman her rights. Then they began leading her away. David knew this was his last chance. He needed to say something that would trigger an unguarded response. He couldn't think of anything. "Your son is a murdering sack of shit."

She turned to stare at him, her hands cuffed behind her. Her face became feral as her lips curled back from her teeth. Everything he needed to know was in that response. "I was helping him. I was protecting my son so he'd have time to get away."

"You helped a killer escape."

"This is a witch hunt. My son would never hurt a fly."

"Your son kidnapped my partner. He held her hostage."

"But did he *kill* her? No! Because he's not a killer! My son is not a killer! And now, by the grace of God, he's been saved. If he was a bad person, God would never have raised him from that coma. My son is good. He's good!"

David almost felt sorry for her. She believed what she was saying. She needed to believe what she was saying.

"And just look. The murders . . . they kept happening even when he was in a coma. How do you explain that?" She was shouting, her face bright red. David was afraid she might have a stroke right there in the kitchen.

"Oh, Savannah!" she said. "I'll bet you money that somebody—the mayor or somebody—put pressure on you to find the killer, and my son was just in the wrong place at the wrong time. He was handy. And yes, I helped him get away. Why? Because he's innocent, and helping him was the right thing to do. I love my son. I'm a good mother."

Ah, and there it was. Because the mothers of killers had a lot of guilt to carry, always wondering if they should have seen the signs, or if they'd done something to create the monster. And many, like Mrs. Francis, simply refused to believe the truth because they couldn't live with it. David had seen mothers sobbing at executions, proclaiming their sons' innocence all the way to the final injection.

"He paid somebody to drive the car here," she said, suddenly eager to let them know just how her son had outwitted them. "I don't know who. The guy just parked it, handed me a letter with instructions, and left in another car."

"Found it." An officer held up a piece of lined paper. Evidence.

"Bag that," somebody said.

"Right now my baby is on a plane to some other country," Mrs. Francis said. "Or on a boat, going far away."

David hoped to hell that was the case, but it didn't fit Tremain's profile. Running was probably the last thing the guy would do. And then David remembered that Elise was alone at the plantation.

CHAPTER 38

After eating the slice of pie, Elise went to the bedroom and lay down on the feather mattress. The medication had kicked in, and she was without pain for the first time in days. What a concept. To simply feel better because she didn't hurt.

She hadn't meant to sleep, but she dropped off, waking up an hour later groggy and disoriented. She checked her phone to find a text from Avery, telling her he'd gotten the mojo bags to the DNA lab. Nothing new from David.

The last text was from Audrey with her flight numbers and departure times. Elise would be relieved when all of this was over, when Audrey was back home and Tremain was behind bars.

When she was working a case, she got lost in it and forgot about her own life. But now, with the finalization of two big concerns, Tremain and Audrey, her focus shifted, and she found herself once again thinking about her life and the path she'd taken. Before long, Audrey would be out of high school and off to college. These few years were so important, and having a mother with her head buried in case files and investigations and death and brutal crimes . . . What kind of life was that for a teenager?

Elise's thoughts shifted to the coffee shop. What would they call it? Sweet Kitty. Yes. And she and Audrey would wear pink aprons with black cats on them, and the latte and espresso foam would have a cat design. And where would David fit in? He'd come to the shop and drink a latte. Maybe he'd tell her about a case he was working, and maybe he'd even consult with her at times.

Propped up in bed, Elise picked up the receiver to the landline phone and began dialing the department to report Anastasia, but she couldn't make herself complete the number.

Police work was black and white, but life wasn't. There was so much gray. And maybe deep down she was glad her aunt was getting away.

Elise returned the phone to the cradle and tossed back the knitted throw. Purple. Soft. Probably made by Anastasia or by someone who'd stayed at the plantation.

Barefoot except for the elastic bandage around her ankle, Elise grabbed her cane and walked down the hallway, turning on a few dim lights as she went, muted bulbs casting a soothing glow on wooden walls. Through the living room, to the pool room. Once there, she opened the door and hit the round dimmer switch, adjusting the overheads to low. The next switch turned on the submerged pool lights, illuminating blue water.

Elise stripped down to black bra and panties, then sat on the chaise longue and unwound the elastic bandage before approaching the water. Careful of her ankle, the cement floor cold, she curled her toes against the lipped edge of the pool, linked her thumbs above her head the way she'd been taught as a child, and dove in.

It was colder than she'd anticipated, and she suppressed a gasp reflex. Eyes open underwater, arms outstretched, she rode the downward momentum, shooting toward the drain in the deep end. And, just as she'd done years ago, she touched the metal ring with her fingers, then turned her body, braced her good foot against the bottom of the pool, and pushed hard. She shot skyward, breaking the surface of the water moments later.

She swam several slow laps, loving the way the water felt against her skin. Sensuous. Relaxing. Finally she turned, closed her eyes, and let herself float.

She thought about Audrey, soon to be up there in the sky, above water, above the Atlantic Ocean. A flight to New York, then a switch to Savannah.

Elise knew she should probably be the mom.

No, David was right. This wasn't a time for discipline. It was a time for honest reaction. When Audrey got off the plane, Elise would hug her, and they would both cry. Mother-and-child reunion.

Elise fanned the water on each side of her, then she did a surface dive, gracefully moving through the water, reaching the bottom once more. This time she stayed down there, thinking of those tea parties she and Anastasia used to have. From below, she looked up through the layers and gallons of water to see the lights on the ceiling above, out of focus and shifting as if being stretched and pulled.

From somewhere in the broken prism, a dark shape emerged. Something beyond the water, near the edge of the pool.

A person.

Elise pushed herself and shot to the surface, expecting to see Melinda. Treading water, her hands moving in quick figure eights, she scanned the room, her gaze freezing when it reached the chaise longue. A person, yes. But not Melinda. Definitely not Melinda.

Her heart began to pound in her head and she gasped, sank, and resurfaced to stare at what she wished to hell was an apparition. But no. Atticus Tremain sat on the chair by the side of the pool, a dark jacket beside him, his hands stacked and resting on the crook of her cane.

CHAPTER 39

A h, there you are," Tremain said, as if he and Elise had casually gone to different areas of the house hours earlier and had now reunited.

The thing about Tremain? He wasn't bad looking. If a woman met him in a dark alley and had to choose between Tremain and a tattered, homeless guy, she'd choose Tremain. She'd *run* to Tremain for help. Many cold-blooded killers had a certain look, something not quite right about them, where even the face itself seemed off. But then there were the ones like Ted Bundy and Atticus Tremain. Those charming and handsome sociopaths who could fool their family and coworkers.

Elise struggled to understand how he'd gotten from northern Georgia to the plantation. David had just texted her an hour and a half ago.

He smiled. "I can see you're trying to figure this all out. Did you do it? Figure it out?"

She continued to tread water in the center of the pool, wishing her heart would slow down so she could think. "You never left Savannah, did you?" she asked. That was the only explanation. He'd never gone anywhere. He'd set a trap, and they'd walked right into it.

"I actually thought you'd go to my mother's house and I would come here and hide while you were gone, but how fortuitous that you stayed behind, because this works out nicely." Tremain looked around, walked over to a small wicker shelf, and returned with a mint-green towel.

He was dressed in baggy black pants, leather shoes, and a rumpled plaid shirt. None of the clothes looked new, and she figured he'd picked them up at Salvation Army or Goodwill. His beard was gone, but the dark hair on his head was long, almost to his shoulders.

"Come out of the water, Elise. I can see you're getting tired. I'll even give you a hand."

"What do you want from me?" It was a ridiculous question to ask a man who was batshit crazy, but she was stalling. She was buying time.

"I want you to recognize your calling, that's what I want. And if you won't do that, I want you to pass the mantle to me."

"I don't have a mantle to pass, and if I did, I'd pass it to my daughter, I wouldn't pass it to some murdering psychopath." Probably shouldn't have said that. "And anyway, mantles can't be taken. They have to be given willingly."

"Then you haven't kept up with your studies. Your power can pass to me if you die by my hand."

"I have no power." Why did everybody keep insisting she had something she didn't have? And she was beginning to suspect David was right. It was all bull anyway. The Black Tupelo body art hadn't protected her. The mojos Strata Luna kept plying her with had done nothing. *Nothing.* Why? Because none of it was real.

"That's what makes me mad," Tremain said, not sounding mad in the least, but rather typically detached. "Your denial."

Growing increasingly tired, Elise slipped, resurfaced, and gasped for air. Realizing she couldn't continue to tread water, she struck out for the opposite side of the pool, away from Tremain, her fingers making contact with the concrete edge. She stuck her elbow in the gutter and anchored herself there, her toes against the wall of the pool.

"There are no accidents," Tremain said. "Everything happens for a reason. Do you remember that night a long time ago? You were maybe ten or eleven, and everybody was down by the river. You were going to go swimming, but I told you not to. I told you there were alligators in the water."

Her mind struggled to grasp what he was saying.

He nodded as he watched the comprehension on her face. "I used to come here," he said. "Years ago. I knew your aunt. In fact, she and I spent a few interesting nights together. And just think, if not for me you'd have been raped. Probably killed. Just to keep you quiet, because rapists do that. I saw the guy pick you up and carry you into the house." Tremain shook his head. "Something told me to go after you, protect you. And I did."

"That was you." She felt a tumbling and shifting in her brain as the pieces fell into place, and she was both horrified and amazed. Amazed to think that the long-ago past was touching today, touching this moment. That knowledge was profound. Her fear receded, not because he wasn't to be feared, but because the song the universe was singing was beyond her control. It would sing the same song no matter what she did.

"I had a different name then," he said.

"Joe."

"Not Joe. Joel. But you called me Joe, and I didn't have the heart to tell you that was wrong. After the murder I changed my name to Atticus Tremain in case your aunt decided to report the incident." He circled the pool as he talked, keeping his eyes on her the entire time. "I wanted a different name anyway. Thought about changing it to Sweet. Kinda wish I had."

Now he was a few yards from her. "There are so many ways into this place. Do you know this was a stop for the Underground Railroad? At least that's what Anastasia told people, but I suspect a lot of what she said was a lie." He unfolded the towel and held it up with both hands—an invitation to let him wrap her in it. "I came from the river. She really should do something about the bars over the tunnel entrance. Anybody can get in." He laughed. "And the little bit of rebar left was painted blue. Like that would stop me."

"Blue paint isn't for humans," Elise said, trying to keep him going while her mind devised a plan. She had to get to her room, to her gun. If she could outrun him . . . "Blue paint is for slip-skin hags, for spirits."

"There was no one here when I arrived," he continued, seeming to relish sharing how well things had fallen into place. "I hid upstairs in one of the rooms and waited for you to come home."

"We could go to the kitchen and have a slice of pie," Elise said shifting to another tactic. "It's really good. I'll bet you're hungry."

"Don't pull that detective stuff on me again. It didn't work before, and it won't work this time."

She was watching him, watching him.

Come closer. Just a little closer.

"Sorry," she said, trying to keep her voice conversational. "I just thought . . . Sometimes pie can fix a lot of things. The ultimate comfort food. You saved me once. I'm grateful for that. I really am."

Odd, to think she could very well be dead if he hadn't been at the plantation that night. And if she'd died . . . no Audrey. And she would never have known David. She liked to think she'd brought some stability to his days. What would have happened to him without her?

Tremain's face softened a little at her acknowledgment of the role he'd played in her life, and she thought maybe she was getting through to him.

"You were cute," he said. "And I knew who you were, even back then. I knew you were Jackson Sweet's daughter. I didn't want him hurting Jackson Sweet's kid."

Both of her arms were out of the water, elbows bent, braced. *Come closer.* "I miss those days," she said softly. "Everything was innocent."

"That was my first kill," he told her. "Think about that. I did it for you. Weird, isn't it? How everything comes around. It freaks you out, I can tell. You started me on this path. And I kind of own you since I killed for you all those years ago. We're practically soul mates. And there's something else. Remember when you came to the hospital?"

"When you were in a coma."

"You touched me, and you talked to me. You woke me up. So see, our connection is strong. There's something between us and you need to quit fighting it. You need to let it happen and accept it."

His expression softened even more as he basked in his delusion. For a fleeting second, he lost focus on the now. She lunged, grabbed his foot, and tugged, pulling his leg out from under him. He landed hard at the side of the pool, but not in it. She'd wanted to pull him in it. Drown the bastard.

She turned to swim away, hoping to reach the other side, hoping to get out of the pool and run to her room, but he was fast.

"Bitch." He grabbed her hair and slammed her head against the side of the cement pool, stunning her. Then he shoved her face under the water and held her there.

CHAPTER 40

Elise didn't want David to find her dead in the water. She imagined him walking in the kitchen door, calling her name, looking through the house until he checked the pool room. And there she'd be. Another water death. Another water murder.

The fear of David finding her body gave her strength. Or maybe Tremain wasn't ready to kill her yet. Whatever the case, he loosened his hold, and her head broke the surface. She sucked air into her burning lungs in one long, gasping breath.

With no hesitation, she grabbed his leg, this time with both hands and even more resolve, and she pulled, her feet braced against the side of the pool. His arms flailed, and he tumbled into the water. Without waiting to witness the result of her attack, she swam away, to the other side. With both hands on the ladder, she pulled herself up and out. Then she ran, ignoring the pain in her ankle, out the door and down the hall.

In her room, she lunged for the dresser and the weapon she'd left there. Coughing, wheezing, struggling to catch her breath, she stared at the empty holster in her hand. Her gun was gone.

From behind her, Tremain appeared in the doorway. Over his wet shirt was the brown jacket she'd spotted earlier on the chaise longue. He nonchalantly reached into a pocket, then brought his hand back out.

"Happiness," he stated, dangling her missing weapon from one finger.

She almost laughed at the way he looked, his wet clothes hanging on him, hair plastered to his head. And maybe she did laugh. She wasn't sure. Because at that exact moment, the moment she would have made an actual sound, he aimed the gun and pulled the trigger.

Headlight beams bounced as David pulled off the dirt road and hit the highway leading back to Atlanta. He pushed the accelerator to the floor, hoping the sedan had some power. It took awhile, but the car eventually topped out at ninety. He checked his phone and was relieved to see he finally had a couple of bars. Earlier, he'd texted Elise to warn her about Tremain and to tell her to get back to Savannah if she was at the plantation, but the text hadn't gone through. Now he hit "Resend."

The sound of the discharging gun and the pain that ripped through Elise's arm hit at the same time. The force of the bullet knocked her backward in a stutter step. She caught herself, then stabilized, her injured arm hanging loosely at her side, blood dripping from her fingers.

"Guns are amazing," Tremain said. "I'm over here, you're over there, yet I'm hurting you. Stopping you. Amazing." He pulled the trigger again. White-hot pain shot through her leg, just above her knee.

"I want to make sure you can't get away this time," he explained. "I don't want you dead. At least not yet. There's something I need to do first."

"The mantle?" she asked in a breathless, snagging whisper of pain. She'd outsmarted him once, but this time was different. This time she had two bullets lodged in her. And this time she knew what he was capable of.

"You have something else of mine," he said.

She could only think of one thing. "The tattoo."

"Smart girl."

Her phone buzzed, and both she and Tremain looked at it. He jumped, snatched the phone from the dresser, and read the message.

"From your partner," he told her. "Texting to tell you that I'm not at my mother's." He laughed. "And to warn you about me. He wants you to stay in Savannah tonight. I'll just let him know everything is fine." He typed a reply, then hit "Send."

David's phone buzzed with a reply from Elise.

Everything is fine here, but I'll stay in Savannah tonight so you won't worry. She ended it with a smiley face.

He let out a sigh of relief, checked the speedometer, and settled on eighty-five miles per hour. There was one more flight from Atlanta International Airport to Savannah that night, and he wanted to be on it.

CHAPTER 41

As soon as David's plane touched down at the Savannah airport, he flashed his badge and pushed past passengers in order to be the first one off. Then he was sprinting down the walkway, running through the deserted airport and past the closed shops to the parking lot where he'd left his car.

Middle of the night and there was no traffic. Both the airport and plantation were north of town, and thirty minutes after stepping off the plane he was pounding on the plantation house door even though Elise's car wasn't in the driveway, and even though she'd told him she was staying in town.

If she was in town, she would have answered when he tried to call. And there was the issue of the smiley face. At the time of the message, he'd just been relieved to hear back from her. But then he started thinking about it. Elise didn't use emoticons. She didn't even use exclamation marks.

No response, so he broke the glass on the door with a large stone, reached through to unlock the dead bolt, and stepped inside.

Flowers in the center of the table. A pie missing a single slice, and a plate with a few crumbs on it. Wine, opened but very little gone. These were the details he absorbed in a second.

He spotted a folded piece of paper. A letter to Elise, from her aunt. He forced himself to take the time to read it in case it held any clues, but it only confirmed his earlier suspicion. The woman had faked her death, most likely for insurance. And now that Elise had discovered her deceit, her aunt had run off.

David tossed the note back on the table, and moved cautiously toward the bedroom where he'd deposited Elise that first day. In the hallway, on the wooden floor, he spotted something dark. He crouched to get a closer look. Freshly dried blood. He followed the drips to the bedroom where upon first glance it appeared nothing had been disturbed. But there on the bed was Elise's black shoulder holster. The weapon itself was gone, and her phone was on the dresser.

He did another scan. On the floor near the doorway were two 9mm shell casings. Elise's gun used 9mm.

He pieced together a scenario that might or might not have been what happened. She'd gone to bed. Something had awakened her, and she'd pulled her weapon. He hoped to hell Elise had been the shooter, and he hoped to hell the blood belonged to the person she'd shot. *And let's be perfectly frank,* David told himself. That person was most likely Tremain.

With his own gun in hand, David moved back down the hall, opening doors as he went, to reveal stale rooms that hadn't been disturbed in years.

He cut through the living room to the pool area. Through the glass, before he opened the door, he saw a pile of clothes on a chair. Elise's clothes. He recognized the shirt and pants. And now his brain put together a new scenario. In this one Elise wasn't the shooter. Instead, she'd gone for a swim thinking everything was okay, thinking Tremain was in custody, or at least soon-to-be in custody. Tremain gained entry, found her gun, and accosted her.

David was pretty sure Elise was no longer in the house, yet he forced himself to check the place from bottom to top, all with great speed, because he knew every second brought Elise closer to death.

As he moved through the building, he tried to calculate when the attack had taken place, how many hours had passed. He was pretty sure the texts he'd gotten from her when they were preparing to storm the Francis house were real. That was, what? Five hours ago.

The first hour was crucial. Even laypeople knew that. After the first twenty-four hours, chances of the person being alive dropped drastically.

He'd been through this before. Done this before. Weeks ago. He was trapped in some loop, some recurring nightmare, he thought, as he ran back to the bedroom to use the landline phone to call Savannah PD.

No dial tone. Cut cord. The guy was thorough.

Back outside to his car where he grabbed a flashlight and did a quick examination of the lane and dirt driveway. It had rained recently, but he could make out tire tracks coming and going, along with a few scattered footprints that might or might not have been fresh.

Where would Tremain take her? *If she's still alive.* She'd gotten away from him once. Could she do it again?

Tremain would know better than to go to his house. No, he'd take her somewhere remote. David was pretty sure of that. Someplace she couldn't escape.

Tremain was smart, and he wouldn't make the same mistake twice. This was his do-over, his chance to get it right. This time he'd make sure he killed Elise before she got away. But he hadn't killed her yet. At least it didn't seem that he had. If she were dead, her body would have been left at the plantation, organ or organs removed. That was his MO.

No, he was infatuated with Elise, and that infatuation would make her harder for him to kill. He would toy with her, savor her, and then, finally, when he'd had his fill, he'd kill her.

David could feel himself unraveling, feel himself falling apart.

Maintain.

Last time, he'd just plain lost it, but this time he had to be the cool-headed FBI agent he'd once been. A long time ago, before his life collapsed. He vaguely remembered that guy. He could be him again.

He got in his car and drove toward Savannah, checking his phone, watching for bars to appear. It didn't take long to get out of the dead zone, and once he had a signal he pulled to the side of the road and keyed in the task-force number. David told the officer working the night shift to get a crime team out to the plantation as quickly as possible even though he knew nobody would show up until morning.

"And we need to get information to every news station in the tristate area," David said. "Every national station that'll run it. I think Tremain is in Detective Sandburg's car. If he hasn't ditched it already, he will. He'll probably avoid major roads. I think he'll be looking for a remote location. I know we're understaffed, but get some people on this as quickly as possible. Get them out of bed. See if there are any remote locations that Tremain is familiar with. Places he used to go as a kid. Anything. And I don't need to tell you that we have to work fast. I don't think he'll hang on to her long this time."

Once he was done talking to the officer manning the task-force line, he called Avery, who answered his phone pretty quickly considering David woke him up.

"He's got Elise." That's all David had to say.

CHAPTER 42

The manhunt for Tremain quickly reached fever pitch, and by nine the next morning his face was once again on every news station, local and national. The police department was aware that time was against them, and they were aware that they'd failed Elise before. It was important for them to solve this, find Tremain, find Elise, and do it fast.

Hotline phones were ringing with calls about Tremain sightings. It was too damn bad he looked so generic.

"Three reported spottings in the area," Avery said when David stopped by the command center. "One report of him lying under a bush in Forsyth Park, another of him strolling around Tybee Island, and the last one from a teenager who said he gave Tremain a ride."

"Get that kid on the phone," David said. "I need to talk to him."

They had to pull the teenager out of class. "He's on the line," Avery said after a wait of ten minutes.

David grabbed the phone and began drilling the kid. But when he got to the question about the exact location of the drop-off, David no longer had any doubts.

"I stopped in the middle of the highway, and he got out," the kid said. "There was this dirt lane that was kind of overgrown, but you could tell cars had been down it recently because the grass was all packed. You know how it looks at a fairgrounds or a concert, when a bunch of cars drive over the grass? That's how it looked."

The party.

"Did you see any buildings?"

"No, it was dark. I asked him why he wanted out there, and he laughed and said he was going to see an old friend."

"Can you remember anything else about him? Any small detail?"

"Not really. I mean, he just seemed like a guy who needed help. I would never have figured him for a kidnapper or killer," he said, sounding freaked out.

"Anything else?"

"He did smell a little weird."

"Weird? How?"

"I don't know. Not bad. You ever go into one of those shops where they have all kinds of incense, and it burns your nose? Like that. He smelled like incense."

"Thanks," David told him. "We're going to send someone by the school to take a statement from you." David made a come-here signal with one hand, motioning for a uniformed officer. "Don't leave the school. Someone will be there soon."

He disconnected. "A solid sighting," he announced. "Let's get more manpower out there to canvas the area around the plantation."

He planned on heading out himself once he made sure no other leads had come in. He was hurrying down the hall to report to Major Hoffman when his cell phone vibrated. He pulled it from his pocket hoping it was Elise, knowing it wouldn't be, but she'd called him before when she'd escaped Tremain.

It wasn't Elise, but close. Audrey. He turned and answered while aiming for his office and privacy. He closed the door just as Audrey began talking.

"I'm at the airport," she said, sounding as if she'd been crying. "Mom told me she was picking me up. She told me she'd get a special pass so she could meet me when I got off the plane, but she's not here. I know she's mad at me." He heard her struggle to contain a sob.

With all that had happened, he'd forgotten Audrey. And judging from what she'd just told him, she didn't know about Elise. There weren't that many television screens in the Savannah/Hilton Head Airport. None in the main waiting area, if he recalled correctly.

"I just wanted to come home," Audrey said. "And now I don't know what to do. I thought about calling Dad, but you know how he is about Mom. He'll make me move to Seattle if I tell him she didn't pick me up when she was supposed to. I'd take a cab home, but I only have ten dollars. Most of my money is still in euros."

"Wait for me in the main drop-off area," David said. There would be plenty of police around. "I'll be right there. Do you hear me?" He wanted to tell her to stay away from the televisions, but that would be a little suspicious. "Don't leave the main entry. Don't go to the Starbucks. Don't talk to anybody. Just wait for me."

"Why? What's going on? You're scaring me. Is something wrong? Did something happen to Mom?"

David didn't want to tell her about Elise over the phone, so he lied. He was doing a lot of that lately. "Your mom is fine," he said. "She just had a last-minute appointment, and she asked me to pick you up."

"Oh, okay." He could almost see her relax. "How long before you get here? Because good Godzilla, I'm tired. I had to sleep in an airport last night."

"I'll be there soon," he said. Instead of going to Hoffman's office, he began walking in the direction of the stairs. "I'm leaving downtown right now."

David reached the airport in twenty minutes. He pulled up to loading and unloading, spotting Audrey with a giant polka-dot suitcase. She wore big black sunglasses and a pink dress with black leggings, along with blue Keds. She looked taller even though she hadn't been gone very long.

David got out and circled the car, went to her, and gave her a hug because she looked like she needed one. Then he hefted her suitcase into the trunk and they were on their way, buckling seat belts as David put the car in gear.

Audrey began babbling immediately. "I don't know why Mom is so mad," she said. "I'm just coming home when I was supposed to. I mean, to begin with, before she got the idea I needed to stay longer."

David knew he should take her somewhere to eat. And once they were done, he should take her for a walk where he could break the news about Elise. But they didn't have the luxury of time. He had to get back downtown and focus on the case.

"I have to tell you something," David said as he guided the car onto Airways Avenue. "It's about your mom."

"She's really mad, isn't she?"

"She's not mad. At least I don't think so."

He should have pulled over so he could look at her. Instead, he had to keep his eyes on the road as he maneuvered in and out of traffic. "Audrey, your mother is missing."

He didn't know anything about teenage girls. Well, he had a sister, and he remembered the drama, but he mostly remembered trying to avoid it. He was sure he was handling this all wrong. But was there a right way to tell a kid her mother had been kidnapped? For the second time?

"Missing? What does that mean? I know Tremain is loose. Is it Tremain? Does he have her again?" She undid her seat belt and turned to face him, sliding her sunglasses on top of her head. "Oh, my God."

"That's what we're presuming."

"Is she okay? Do you know if she's okay?"

He shook his head. "We're doing everything we can to find her. Hook your seat belt."

"You mean like you did everything you could to find her before?"

"We know more about Tremain now. We have more to go on."

"This doesn't seem real. This seems like a dream. A nightmare." She dropped back in her seat, facing forward, tugged at the seat belt, and latched it. "What is that hula girl doing there? Why do you have that on the dash? You shouldn't have that. Not now. Not today."

He tried to remove it, but it was stuck fast. "Sorry," he mumbled as the hula girl danced.

Audrey shot questions at him, many he couldn't answer. How did it happen? Why? When? Where? Poor kid. It was obvious she was running on adrenaline. Her brain finally caught up with her surroundings, and she asked, "Where are we going? This isn't the way to my house."

"You can't go home. And anyway, it's still under construction."

"This isn't the way to your place."

"You can't go to mine either because I won't be there. I'm not going to sleep until we've found your mother. I have to take you someplace where you'll be safe."

"What difference does that make? This isn't about me. It's about Mom."

"She'd want me to make sure you're okay."

He turned right onto Martin Luther King, Jr. Blvd. Five more minutes and they were pulling to a stop at a wrought-iron gate. He pushed the intercom button. "It's David Gould," he said when a male voice answered. "I need to see Strata Luna."

The gate opened, and the car shot forward.

"Strata Luna?" Audrey said. "Are you freakin' kidding? Me, staying with the owner of an escort service? That's like staying with a pimp. Mom is not going to like this."

David put the car in park and cut the engine. "I don't have time to argue. I have to find your mother. This is the safest place for you. The end."

He got out, unloaded her suitcase, and began walking toward the mansion. Audrey followed at a distance.

"I'm taking you up on your earlier offer," David told Strata Luna when she met them at the door. She wore a bright blue scarf tied around her head, the only color David had ever seen on her, and it made him wonder if the black was just for show. Maybe she had this closet of brightly colored clothes that she only wore when nobody could see her.

"The offer was for Elise, but I'm perfectly fine with Elise's baby," Strata Luna said. "Come on in, sweetness. I'm sorry 'bout everything, child. I been working a protection spell, and you can help me. I can use your hair, and maybe you've got some article of clothing that belonged to your mother." Strata Luna put a long-nailed hand on Audrey's shoulder and urged her inside. Then, to David, she said, "Go. Find Elise. I'll take care of this baby girl. She'll be fine here, because Strata Luna will guard her with her life."

CHAPTER 43

I n the evidence room of the Savannah PD, David pulled out his phone to photograph one particular item in Tremain's sketchbook—the drawing used as the template for Elise's tattoo. David had the photo he'd taken of Elise's back, but the drawing was a clearer image.

Finished, he pocketed his phone, rebagged the sketchbook, signed and dated the chain-of-evidence tag, and returned everything to the shelf. Then he peeled off his latex gloves, tossed them in the container near the door, and headed upstairs to the task-force room.

"Somebody get the name and phone number of the best historian in the area," he announced.

Keys clicked, and Meg Cook, the young blond woman who was proving to be invaluable, brought him a list of three experts. He called the first one, a man named Bartholomew Gordon, who'd written several books on the history of Chatham County. David introduced himself and told the man about Elise.

"I heard the news," Bartholomew said. "It's horrible." He had a beautiful Georgia accent, the kind that was almost like music. "But I don't understand why you're calling me."

"I'm hoping you could identify some landmarks. Landmarks that might help us find Detective Sandburg."

"I'll do anything I can."

"Okay if I e-mail an image to you?"

Gordon gave him his address.

David hit the loudspeaker button on his phone so he could talk and operate the keypad at the same time. "I probably don't need to tell you, but speed is of the utmost importance. I'm e-mailing the photo to you right now." David attached the best image and hit "Send." "Please look at it and call me back at this number as soon as you identify anything. I'm particularly interested in the church and the cemetery, but there's also a building in the background that's probably too generic for identification. Please take a look at that too."

"I'd be honored."

They disconnected, and David began to pace as he waited for the return call. He was thinking about contacting the next name on the list when his phone rang. He hit "Answer." "Yes?"

"I was able to identify the cemetery right off. Kind of surprised you didn't recognize it, but of course it's just one tomb. I'm fairly certain that's the grave of Lavinia Lafayette, a voodoo priestess. It's located in Laurel Grove Cemetery on the northeast side of Highway 204, near Sycamore."

"How certain are you of this?"

"Ninety-nine percent."

"What about the other landmarks?"

"I'm going to have to get back to you on that. I think I know the church, but I have to make sure. The building . . . that's going to take longer, if I can figure it out at all."

David thanked him, disconnected, and grabbed his jacket. "I'm heading for Laurel Grove Cemetery. Who's coming with me?"

Avery stepped forward. The man was becoming David's BFF.

"We'll call for backup if we find anything," David said. "In the meantime, keep taking calls. Oh, and Meg? Contact the other two men on the list, and send them the image I just e-mailed to the whole team. See if they can identify anything."

She nodded and got to work.

David and Avery left, almost running down the hall, taking the stairs instead of the elevator. In the car, David drove over the speed limit, but not much. He didn't want a patrol officer stopping them for speeding, didn't want a siren announcing their arrival at the cemetery.

Once there, David parked the car and both men got out.

"I don't know anything about this place," Avery said as they walked down a narrow dirt road. "My wife's into all that ghost stuff, done all the tours. She's tried to get me to come along, but I always manage to get out of it."

David made a small sound of sympathy, spotted something, and pointed. "That could be it." In the far distance, under a live oak draped in Spanish moss, was an aboveground tomb covered with offerings, glass and metal reflecting the sunlight.

"Look at all this," Avery said in disbelief as the two men approached the cement slab.

Small gifts and offerings weren't at all unusual in the South, but David had never seen so much stuff. Beer bottles and shoes and Popsicle sticks bound together with string. Money and buttons, and what had to be dozens of candles, most burned completely down to the metal that held the wick, but some were waiting for a match.

Scattered among the candles were sticks of incense, packets of incense, incense burners, matches, cigarette lighters, articles of clothing. Pink baby rattles, a nasty pink baby blanket that might have been there for years. But the thing David and Avery were both staring at, their mouths agape? Propped up in the center of the entire mess was an eight-by-ten color photo in a gilded frame. But the photo wasn't of Lavinia Lafayette. The photo was a head shot of Elise.

"Holy hell," Avery said, hands on hips. "It's a damn shrine to Detective Sandburg."

David hadn't believed Elise when she'd told him her body was probably worth a lot of money. But judging by the amount of traffic that obviously came through here, she had a large following. "We need to put a twenty-four-hour watch on this grave," David said.

Had Elise known about the shrine? Had she ever come here out of curiosity? She was so secretive about that part of her life. Well, maybe not secretive, but it was painful for her to talk about. He knew that much.

His phone vibrated. He checked the screen. Bartholomew Gordon.

"I think I've identified the two other places," Bartholomew said. "The church is located on St. Helena Island in South Carolina."

St. Helena Island, where Elise's father was rumored to have been buried. Given Tremain's obsession, it made sense that it would be included in the visual history.

"And the other building . . ." the historian continued. "I had to get out a magnifying glass, but I'm eighty percent certain it's the old Broder Plantation long before it went through a fire and restoration. Later it was bought by some hippie woman and she turned it into kind of a commune. It's somewhere northwest of town, I believe. On the Ogeechee River."

CHAPTER 44

"We could go away together," Tremain whispered, his body pressed against Elise's back, his breath hot against her cheek.

Elise continuously drifted in and out of consciousness, welcoming the nothingness. But sometimes, like now, she'd wake up to find Tremain on top of her.

The only light in the cramped, windowless room came from the lantern on the floor, and the battery seemed to be fading. Or was that her vision? She didn't know where she was, and she didn't know how long she'd been there. It could have been hours or it could have been days. It almost seemed she'd always been in this room that smelled of mildew and sweat and old wood. This bed . . . no, not a bed, just a pallet or bed frame that bit into her skin. She was bound, facedown, her wrists and ankles tied. She'd lost feeling in her hands and feet.

Was she wearing clothes? She didn't know—that's how disconnected she was. Sometimes she thought she was naked, but other times she thought she might have felt the weight of fabric against her back and legs. A blanket?

She was shutting down. That much she knew. In the deep recesses of her mind she attributed the shutdown to shock, but did it matter where it came from?

Last time Tremain held her hostage she'd played the part of her own negotiator and had tried to reason with him. This time nothing he said or did touched her. Had she given up? Maybe. Or maybe her brain was simply misfiring and she was unable to form the complex thoughts needed to bargain with him. More likely.

But there was a price to pay for unconscious escape, because the shock of coming back around and finding herself in this space, with Tremain breathing in her ear . . . it was unbearable. His slobbering kisses against her neck, her mouth. She would turn away and gag, and he would punch her in the face.

He was all about torture and violation, but sometimes he lapsed into groveling regret after a brief glimpse of himself, maybe feeling sorry for what he'd done to her. He would rouse enough from the depths of his obsession-driven insanity to frighten himself, at least a little. Whenever that happened, his persona shifted, and he began talking about how they could be happy together.

Once a murderer committed to the kill, to the twisted rationality of what he was doing, he shouldn't step back. He had to keep charging forward, without question, without self-examination.

Elise had seen murderers falter, seen murderers look at themselves and recoil. That was when they went full-blown crazy. Those were the people who took out random strangers, who went on shooting rampages, because the alternative, the thinking, the realization of what they'd done, was intolerable. They needed the noise and violence and shock and commitment to cover up the bad.

"Kill me." Her words were spoken in a harsh rasp, with a voice she didn't recognize.

What about Audrey? Yes, there was Audrey, but Elise was dying. This she knew. Of this she was certain. She could feel herself fading. And since she was going to die, she'd much rather it happen sooner than later. Yet Tremain seemed unwilling to let her go, unwilling to take that final step. Once she was dead and his obsession was gone, what would he have left?

She could feel the bullets lodged in her body, and she visualized hot metal embedded deep within raw flesh. When she moved, blood oozed from holes. She tried not to move.

"It's this thing on your back. That's what it is," Tremain said.

He'd mentioned the body art before. She had a vague recollection of his trembling fingers as he traced the outline of the Black Tupelo design.

"It's protecting you," he said, and now the tremor was in his voice. The design scared him. "It's keeping you from opening up to me."

"It's Strata Luna's," Elise said. "You know that, right?"

The Gullah woman's name evoked fear in most men and women, and Elise wasn't disappointed in Tremain's reaction. He sucked in a breath, and muttered something about an evil priestess.

His fear inspired her, and she began to chant the words of a spell she'd learned years ago, a spell she no longer believed in. All of it was nonsense, just as David said, but if Tremain believed . . .

"Bones of anger, bones of dust,
Full of fury, revenge is just—"

"Don't!" He clamped a hand over her face, stopping her words, pressing hard, his fingers biting into her cheeks, covering her nose and mouth. He didn't let go, and she finally lost consciousness.

Minutes or hours or days later, a stabbing pain in her back brought her around. The pain began slowly, then increased until it swallowed her. She felt liquid warmth run down her hip and drip to the floor.

"I'm going to get rid of this damn thing," Tremain said.

That's when it dawned on her that he was removing the Black Tupelo design, cutting it from her body with a knife or scalpel.

After creating a slit, he worked his finger beneath the skin. Then, with one terrific pull, he ripped the piece from her back.

She screamed. Even though she knew he liked the sound, she screamed.

Tremain dug his fingers into her hair and jerked her head up. "Look at this!" he shrieked. "Look!"

She opened her eyes. Through a red haze of pain, she saw Tremain's hand in front of her face. Between his bloody fingers was the very thing meant to keep this from happening.

"It can't protect you anymore," he said, tossing the implant to the floor. "Nobody can protect you. Nobody is coming for you, because nobody knows you're here. It's just you. And me."

He wasn't satisfied with ripping it out. Or maybe he hadn't gotten it all. Or maybe he just wanted to hear her scream once more. Whatever the reason, he began cutting her again. She bit her lip and squeezed her eyes shut. Then, mercifully, she blacked out.

CHAPTER 45

Night was the toughest, when nothing happened and most of the city was asleep, leaving David to obsess over the mistakes he'd made, his latest being the tattoo hunch that had proven to be a waste of valuable time and manpower, an area search and door-to-door canvass of St. Helena Island having turned up nothing.

There was no way David could go to bed, so he drove around for hours, as if he would somehow stumble upon a clue. Or better, stumble upon Elise, alive and well. He drove past her house; he drove past all of the locations Tremain's victims had been found. He parked outside Tremain's house, waiting and watching even though the place was already under surveillance. About 4:00 a.m., he drove to his apartment, fed Isobel, pet her, sweet-talked to her in a way that would have been embarrassing if anybody had caught him, slept on the couch for an hour, took a shower, and returned to head-quarters to see if any tips had come in.

He was in the break room pouring a cup of coffee when Meg Cook stuck her head in the door. Over twenty-four hours had now passed since Elise had gone missing, and David was trying not to fixate on the twenty-four-hour thing.

"They found her car." Meg rattled off the location, which was roughly ten miles from the plantation. "A photographer was out early this morning trying to get some sunrise pictures when he saw what looked like the top of a vehicle submerged in a marsh. A rescue diver reports that the vehicle is empty, and we've confirmed that the plates belong to Detective Sandburg. A wrecker is on the way there right now." The rest of the pertinent information was spoken as she tried to keep up with David as he ran for the stairs.

David arrived on the scene just as Elise's yellow Saab was being dragged from the marsh, brown water and mud gushing from every crevice. A couple of cop cars were on site, along with a wrecker and three civilian vehicles. No media coverage. He spotted a man in a mud-covered wetsuit, flashed his badge, and asked, "Any chance someone escaped from the car after it went in?"

The guy shook his head. "Pretty sure it was empty," he said. "Windows were up and doors were closed."

"Thanks." David had to walk away, and when he pulled out his phone to call Meg Cook, he realized his hands were shaking. "Pull up Blaine Johnson's statement," David told her. "The kid who gave Tremain a ride."

"Got it right here," she said.

"I'm looking for time of day and direction he was traveling."

"Time of day . . . Oh, that's weird. I don't see anything about it in his statement. And as far as direction . . . we don't have that either."

In a very distant part of his mind, David realized it was starting to rain. "Call him. Find out."

Minutes later, she was back with the information.

All along they'd figured the teen had picked up Tremain *before* Elise was kidnapped. Instead, he'd picked him up after. And why would Tremain dispose of Elise's car so quickly, then get a ride *back* to the plantation? Only one reason David could think of. He'd left Elise there. Maybe the tattoo hadn't been a false lead after all.

"This is why small details matter," he told Meg. "I don't know who took Johnson's statement, but he needs to be more thorough." David also faulted himself. He'd missed it too, and there was zero margin for error right now.

Leaving the young officer with instructions that she call with anything that seemed relevant no matter how small, David drove the ten miles to the plantation through what had now become a torrential rain. At the plantation house, David dove from his car and ran for the cover of the porch. He broke the yellow seal left by the crime-scene team, ripped off boards, and went inside.

The pie was soggy, and fruit flies had gathered. The flowers were wilted from lack of water. How quickly things died.

With wet hands and rain dripping from his hair and coat, David pulled out his phone to call Meg. One bar, so he sent a text message telling her to get all she could on the plantation. History, but especially floor plans, if any existed. He hit "Send," then continued through the house while deep thunder rattled windows.

The pool room looked the same as it had twenty-four hours earlier. Back through the living room, down the hall, to Elise's bedroom. Undisturbed except the shell casings had been collected and there were signs the room had been dusted for prints.

And now he started to think that this was another dead end, another of his mistakes and misplaced hunches born out of desperation.

He moved through the building as silently as he could, his heart sinking a little more with each step, the conclusion to this drama already foretold. He imagined going to Strata Luna's house, taking Audrey aside, telling her that her mother was dead, all the while unwilling to believe it himself.

Up the stairs to the second story, visually examining bedrooms that had been stripped of fabric and plaster. On the third floor, he took fresh note of the weird room that had obviously been occupied recently, but there was no sign of anybody today. He was trying to make sense of it when he thought he heard the faint sound of a car outside beneath the noise of the storm. He listened, the unmistakable slam of a car door serving as confirmation.

With gun drawn, David made his way downstairs, wincing with every creak. Once he'd traversed the hallway, he swung himself into the kitchen, gun arm extended and braced.

The door opened and a woman in a red raincoat and purple tights let out a shriek, dropped a paisley bag to the floor, and raised her hands high.

CHAPTER 46

David didn't lower his weapon. "You're Elise's aunt, right?"

She nodded while continuing to look at him in horror.

"What did you have to do with her disappearance?"

"Why is everybody so eager to paint me black? To think so poorly of me?"

"For one thing, you committed a felony. I did some research," he added, by way of explanation. "And then there's this." He held up the note she'd left for Elise. "You were running."

"I'll admit I was ready to leave the country, ready to start a new life as an expatriate, but then I saw the news about Elise." She slowly lowered her hands, wiped at her wet face, and shook rain off her arms. "I don't know if I can be of any help, but I had to come back."

He tossed the paper aside. "Do you know Atticus Tremain?"

"I'd never heard of him until all this awful stuff started happening."

"Tremain wasn't always his name. He changed it. He used to be Joel Francis."

She put a hand to her throat and her eyes got big. "Joel Francis?"

He lowered his gun. "Heard of him?"

She looked around the room, her gaze dropping to the table. "My poor pie," she said forlornly, in an obvious attempt to derail the conversation.

"Did you know him?" David asked.

"There was a Joel Francis who used to come here years ago. Elise called him Joe, but his real name was Joel. You have to realize that a lot of people came and went back then. The plantation was always open, and I never turned anybody away." She looked nervous and flustered and uncomfortable, and none of those reactions seemed to have anything to do with David and his gun.

He returned the weapon to his shoulder holster. "What are you not telling me?"

"If Tremain is who I think he is, then he stayed here one summer when Elise was visiting."

Wow. David wasn't expecting that.

"He seemed like a nice young man. He wrote these folksy songs, and we recorded some of them. He was going to shop them around, try to find a record label."

"What about Elise? How does she fit into this?"

"Well . . ." With both palms flat on the table, Anastasia lowered herself into a chair. "The whole thing is kind of fuzzy. There was a party." She jumped tracks, and her face lit up. "Wasn't that a lovely party the other night?"

"Yeah, but let's hear about the one that took place years ago."

"I feel funny talking about this to a detective. I think maybe I should discuss it with a lawyer."

"Let me point out that every second that passes brings Elise closer to death," David said. "Holding back information right now could very well result in her funeral." Brutal, but he didn't have time to be nice.

Anastasia pressed her lips together and nodded. Then, like someone waiting in the wings preparing to go onstage, she lifted her chin and took a deep breath. "My parties were . . . well, not really for children. People ran around naked, and we smoked a lot of pot. Really good stuff that I suspect was laced with something, because wow. Anyway, I was really stoned that night. Normally I put Elise to bed before things got so wild, but I remember going for a swim in the river and getting out of the water to see Elise standing there. People were drunk and high and making out. I think I said something about Elise needing to go to bed. One of the regulars, a man named Scott, said he'd take her upstairs. He left with her, and Joel followed. I do remember that, and I thought it was strange. So I got dressed and I went after them, just to make sure Elise was okay. I thought I would tuck her in the way I usually did. But before I even stepped outside, I heard the sounds of fighting and broken glass . . . and then nothing."

"Tremain."

"This is where things get really fuzzy for me. I think I may have blocked it out. Maybe some kind of post-traumatic stress, but once I got upstairs, I remember seeing Joel—or Tremain, as you know him—standing over a body, and poor little Elise—" She let out a single long sob. "Oh, poor thing, poor thing. With her nightgown pulled up, and her panties ripped off."

David reached blindly for the table and dropped into a chair.

"I think Joel, or rather Tremain, got there in time," she rushed to add.

"Are you saying Tremain killed a rapist and pedophile?" David asked in disbelief.

She nodded. "Tremain was hardly more than a kid. I'm guessing maybe twenty, twenty-one. I never asked people their age. I didn't want to know." She picked up a petal that had fallen from the bouquet of flowers, and she began fiddling with it rather than looking at David. She swallowed, then continued: "I know it was wrong, but we hid the body. He was just a kid. I didn't want him to go to prison. And I can tell you that the people around here were looking for a reason to shut me down. Just a month earlier we'd had an arson attempt. I couldn't lose the plantation."

David's profiler mind kicked into full gear. That night the secret murder most likely triggered the killer instinct in Tremain. Hard to say what he would have become if it hadn't happened. He still might have taken a dark path. Different circumstance, different trigger, and probably a different dark path, but a dark path all the same. This one led him directly to his obsession with Elise. He'd saved her. God, it all made bizarre sense now.

"Was he interested in tattooing at that time?" David asked.

"I had a fairly famous tattoo artist staying here that summer. He was offering classes. Totally forgot about that until you mentioned it. Tremain was one of his better students. Tremain ran off that night, the night Scott was killed. I never saw him again."

David suspected some historical revision was going on, but at the same time her story made sense. In fact, it fit like a puzzle piece.

"An hour ago I was convinced Tremain and Elise might still be here, but I've gone through the house top to bottom," David told her. "Did I miss something? Any place he could be hiding?"

"I've been told this plantation was once part of the Underground Railroad because there's a tunnel to the river. Others say it was used for rum running or trafficking of women for prostitution. I prefer to believe the Underground Railroad story, plus the house itself supports that theory.

"Over the years I've done a lot of restoration and remodeling, and during reconstruction we found false walls and false floors and secret passageways with stairs. Much of the house has double walls, which made it a great place for musicians to record."

"Would Tremain have known about the passageways?" David asked.

"It's possible. We remodeled the living room the summer he was here, and I'm pretty sure he helped with it. And whenever a wall was torn out, we always uncovered something interesting. It's like there's a whole other house living in the shadow of this place."

The storm intensified. Thunder crashed, and lightning lit up the sky. "Show me these passageways," David said.

CHAPTER 47

Elise was pretty sure she had a fever. Maybe that was a good thing because nothing seemed real. The pain of the body art removal was a burning memory, but the bullets still lodged in her arm and leg hurt with every breath.

Tables had turned, and Tremain was the one trying to engage her in conversation. It was like he wanted her in his head. He wanted to live and breathe her. But occasionally something he said would stir her curiosity, pull her from her stupor.

"Why did you choose the name Atticus Tremain?" Her words were slurred and slow, and her tongue was thick. Neither name seemed sinister. Not until he'd made them that way.

"*To Kill a Mockingbird* was one of my favorite books growing up," he said. "And Atticus Finch was a strong man. A good man."

"And Tremain?"

"From *Johnny Tremain.*"

"You read a lot."

"Not really, but I liked those books."

Interesting that Tremain had gone so far as to name himself after fictional heroes.

"I saved you years ago so you could grow up to realize your full potential," Tremain said, turning the conversation back to her the way he'd been doing for the past several hours. "But you squandered your life. You took what was a gift, from me and from your father, and you turned your back on it. I shouldn't have saved you that night. I should have let that guy rape and kill you. And now I have to take what you won't willingly give. The mantle has to be passed."

Her biggest fear was that he'd remove the tattoo from her back while she was still alive. After that, he'd kill her and harvest her organs. She hoped he killed her first, but knowing Tremain it didn't seem likely.

"You try to make yourself sound so noble," she said, "but you're nothing but a criminal trafficking in body parts. What about the people you've killed? What do they have to do with any of this?"

"A guy has to make a living."

She may have drifted off; she may have lost consciousness. When she came back, she was still thinking about what he'd said. And the thing was, he made sense. Was the abyss looking back at her? Or had he touched on the very heart of her own self-doubt?

"I've questioned the choices I've made," she said. And wasn't it strange that a man who'd saved the child was going to kill the adult? It seemed right. Or was that the fever talking? No, she'd had similar thoughts. Not about Tremain killing her, but the wrong turns she'd taken. And now she suddenly saw him as her confidant, her savior, protector, killer. All of those things.

"Will it be fast?" she asked. "When you kill me?"

"I don't want to talk about that."

"Will you cut my throat? And where will you do it? Here? Or maybe the grave where I was left as a baby."

"You'd like that, wouldn't you? If I took you someplace that's probably crawling with cops."

It had been worth a try. "When I'm gone," she said, "what will you do? When I'm no longer around? I've been your obsession. I think you might miss me."

"I hadn't thought of that," he said slowly, with a disturbed tone entering his previously smooth voice. "I don't want to think about that."

"You have to think about it. Dead is dead. You'll miss me when I'm gone. You'll have no direction."

"No. I'll have what you've given me."

They both heard a far-off noise, maybe a slamming door, maybe just the wind. Tremain clamped his hand tightly over her mouth. "*Shhh*. Make a sound, and I'll cut your throat right now. You'll be dead, and I won't miss you."

CHAPTER 48

Anastasia produced two lanterns and handed one to David. Then she led him down the hall to a closet. Inside, she pushed at the back wall, and a secret door opened.

She paused to whisper over her shoulder, brushing cobwebs from her hair. "I've only been this way a couple of times, and that was years ago. But I want to show you this one place if I can find it."

The space was tight and smothering and claustrophobic. They wound around, up and down, until David lost all sense of direction, until he began to wonder if the whole thing was a trap, set by this crazy broad and Tremain. Think about it. The way Elise had been lured there to begin with.

She stopped, and he stopped. They seemed to have at least reached their goal. In the distance, he saw a wooden door that stood ajar. Anastasia pressed against the wall so he could squeeze by.

He pulled his gun and motioned for her to stay back.

David approached the door with caution, then pivoted into the room, doing a quick scan with lantern and gun. The space was empty except for a wooden pallet that had probably served as a bed.

"Can you imagine?" Anastasia said from behind him. "Staying down here?" He could feel her breath on his neck, and he half expected her to crack him over the head with the lantern.

"The passageways look like something used by the Underground Railroad," David said. "They would have hidden and rested in here."

But right now David didn't care about the Underground Railroad; he was looking at the stains on the floor near the pallet. He brought the light closer, and Anastasia let out a gasp.

"Is that blood?"

"Yes."

"There's so much."

She was right. Some dried, some thick and coagulated, and some fresh. "Fresh blood means the person is still alive." What he didn't say was that they had no idea who that person was. It could very well be Tremain's blood. Maybe Elise injured him. Then again, maybe Tremain killed her, dumped her body. Maybe he came back here to hide.

"Why didn't we hear anything?" Anastasia asked.

"The storm would have covered up any noise, plus with the false walls and the sprawling nature of this place . . . " David spotted something else and bent down to pick it up, bringing it close to the lantern.

A bloody piece of Teflon with skin hanging from it. It was the Black Tupelo design, which could only mean one thing: Elise *had* been there.

"Did you say there's a tunnel leading to the river?" David asked.

"Yes, but it's sealed."

"I'll bet it's not."

And now he saw what he'd missed when concentrating on storming the room: a faint trail of blood.

He pulled out his phone. No signal. "Go back upstairs," he told Anastasia.

"I'm coming with you."

He didn't have time to argue.

They followed the trail down a sloped passageway that eventually turned from wood to stone, until they saw light in the distance and could hear the sound of rain and rushing water. A minute later they were at the mouth of the tunnel. The metal gate across the opening had been cut and bent, and they were able to slip through the rebar. Once outside, David regained his bearings when he spotted the plantation house looming above them through the trees.

The blood trail ended where the rain began, but there were footprints in the mud around the riverbank.

"Look!" Anastasia pointed.

They were buffeted from every direction: rain from the sky and water from the river. Through the gale, he could just make out a small blue boat at the edge of an island. While he watched, the rope holding the bobbing boat to the tree snapped and the craft broke free, spun in a circle, and was swept downstream.

"On that island"—Anastasia shouted against the wind while holding her hair away from her face—"on that island is a little cabin. We used to have picnics there. And parties."

David pulled out his phone. Now that they were no longer in the tunnel he had one bar that came and went. He typed a message to Meg Cook and hit "Send," hoping it would go through. Then he slapped the phone into Anastasia's hand. "The landline at the plantation has been cut. Get in your car and drive until you get a signal, then call this person, Meg Cook. Fill her in on the details, then go back to the house and wait for the police so you can bring them here." He didn't say he might be dead by the time they arrived, and she might be the only person who could tell them what had transpired over the past two days.

She nodded, turned, and ran up the hill in the direction of the plantation.

CHAPTER 49

David stared at the island. And he stared at the river churning between him and the island.

Jesus.

The current was moving fast, and he wasn't a great swimmer even under normal conditions—and he'd just witnessed what had happened to the boat.

He ran along the shore, shrugging out of his jacket as he headed upstream where he kicked off his shoes. Then, before he could think about all of the reasons this was a bad idea, he dove in, the cold taking his breath away. He both fought and used the current, striking out with strong strokes as the wind beat the water into whitecaps and waves washed over his head, obliterating his vision.

Progress seemed impossible, and for a long span of time he thought he'd failed, that he physically couldn't make it. But ten minutes after diving into the water, when it looked like he'd overshoot the island and be swept downstream, his legs made contact with shallow shoreline.

On hands and knees, he took a moment to stabilize, then dragged himself from the water, his breathing coming in tight bursts, his body shaking from the cold, his saturated pants hanging on his hip bones, falling over his bare feet, socks lost. Moving stiffly, his wet clothes making slapping noises, he slipped through dense shrubbery to finally locate the cabin Anastasia had told him about.

Windows were broken, the wooden door hung on one hinge, and the ever-tenacious kudzu vines made the structure look more like a product of nature than of man.

With numb fingers, David unsnapped his leather holster and drew his gun as he scanned the surroundings, cold rain beating down. He could call Tremain out, which seemed like a bad idea, or he could take him by surprise.

There was no decent cover near the shack. Crouching, David ran straight for the building.

Tremain was waiting. Shots rang out, and bullets sprayed. White-hot pain ripped through David's shoulder, knocking him back. He staggered; he caught himself.

He didn't dare return fire for fear of hitting Elise if she was inside. Head down, he continued his charge while bullets chewed the ground around him until he reached cover. He stood, breathing hard, back pressed to the building, door to his left.

How many shots had Tremain fired? A lot. Did he have a gun other than Elise's? Was there any chance he was out or almost out of bullets? No way of knowing. If he was out, he could be reloading right now. Time to move.

Without hesitation, David swung into the half-open doorway, gun braced, and in a fraction of a second he processed the situation.

Elise, lying on the floor, hands tied behind her back, feet bound at the ankles. Wearing black panties and a black bra. Nothing else. Unlike him, she wasn't shaking from the cold. She seemed beyond that. Alive, but not entirely conscious, her hair falling across her face, covering her eyes, her lips blue.

And there was Tremain, straddling her like some proud hunter standing over his trophy. That was the thing about Tremain. In his mind, he owned Elise, and he was now finally and truly claiming what was his.

David took a step inside, keeping his gun trained at Tremain's head. "It's over," he said.

The wind and waves and pounding rain combined to create a roar that seemed part of the small room, but beneath it David thought he recognized the sound of a siren. And not one siren, but many. Tremain heard it too. Fewer than thirty minutes had passed since David sent the message to Meg Cook.

"See?" David said. "Over."

It was Elise's gun Tremain held in his hand. And it was obvious from the way he held it that he was an amateur. And amateurs tended to empty the magazine in one long adrenaline rush.

"It's wet," Tremain said. "Your gun is wet."

"You think that matters? This is a forty-caliber Smith & Wesson. It's never misfired, wet or dry."

"You would say that."

But David could see the hesitation in that comment. The doubt.

"You don't know much about guns, do you?" David asked.

"You can't kill me. You have to arrest me."

"I know it's weird," David said in a conversational tone. "I'm really kind of a pacifist, but if a person hurts somebody I care about, I don't give a shit what the law says."

"You're a cop."

Tremain, trying to remind David of his sworn duty. To hell with that. "Being a cop doesn't mean I can't think for myself. It doesn't mean I always follow protocol." *I'm warning you.* "Move away from her."

"How did you figure it out?" Tremain asked. "Was it my mother?"

"Your mother will always consider you an innocent victim. No, it was the tattoo. I really expected to find you in the cemetery, but when you weren't there . . . Have to admit, the plantation was the last place I thought you'd go. Doubling back. You had me for a while. And I suspect you were in the house when I stopped the first time."

"Hiding in a secret room. And I still plan to go to the cemetery," Tremain said. "This is just a little delay, that's all." He placed his booted foot on Elise's head while continuing to keep his weapon trained on David. "Put the gun away or I'll crush her skull." Another indication that he was out of ammo.

"Interesting about the cemetery," David said. With absolutely no bluff, he stared at Tremain. He thought about how he should have smothered the guy when he was in the hospital, and he thought about how he'd intended to kill him up in northern Georgia. Now, without hesitation, David squeezed the trigger. The Smith & Wesson fired, as he knew it would, the bullet striking Tremain in the head. Blood flew and the man jerked, then he dropped like a stone.

Kill shot. Over, just like that. And yeah, Tremain was going to a cemetery, all right.

David staggered to Elise and shoved Tremain's body aside. She was still alive, breathing shallowly, eyes closed. He began working on the rope around her wrists. How he would love to savor finding her, but she wasn't out of danger yet.

"What day is it?" Elise's voice was thick and slurred. Her eyes, as she opened them and struggled to focus, were glassy.

With the bindings gone from her wrists and ankles, he put a hand to her forehead. She was burning up. "Today is the day we finally got Tremain. That's what day it is."

She tried to pull her thoughts together. "No, the execution. Did you miss it?"

She wasn't as out of it as he thought. "That's okay," David said. "I can go to an execution any old time." One of his weaker jokes, but when hypothermia was setting in and he had a gaping hole in his shoulder, it was hard to be sharp. "I didn't need to see it."

"No, you didn't." She closed her eyes, and at first he thought she'd slipped into unconsciousness. But then she spoke. "It would be kind of funny if we both died."

"Hilarious," he agreed.

"Audrey?"

"I picked her up from the airport and she's in good hands." He wouldn't mention Strata Luna just yet.

"How did you get here?" she asked.

"I swam. Or swum. Or swimmed."

"I thought you didn't swim."

"I can swim; I just don't like it."

Then, a few moments later: "Do you think anybody's coming for us?"

"They'll have to wait out the storm."

The words had barely left his mouth when he heard something that sounded like an engine. Nah. But there it was again.

He shoved himself to his feet and stumbled to the door to see a man, head bent into the driving rain, hurrying toward the shack. Once inside, he slammed the broken door and pulled back the hood of his rain gear. Avery. David was really starting to like Avery.

"Got a call from a woman telling us you were out here on the island. Found a crazy guy named Don with a boat, and here we are." From outside, came the sound of a laboring motor. Avery scanned the room, spotting Elise and Tremain. "Jesus." The word was an exhale. "Is she . . .?"

"No, but we need to get her to a hospital."

"And him?"

"Dead."

"Dead is good."

Avery walked over to Elise and knelt down next to her. "Hey, boss," he said gently.

Her eyes opened. "Boss?" she asked.

"I heard through the grapevine that you're being promoted to head homicide detective."

She groaned. "No."

"Two gunshot wounds," David said. "Arm and leg."

"No vitals?"

"I don't think so."

"I was going to quit," Elise said. "I planned to open a coffee shop. Audrey was going to work with me, and we were going to wear matching aprons."

"And I'm going to leave homicide to pursue a career in ballet." Avery grabbed Elise's uninjured arm. "I hate to do this to you, but—" Bent at the waist, he slung her over his back in a fireman's carry. She let out another moan, then went silent.

David and Avery looked at Tremain, looked at each other, David shrugged, then they headed out the door into the storm.

CHAPTER 50

What was it about the combined sound of cutlery and conversation that evoked such a sense of well-being? Just silverware and glasses and that low drone of people talking. Somebody should make a mojo from this day, Elise thought as she sat at the dining room table surrounded by people she cared about, people who were important to her. Somebody should throw a butterfly net over the air in the room and grab the magic of the moment, put it in a tiny bag, and pull the string closed so it wouldn't escape.

"How you doing?" David asked, a bite of turkey on his fork.

Her body had taken a pounding. Her ribs and ankle had been reinjured, and the gunshot wounds sent a bolt of lightning through her whenever she moved. She smiled. "Fine."

"Liar." He wasn't moving all that fast either, but the bullet he'd taken in the shoulder had gone straight through and he was expected to heal without any complications.

Ten days had passed since the abduction. It was Thanksgiving, and they were in Elise's house. Thick plastic that rattled and whispered hung in front of doorways, and the upstairs bathroom had no toilet, no sink, and no shower. But Audrey's room was finished, even down to the painted walls, thanks to Strata Luna sending over Javier to help.

The bond between a homicide detective and the owner of an escort service might be considered an unwise and unethical alliance to some. So be it. And anyway, this was Savannah, a place that lived by its own set of rules, and Strata Luna kind of *was* Savannah, the mystery and mystique she carried and nurtured seeming a part of the city itself.

The rest of the house was still unfinished, but livable. The kitchen stove worked, and the dishes could be washed in the sink. The floor was a plywood base Elise was actually beginning to like. The downstairs bathroom was done, along with the guest bedroom where Elise was staying until it no longer hurt to go up and down the steps.

Home sweet home. It felt good to be here. It felt right, and nothing had felt right in quite awhile.

David had arrived early that morning to help with the meal. He, Elise, and Audrey had stuffed the turkey and made the dressing and even managed gravy that wasn't too lumpy. And now Elise looked down the table where candle flames reflected off the vintage china given to her by Anastasia. "I won't be using them where I'm going," her aunt had said.

An odd crew. Seven people in all, three on each side of the table with Elise at the head. On her left sat Strata Luna. Today she wore a narrow black skirt, but instead of her usual black top she'd opted for something festive and bloodred. Beside the Gullah woman was Medical Examiner John Casper, along with his fiancée, Mara. On the opposite side of the table were Audrey, Anastasia, and David.

"How wonderful to be here," Anastasia said with a sigh.

Nobody mentioned that this would most likely be Anastasia's last free Thanksgiving for a long time. She was scheduled to appear before a judge and receive her sentence for insurance fraud, but the concealment of the body was their biggest concern. The man killed that night at the plantation had been identified as Scott Priesman, someone who'd been on the missing persons' list since the murder. There would be an inquiry, followed by a trial. Elise hoped the jury would go easy on her aunt.

Whatever happened, it looked like the plantation might be waiting for her when she got out of prison. A group of artists in Savannah had started a fund-raising campaign and within a few days it exceeded their expectations, donations flooding in from all over the country, many from artists who'd once stayed at the plantation and had made it big.

Elise's mother took full credit for exposing Anastasia.

"I knew something was fishy," Grace said when Elise called with the news. And sadly, she didn't seem at all happy to discover that her sister was still alive.

The DNA samples supplied by Strata Luna had confirmed the worst. Pure, primo, uncut body parts were being ground and sold for root work and mojos. As the Gullah woman suspected, the ingredients were indeed human. That was enough for her to share the source, and the supplier was arrested and shut down. But, as Strata Luna said, it wouldn't stop the trafficking. People would continue to look for mojos to make them strong and beautiful and rich. And if it meant killing to do it, people would be killed.

"I'm not going to put anybody on the spot and ask you what you're thankful for," Elise said.

What was she thankful for?

For this moment. She was thankful for this moment.

What would they say if pressed?

Chin down, Strata Luna was looking at Elise with a knowing smile on full red lips that matched her top and the wine in her glass. If the woman were honest, she'd probably say she was thankful for herself. And John Casper would be thankful for his fiancée, because it was obvious he was smitten. And his fiancée would be thankful for John, because they could both share a life in which they could discuss dead bodies over dinner and it wouldn't seem at all strange. And Anastasia . . . she probably wasn't thankful for being found out, or thankful about the hidden body being discovered, but she had to be relieved it was all over.

David. What was he thankful for? That his pumpkin bread was every bit as good as he'd hoped? Thankful that his ex-wife was finally dead? Thankful that Tremain was at the bottom of the river, being eaten by alligators? Because, unfortunately, Tremain's body was gone when the police returned to retrieve it, and drag marks to the water's edge indicated an alligator had most likely claimed him. Elise was trying not to dwell on it, but a body would have given her more closure.

And Audrey—Elise was sure she was just glad she wasn't in trouble, and glad Elise wasn't dead.

And Elise? Even murderers could teach a person lessons. What had Tremain taught her? Had there been some truth about her unwillingness to accept who she was? Yesterday Audrey asked if she planned to get the tattoo removed.

Elise told her no.

"Because it's so big?" Audrey had asked. "And it will cost a fortune and take forever and probably really hurt?"

"None of those things," Elise told her.

Yes, the tattoo represented a bad event, a dark event, but maybe Tremain did her a favor by leaving her with a permanent record of her heritage. No more denying where she'd come from. No more denying that she was the daughter of a root doctor, a conjurer. And no more kidding herself about owning a café. That wasn't who she was. She could look at those coffee-shop people and imagine herself living that life, but it wasn't her. It was a nice dream, but that's all it was, a dream. She had to figure out who she was and remain true to that self, and part of the secret would be accepting her heritage. Maybe even embracing it.

Heritage . . . People spent their lives trying to leave it behind, hang on to it, or find it.

Was there anything to root magic? Maybe. Maybe not. But she owed it to herself and Audrey to explore the possibilities. Head of homicide and a conjurer's daughter. Who would have thought?

Yesterday she'd called Major Hoffman and accepted the position as head detective. She would take the job and Audrey would be fine. They would both be fine. They would all be fine.

"This pumpkin bread will blow your mind," David said as he held the plate high for everyone to see before he passed it. "I used fresh pumpkins this time."

Halfway through the dinner, Audrey announced, "While I was at Strata Luna's we made mojos." She ran off to reappear with a handful of small velvet bags in different colors. "I have spells for love, I have spells for wealth, and I have spells for happiness."

"I'll take love," John Casper said.

His fiancée play-punched his arm, and he fake-grimaced. "You already have love," she said.

"I just want an extra helping of it."

"I'll take happiness," Elise said.

Audrey handed her the blue velvet bag. "No body parts."

"I'll take love," David said. "Because someone shredded my last one." Audrey dangled the bag in front of him, then dropped it in his hand. "There's name paper inside," she said. "And instructions."

He smiled and nodded and shot a look at Elise. Later she would take him aside and tell him not to write her name on that paper. And he would laugh at her again, because he didn't believe.

"We got in an interesting body this morning," John said. His fiancée nodded with the kind of enthusiasm most young women saved for clothing or really good food.

Mara smiled. "We unzipped the bag and the smell of almonds almost knocked us over."

"Poison," David and Elise and Strata Luna said in harmony.

"I did a bit of research," John Casper told them. "And the decedent was a fairly well-off elderly guy. Recently married to a younger woman. We put him back in the cooler. We'll do the autopsy tomorrow."

And the conversation turned to bodies and murders and black widows who preyed on elderly men.

"Who wants more turkey?" David asked as plates began to show empty spots. He lifted the platter and passed it to Audrey.

"Good Godzilla." Audrey paused, platter in her hands as she stared at the turkey carcass. "Is that the wishbone?"

The doorbell rang and everything stopped.

"You expecting someone else?" David asked Elise.

"Melinda is stopping by later this evening."

Audrey pushed away from the table. "I'll get it."

She ran off, then reappeared a minute later. "There's some old guy here." She made a strange face. "Says his name is Jackson Sweet."

Strata Luna's wineglass slipped from her fingers and crashed to the floor, her eyes wide as she stared in the direction of the living room.

Finally, after what seemed like minutes but had probably been only seconds, David spoke. "I'd suggest a swab of his mouth and maybe a hair sample."

A murmur of agreement went around the table. Strata Luna grabbed the wine. Since her glass was broken, she took a swallow straight from the bottle.

And then the man in question, the very man who'd visited Elise that night at the plantation, appeared in the arched entry that separated the living room and dining room.

Strata Luna made a choking sound—a kind of sob. Everything about her said the man standing there was none other than Jackson Sweet, the person responsible for the darkness in Elise's life. The whispers at the police station, the fear in her stepmother's eyes, and later the rejection. She was an outcast because of him, and she'd been kidnapped and tortured and shot because of him. And now, here he was, showing up on Thanksgiving.

No need of a DNA test to identify him as Jackson Sweet. The expression on Strata Luna's face was confirmation enough. Elise tossed down her napkin, ready to tell him to get the hell out.

David rubbed his hands together with way too much enthusiasm and said, "Grab a plate and pull up a chair."

ABOUT THE AUTHOR

Anne Frasier is the *New York Times* and *USA Today* best-selling author of twenty-five books and numerous short stories that have spanned the genres of suspense, mystery, thriller, romantic suspense, paranormal, and memoir. Her titles have been printed in both hardcover and paperback and translated into twenty languages. Her career began in 1998 with *Amazon Lily*, a cult sensation and winner of numerous awards. Her first memoir, *The Orchard*, was a 2011 *O, The Oprah Magazine* Fall Pick, number two on the Indie Next List, and a Librarians' Best Books of 2011. She divides her time between the city of St. Paul, Minnesota, and her writing studio in rural Wisconsin.